"Is he handsome?" Eliza prodded with a grin.

"Quite." Laura laughed. "Also quite dismissive of Society ladies. He thinks we are all empty-headed and frivolous."

"You'd be the lady to convince him otherwise," Maggie said. "Laura the mathematician. Not that you need to win his favor, of course. A banker's rich *daughter* may find an aristocratic husband, but a banker's *son* would be entirely ineligible as a match for you."

"How fortunate I am not angling for a husband," Laura retorted. No matter how appealing she might find the admittedly unsuitable Mr. Rochdale.

Author Note

A Society veteran in her second Season, with her two best friends unavailable, Lady Laura Pomeroy befriends merchant heiress Susanna Rochdale. To help the shy banker's daughter cope with the demands of the Season, Laura offers to give Susanna lessons in conversation and the gentle art of flirtation.

Susanna is enthusiastic, but her protective brother, Miles, is horrified by the idea that Lady Laura might turn his sweet sister into a heartless Society flirt like the one who led him on and broke his heart. To protect Susanna from Laura's destructive influence, he offers to join in on the lessons, ostensibly to learn to better court the daughter of a business associate both families expect him to marry.

The two begin as wary adversaries, but as the lessons progress, they discover they have more in common than they could have imagined. Strongly drawn to each other, they indulge their desire to become better acquainted, each confident that as they inhabit two different worlds, their association will be short-lived. But soon, they begin to wonder the unthinkable: Is there any way for the aristocratic daughter of a marquess and the commoner son of a businessman to end up together?

I hope you enjoy Miles and Laura's story.

JULIA JUSTISS

A Season
of Flirtation

HARLEQUIN®
HISTORICAL™

Recycling programs
for this product may
not exist in your area.

ISBN-13: 978-1-335-72366-6

A Season of Flirtation

Copyright © 2023 by Janet Justiss

For questions and comments about the quality of this book,
please contact us at CustomerService@Harlequin.com.

Harlequin Enterprises ULC
22 Adelaide St. West, 41st Floor
Toronto, Ontario M5H 4E3, Canada
www.Harlequin.com

Printed in U.S.A.

Julia Justiss wrote her first ideas for Nancy Drew stories in her third-grade notebook and has been writing ever since. After publishing poetry in college, she turned to novels. Her Regency historicals have won or placed in contests by the Romance Writers of America, *RT Book Reviews*, National Readers' Choice Awards and the Daphne du Maurier Award. She lives with her husband in Texas. For news and contests, visit juliajustiss.com.

To the Zombie Belles,
who always make time to brainstorm through
a sticky plot, commiserate over difficulties, rejoice
with the victories, cajole me to keep going when
I'm flagging and generally make this writer's life
a more beautiful place. I love you guys!

Chapter One

'Thank you, Haines, I can escort myself in,' Lady Laura Pomeroy said, smiling over her shoulder at the butler who'd ushered her to the door of her friend Susanna Rochdale's parlour. She turned back to enter the room—and collided with the tall man who was just exiting.

Knocked off-balance, she stumbled. Strong hands reached out to catch her wrists, steadying her. About to offer an apology, she looked up into ice-blue eyes so arresting she caught her breath.

The rest of the gentleman, she thought, giving him a covert glance from under her lashes, was equally worthy of admiration. A wide forehead brushed by sable locks, high cheekbones and a strong chin combined into a pleasingly handsome face. Broad shoulders set off a well-tailored dark blue coat that, while not in the latest kick of fashion, was made of expensive wool, as was the waistcoat beneath it, while the shirt was pristine and neck cloth expertly tied. The long legs outlined by buff trousers were shapely as well.

In addition to his good looks, the man radiated an aura of command and potent masculinity that prickled her skin with awareness. Even with gloves on, the feel of his hands on her wrists seemed to burn her skin, radiating heat up her arms and throughout her body.

'Excuse me, sir!' she said belatedly, a smile curving her lips at this vision.

It took her a moment to realise her smile wasn't being returned. Indeed, an expression of annoyance passed over the man's countenance.

'Undoubtedly my fault,' he said as he released her and stepped back. 'One should always avoid ladies who don't look where they are going. You must be Lady Laura Pomeroy. I'm Miles Rochdale, by the way.'

Without being immodest, Laura knew she was considered pretty. Her looks combined with her breeding and elegance generally won her appreciative masculine attention. Or at least courtesy.

Miles Rochdale was barely civil.

She made him a curtsey, to which he bowed. 'I shall endeavour in future to do a better job of looking, Mr Rochdale,' she replied, an edge to her tone.

'I'm sure my sister will be down directly, if you would care to await her in the parlour,' he said, gesturing into the room. 'Unfortunately, pressing engagements prevent my lingering to entertain you.'

Implying that she was too lack-witted to amuse herself for a few moments? Her own annoyance deepened. How regrettable, she thought, staring back up into Miles Rochdale's remarkable eyes, that it was considered un-ladylike to strike a gentleman. It would be immensely satisfying to slap that faintly patronising look off his far-too-handsome face.

'Oh dear, how disappointing,' she replied in the brightest, most vacuous tone she could manage. 'However shall

I endure the boredom of sitting alone with nothing to divert me?' She gave an elaborate sigh. 'But I suppose I can tolerate it for a few moments.'

'Only for a few. Your servant, my lady,' Rochdale said, giving her a bow.

He'd been anything but, Laura thought, disgruntled, watching him walk away. She really should have resisted the temptation to play the shallow ingénue he obviously thought her. But his dismissive attitude, which she had done nothing to deserve, had been *too* annoying.

How dared he sum her up as *lacking* after exchanging barely a few words?

At the same time, she was conscious of an illogical disappointment. Not that she would expect the son of the house, having encountered her by chance, to delay his departure to converse with her. Besides, why would she wish him to?

Of course she wouldn't. Not if he were going to imbue every remark with that irritating undertone of disdain. No matter how commanding his form or mesmerising his ice-blue eyes.

Even more irritating was the realisation that, despite his unappealing personality, his physical presence had left her nerves simmering.

Maybe she *was* as shallow as he'd assumed her to be.

She'd taken two agitated turns around the room when her friend Susanna rushed in. 'So sorry to be late!' she cried, coming to exchange a hug with Laura. 'I didn't mean to keep you waiting.'

'I bore the delay with fortitude,' Laura said drily. 'As I assured your brother I was capable of doing.'

'Oh, you met Miles? I'm sorry I missed him! I knew he was to be home this morning and hoped I'd be able to introduce you. He's so busy, always at the bank or the exchange or the stock market. He's hardly ever here. And, though he occasionally gets invited to *ton* events, he never attends. I so wanted you to meet my dearest, most considerate brother.'

Dear? Considerate? Laura gave her head a tiny shake. Either her friend viewed her brother through a lens of sisterly blindness, or his behaviour with a chance-met stranger was quite different from his treatment of his family.

Still, even a chance-met stranger could have expected to be treated with more courtesy.

'You're frowning,' Susanna observed. 'Did Miles upset you? He…he can be abrupt.'

'Oh, no! I love being dismissed as empty-headed and frivolous.'

Susanna gave a peal of laughter. 'I'm afraid he does tend to view all females that way. He was probably impatient, on his way to some meeting or other. Since Papa turned over the running of the bank to him, he's had to shoulder a staggering amount of responsibility. But Papa says he's wonderfully competent and fully capable of taking charge, despite his young age.'

'Your papa must be young, too. I'm surprised he's ready to retire from business.'

'Some of his cronies want him to stand for Parliament. They're always in meetings, talking about boroughs and hustings and I don't know what. Getting elected seems to be somewhat complicated.'

'Not complicated—simpler, and fairer too, since the Reform Act passed. No more pocket boroughs that can be bought or controlled by…' At the slightly glazed look in her friend's eye, Laura squelched her enthusiasm about matters political and let the sentence trail off. 'But I dare say you've no interest in the inner workings of Parliamentary elections! Shall we discuss something else?'

'Something more pressing, like Lady Ashdown's upcoming ball?' Susanna said. 'I must admit, I view the prospect with as much dread as anticipation.'

Shaking her head, Laura took her friend's hand. 'You really mustn't let the old beldams intimidate you. Hold your head up, smile and show you believe you've a right to be among them—as you do!'

'The society doyennes are frightening enough. But the gentlemen...' Susanna's sentence trailing off, she sighed. 'I find them even more alarming. The top-lofty ones terrify me so much I can't manage to utter a word. And I never know how to respond to the ones who are *gallant*. Sometimes I wish I'd just refused Lady Bunting's offer to sponsor me. Except Mama would have been so disappointed. Between you and me, I don't care whether or not I make the great match she hopes for. But I did promise to do my best, so I suppose I must continue on until the bitter end.'

'Wise of you not to be anxious to make a match,' Laura said approvingly. 'You are young yet, very lovely and possessed of a handsome dowry. You've no need to accept the first offer that comes your way. You should refrain from marrying unless or until you meet a gentleman with whom you feel you could be happy for a lifetime. I know I shall not be forced into a choice. No matter how many Seasons I must remain on the Marriage Mart!'

The more Seasons, the better, she thought. Her indulgent papa, in no hurry to see her married, allowed her far more liberty to pursue her mathematical interests than a spouse likely would. To say nothing of the demands that would be imposed by acquiring a husband and children.

'The beautiful daughter of a marquess will always be able to take her pick,' Susanna was saying. 'Though I am just the offspring of a humble banker, I intend to be equally discriminating.'

'With your whole life's happiness dependent on choosing wisely, I should hope you plan to be discriminating!' Laura retorted.

Susanna grinned. 'When one can barely manage to speak a word to gentlemen, it does make it easier to discourage them. So perhaps my social ineptitude has its advantages.'

'It won't be an advantage when you meet the gentleman you do wish to encourage.' After studying her friend, Laura shook her head. 'You must conquer your shyness. Learn what to say, how to communicate without speaking—even to flirt.'

Her eyes widening in dismay, Susanna said, 'I wouldn't wish to be forward!'

'Not forward. You just need to know how to converse with eligible gentlemen. How to politely depress the attentions of ones who don't attract you and encourage those who do. Also, how to stand up to those who would try to intimidate you, gentlemen or ladies.'

'Not being gentry-born, I'll never be truly accepted by the *ton*,' Susanna said. 'Which is the main reason I wasn't keen to have a Season and would rather not marry a titled gentleman. My fortune might be prized, but my person would be disdained.'

Having been recently disdained herself, Laura felt that remark strike home. Frowning to shake off the memory of her encounter with Susanna's brother, she said, 'You simply ignore the discourteous and concentrate on those who treat you kindly. And with those gentlemen, you really do need to be able to carry on a pleasant conversation. Besides, knowing what to say and when will make attending social events a pleasure, rather than something you dread. Even if you don't end up finding the man you wish to marry.'

'Shall we stop by Hatchard's after we visit the dressmaker and purchase me a book of instructions?' Susanna asked, laughing. 'I doubt such a thing exists!'

Laura grinned. 'No need to visit Hatchard's. I shall teach you. I can't always be around when you go into society, and I don't want you to feel uncomfortable ever again.'

'I do admire how you always seem to know just what to say to everyone! But can such skills be taught?'

'Of course. Now, I don't mean to imply that I know *everything*—but I have learned a few useful techniques after weathering my first Season! For instance, there are certain conventions—ways of holding a fan and the language of flowers—that allow you to send and receive messages without saying a word. Then there are general situations to which you can practise the appropriate responses, so that the correct reply comes to you automatically, without your having to think about it. A very helpful skill, I can assure you!'

'It would be wonderful to feel more at ease in company,' Susanna admitted. 'Do you really think you can teach me?'

'Absolutely! Are you free this afternoon?' At Susanna's nod, Laura said, 'I am as well. I shall have to return home briefly after our shopping expedition, but after that I could return here and we could begin this very day. With Lady Ashdown's ball only two nights away, there's no time to lose! After a bit of practice, you'll be ready to take on the *ton*!'

Susanna shuddered. 'I quail at the prospect. But if you truly wouldn't mind, I would be vastly grateful. Imagine not having to dread every encounter with a Lady Arbuthnot or a Lord Sinclair! Or Miss Arsdale or Miss Wentworth.' She added the names of two of the most elegant—and snobbish—diamonds of the current Season.

'All are best avoided, if possible. But if you must meet them, we shall prepare you something appropriate to say. Now, if we're to have time for a lesson later, we should skip having tea and head to the dressmaker immediately. We don't want to rush through choosing fashions.'

'That endeavour I can genuinely enjoy,' Susanna said. 'I'll run upstairs to get my pelisse, summon my maid and meet you back here directly.'

'Excellent. I spied some pale green crepe when I visited the modiste last week that I think would look wonderfully on you. I can't wait for you to see it.'

After giving her a quick hug, Susanna hurried out. Laura gazed after her, smiling faintly. Some in Society questioned why she'd chosen to befriend a banker's daughter with nothing to recommend her save a vast dowry. As unimpressed by grand titles as she was by centuries of breeding that often produced self-important individuals of great pride and little compassion, Laura couldn't understand how any sensible person could not be beguiled by Susanna Rochdale's sweetness, innocence and gentle charm.

With the two close friends she'd made in her debut Season unavailable—Lady Margaret D'Aubignon banished to the country and Eliza Hasterling more often than not preoccupied by family concerns—Laura had been drifting through her second Season bored and lonely. She'd been immediately drawn to Susanna's shy smile, and the genuine friendship that soon blossomed between them was brightening what she'd feared would be a sad, dull Season like the first daffodils of spring bring cheer at the end of a long dreary winter. To be able to repay that warmth by equipping her friend to better deal with the Society into which she'd been thrust would be a delight.

She had a sudden memory of a pair of icy, mocking blue eyes. Tutoring Susanna might mean more encounters with her dismissive brother. While preparing her friend to face Society, perhaps Laura ought to prepare herself by coming up with a conversational way to wipe the condescending look off Miles Rochdale's handsome face.

A few hours later, Miles walked back from his office to return the book he'd borrowed to the parlour. As his hand touched the door latch, he paused, remembering his encounter from this morning.

It wasn't often that a lovely young lady fell into one's arms. For a startled moment, he'd simply gazed at her.

She'd been well worth gazing at. A gamine, heart-shaped face, eyes bluer than a summer sky in June, blonde curls that the sunlight streaming through the glass transom over the entry door had shot through with silver and a deliciously curved figure… He might push himself, working tirelessly for long hours, but he was still a man, and couldn't help his automatic response to such feminine beauty.

Fortunately, before he'd become too enraptured, she'd looked up at him and smiled—a teasing, tempting sort of smile he remembered all too well. A smile that had made his heart contract painfully and stabbed him in the gut, calling up the bitter memories he thought he'd put well behind him.

Lady Laura might be blonde rather than brunette, tall rather than petite, but that practised look she'd fixed on him had been designed to allure, just as Arabella's had been. On his guard now, had she not needed his help to recover her balance, he would have shoved her away.

At the same moment, he realised this tempting damsel must be the Marquess's daughter who had unaccountably taken up his sister. He frowned again at the thought.

She looked the part of an elegant young Society lady. He didn't know much about feminine fashion, but even he recognised costly fabric and expert tailoring when he saw it. Her mass of golden hair had been pinned up in elaborate curls, exposing dainty ears that sported expensive sapphire drops, their blue hue echoed in a matching necklace and bracelet.

Fortunately, this time he encountered a Society charmer, he was older, less impressionable and on his guard.

He'd probably been rude, he thought with a sigh, but he hated the idea of his sister spending time with a woman like that. Bad enough that Mother had lunged at the chance when an old friend whose husband had been ennobled had offered to present Susanna to Society. He'd tried, without success, to talk his mother out of accepting Lady Bunting's offer. The last thing he wanted was for his sweet sister to be dazzled by one of the idle sprigs of gentility whose fathers came into the bank needing loans to fund their extravagances.

All those men were gentlemen—of a sort—and he'd insisted that Susanna be well-chaperoned, so he didn't fear she'd come to any physical harm. But he knew only too well how, out of boredom and a desire to pursue some novelty, an aristocrat might encourage her, trifle with her affections and end up breaking her heart when he lost interest and abandoned her.

Arabella had done a masterful job on him.

Naïve, trusting and dazzled as he'd been, it hadn't taken much encouragement for him to fall for her. To believe the relationship she'd beguiled him into was genuine when on her part it had been all pretence, a mere toying with him to practise her charms. His face flushed again in anger and remorse as he recalled her scornful rejection of the offer he'd thought she'd invited and desired.

But in his sister's situation it would be worse if, intent on securing Susanna's dowry to fund a life of idle indulgence, some aristocratic suitor *did* convince her to wed. Such a marriage could only mean misery for her, always an outsider in the world of the husband who'd ignore her while he frittered away her money on cards, gambling, horses, finery and mistresses.

Miles had no idea why Lady Laura Pomeroy had decided to befriend his sister, a girl with no pretence of being gently bred. Likely as fickle as her masculine counterparts, she too could wound his gentle sister, dropping her after the newness of whatever had appealed to her about Susanna wore off.

Until it did, he was equally worried about the influence of this woman he knew his sister admired. He didn't want Lady Laura turning his sister into a vain, frivo-lous Society debutante, a self-centred flirt who played with men's hearts.

Much as he wanted to discourage the friendship, he wasn't sure how to go about it. Looking up to Lady Laura as she did, Susanna was sure to defend the woman if he tried to disparage her.

Sighing again, Miles walked into the parlour and put the book back on the shelf. He just wanted his little sister to marry a man of her own class who would value her for herself, take care of her, make her happy and keep her safely among her own kind. If he had to, he might force himself to go out into the *ton* he normally avoided in order to watch over Susanna and make sure she was not beguiled by some aristocratic ne'er-do-well like the many he'd encountered during his years at Oxford.

And at the same time, prevent her from being led into copying the attitudes and habits of her would-be *ton* friend.

Chapter Two

Miles was about to return to his office and finish going over the ledgers before heading to the bank when he saw their butler ushering Susanna back into the house. He paused, smiling, while she hurried towards him, followed by her maid carrying a number of boxes. Catching her in a fond hug, he leaned over to kiss her cheek.

'Hello, Sunshine! You've been shopping with your friend, I see. I hope she hasn't led you into too much extravagance.'

'Never! Lady Laura advises that I purchase only the minimum number of gowns required to make an acceptable appearance. Styles change quickly, she says, and, even if I avoid following every whim of current fashion, some of my purchases will doubtless seem so outmoded by next Season, I won't wish to wear them again. She's quite right in believing it wasteful to buy too many.'

'Lady Laura advised prudence and economy?' he asked, surprised.

'Yes. Despite her elevated birth, she's quite down to earth and sensible.'

Miles bit back the reply that she'd played the part well

so far, but it was early days to believe her the repository of all virtue. He had to admit, though, insincere as her advice might have been, it was sound.

'She's not at all frivolous or self-absorbed.' Susanna angled her head and gave him a look of reproof. 'Which, however, is apparently what you implied when you met her. Were you going to tell me about it?'

Annoyed, Miles said, 'Did she come whining to you about how I treated her?'

'No, she did not—and what an unhandsome thing to say!' Susanna tossed back. 'You seem to have taken a dislike to her, though I can't imagine why!'

'I didn't dislike her,' he fibbed, telling himself that admitting his prejudice wouldn't help accomplish his aim of distancing his sister from the woman. 'I didn't mean to seem unfriendly, if in fact I was, but I was... preoccupied.'

To his relief, that explanation seemed to satisfy his sister. Her smile returning, she squeezed his hand. 'I knew that must be why you seemed uncivil! I imagine you must head to the bank soon, but walk me to my room, won't you? I must change before Lady Laura returns to join me.'

Wasn't one visit today enough? Miles thought, irritated by the idea of his sister spending yet more time with the lady. But, offering his arm and a smile, he said, 'I'd be delighted to escort the loveliest lady in London.'

'Flatterer,' Susanna said, smiling affectionately at him as they headed down the hall towards the stairs. 'Lady Laura has been such a help, befriending me when most of the *ton*'s young ladies barely deign to acknowledge my existence. I would so like the two of you to be friends.'

When pigs fly, Miles thought. But returning her smile, he said, 'Anyone who makes my little sister happy, I must approve.'

'I believe I'll be even happier after some lessons.'

'Lessons? What sort of lessons? You are perfect as you are.'

As they turned the corner and started up the stairs, Susanna squeezed his arm. 'You are far too indulgent, dear brother! You know how tongue-tied I become in company. Or you would, if I could ever convince you to go into Society with me. I know you encountered indifference, even hostility, from the aristocrats you met at Oxford, and I expected to face the same. Lady Bunting, as you know, is not very discerning and seems oblivious to slights, but I feel them keenly. I'm not so brave as you. They make me uncomfortable, and I never know what to say or do.'

His anger igniting, Miles said, 'There's no need for you to be made uncomfortable! If Society isn't wise enough to welcome and appreciate you, we shall just tell Lady Bunting that you have no further desire to participate in it.'

'We could tell her that, but after all her kind efforts on my behalf, it would be most discourteous. Mama would be so disappointed, too, if I were to withdraw now. And I would feel like…like I'd let myself be defeated by those whose approval I neither seek nor value. No, better that I become equipped to master to the situation.'

'Ah, you plan to fight back. How do you propose to do that, my brave warrior? With swords hidden in your skirts? Pistols in your reticule?'

'Nothing so violent. Proper words and appropriate manners will suffice,' Susanna said.

'How do you mean to acquire those? Lady Bunting is the soul of kindness, but she isn't very clever. I can't see her being of much assistance.'

'No, she's of no use whatsoever. Which is why I was thrilled when Lady Laura offered to teach me how to act and what to say when some Society person makes slighting remarks or ignores me.' Susanna gave him a mischievous look. 'Just as important, she will teach me how to respond to gentleman who show interest in me. How to subtly encourage or discourage them. In short, I'm going to learn how to flirt!'

The very idea confirming his worst fears, Miles had to bite his tongue not to voice his dismay. Trying to keep his voice light, he said, 'Lord protect us! You are dangerous enough as it is. Flirting is the last thing you need to learn. I shall lock you in your room if necessary to prevent it.'

Susanna punched his arm. 'Silly! You must acknowledge that it will be very useful for me to be at ease and feel confident about my ability to respond to gentlemen. I want to appear calm, poised and self-assured. Not as cowed or intimidated as I truly feel, and certainly not tongue-tied. Practising conversation will relieve much of my anxiety so I can, as Lady Laura said, enjoy my time in Society rather than just endure it. In any event, she's returning this afternoon to give me my first lesson.'

'You're sure I can't talk you out of this?' Miles asked as he escorted her through the door into her chamber.

Susanna shook her head. 'Indeed not. It's the best idea I've heard since I felt obligated to agree to a Season,' she replied, halting beside her dressing table.

Looking suddenly thoughtful, she studied him. 'You could benefit from some tips yourself, you know. You and Charlotte have known each other practically since the cradle, and you treat her almost the same as you do me. I know nothing official has been set yet, but everyone expects you'll probably end up married. She deserves to have a little wooing before she settles down to married life.'

'Yes, we've been acquainted for ever—which is an advantage. We're both sensible and know what to expect. There's no need for flowery speeches or extravagant emotional displays or any of that romantic nonsense.'

'Romantic nonsense?' Susanna echoed. 'Surely you don't intend to treat matrimony as if it were one of your banking transactions?'

'It's the best way to regard it. An investment of time and attention that yields benefits of comfort and stability for both parties.'

Susanna shook her head wonderingly. 'I can't believe you would reduce marriage to a prosaic exchange of value! Well, here's hoping you fall desperately in love and are made to eat your words!'

He'd thought himself desperately in love once—and suffered the consequences. He wasn't likely to volunteer for the experience again.

No, he'd make a sensible alliance with a woman of his own class whom he knew well and respected. And leave falling in love to the rash or foolish.

'I hope you, little sister, will make a match with a kind gentleman who will cherish and provide for you rather than strike dramatic poses while reciting bad verse in honour of your eyebrows.'

'One doesn't have to preclude the other,' she countered.

'Perhaps not,' he said, unwilling to fight her on this

point. He'd rather prevail on a much more important one—the proposed lessons with Lady Laura. 'Since you know so much about this courting business, why do you need to have lessons?'

She rolled her eyes at him. 'Knowing about it and being able to confidently participate in it are two different things! If I am to attract the kind gentleman who will cherish and provide for me, I shall probably need to be able to converse with him. Not sit in his presence mute as a post.'

'If he is someone with whom you've been acquainted for some time, you'll already be easy with him,' he countered.

'Perhaps, but I can't envisage marrying any of the men I've encountered thus far.'

'You haven't set your cap on a title, I hope,' he said, trying to keep his tone light despite his dread of the prospect.

'I haven't set my cap on anyone in particular—yet,' she said, sitting at her dressing table and picking up her hairbrush. 'But when I do meet the man whom I wish to court me, I want to know how to encourage him. And flirt,' she said, giving him another mischievous look.

Miles pressed his lips together to keep from making a sharp retort. He truly didn't want her learning anything from Lady Laura, but pushing any harder against the plan would be more likely to annoy than persuade her. Even though the prospect of having the Marquess's daughter turn his sister into a copy of Arabella nearly made him physically ill.

He'd been considering escorting her in Society to protect her from that possibility. Maybe he should seize the excuse she'd offered and agree to attend the lessons. Not to learn how to woo sensible Charlotte, of course, but to judiciously counter Lady Laura's instructions.

Even though the last thing he wanted was to expose himself to more of the lovely blonde Society beauty's practised charm. He was wise enough now to resist her allure, he assured himself. And gentleman enough to resist the impulse to lash out at her, no matter how much her advice might provoke him. He'd be courteous, attentive and prepared *subtly* to turn aside any recommendations that struck him as detrimental to his sister's character.

'Perhaps you're right,' he said at last. 'Maybe I should join your lessons.'

Susanna's eyes widened, her hands with the brush stilling. 'You will? I admit, I was only teasing, but that would be delightful! I see so little of you now. Are you sure you can spare the time?'

'What, spare the time to watch my little sister turn into a *femme fatale*?' he teased. 'How could I miss that?'

Susanna chuckled. 'Maybe my big brother will be turned into a *gallant*.'

Miles laughed. 'That's hardly likely.'

'It's more likely than shy little me becoming a *femme fatale*. But I'd love to share lessons with you! I like Laura so much, I want you to like her too. Spending time with her will be the best way for you to see just how lovely, clever and admirable she is.'

'If you say so,' he said drily. 'When are these lessons supposed to start?'

Susanna glanced at the mantel clock. 'Laura will return in an hour. We'll meet in the parlour. Can you join us there?'

He really needed to get to the bank, but he would

postpone that until after the 'lesson'. It was more important to stay home and safeguard his sister.

Despite the leap in his pulse when he considered the prospect, he was not, he told himself firmly, at all looking forward to seeing the beguiling Lady Laura again.

As Miles walked back down the stairs, apprehension swirled in his gut. What had he just got himself into?

He felt a sheen of sweat form on his brow as he headed into his office. Initially intending to go to his desk, he paused on the threshold, then detoured to the sideboard to pour himself a drink.

How was he to deflect Lady Laura's advice without appearing uncivil?

A sudden vision of her recurred in his memory…the feel of her slender arms under his hands, the warmth of her body almost touching his, the scent of roses rising from her golden curls. Once again, his body stirred.

Muttering a curse, he downed the drink in one swallow. Surely, maintaining his guard against her, he could resist that physical appeal?

He'd find out soon enough.

She'd be here in an hour.

At the thought, he refilled his glass.

Chapter Three

A little more than an hour later, Laura knocked on the door of the Rochdale townhouse. She'd dressed with care, changing into her least frilly and frivolous afternoon gown—not an easy task, given the current fashion for extravagant sleeves and an abundance of lace trimming. Though Susanna had said her brother was seldom at home, there was always a chance Laura might encounter him. She wanted to appear as sophisticated and mature as possible if she did.

Smiling at Haines, who took her pelisse and ushered her towards the parlour, she caught a glimpse of herself in the mirror over the hall table. With sleeves of moderate fullness gathered into cuffs at her wrist, a high collar and a trim shirtwaist skirt below her plain belted waist, she might pass as a governess—or a banking house clerk, she thought wryly.

Just as well she looked serious and intellectual. She hadn't yet thought of anything properly repressive to say to Miles Rochdale if she should meet him. Hopefully her plain garb would make a suitably sober impression while she waited for inspiration to strike.

She'd brought fans with her. Since Susanna had said she was often too intimidated to speak, Laura would start by acquainting her with a non-verbal form of communication. That should boost her confidence, after which they could move on to practise conversation.

Walking into the parlour, she began, 'Susanna! Are you ready…?'

The rest of the sentence froze on her lips as she spied not just her friend Susanna, but also her friend's brother rising to greet her.

Shock held her speechless—belying Susanna's recent praise that Laura always knew what to say in every situation. As she stood motionless, the potent wave of attraction that tingled through her as she gazed at Miles Rochdale proved her previous strong reaction to Susanna's brother was unfortunately not a fluke.

While she tried to master her unexpected response, Susanna came over to give her a hug and Miles Rochdale stood, making a game effort to smile. A moment later, the automatic words of courtesy came to her lips, despite how unsettled she felt—reinforcing how useful it would be to teach Susanna to be able to rely on such conventions.

Despite the connection sizzling between them, somehow she sensed that Miles Rochdale's smile was as false as her own. But why was he here, if disliked her?

'Allow me to introduce you properly this time,' Susanna was saying. 'Lady Laura, may I present my brother, Miles Rochdale? Miles, Lady Laura Pomeroy.'

After bows and curtseys were exchanged, Susanna led Laura to the sofa. Fortunately for her still-shaken poise, Mr Rochdale settled in the wing chair beside it rather than take a seat next to her.

Even several feet away, she was still conscious of his disturbingly masculine presence.

Did he feel a similar pull towards her? A covert glance at his face gave no indication that she affected him as strongly.

Disgruntled, she told herself to stop acting like a looby and subdue her own responses.

After clearing his throat, Mr Rochdale said, 'Susanna tells me that you thought me rather uncivil at our first meeting. I apologise, as that was certainly not my intention. I can only plead my lamentable preoccupation with business matters. I do hope you will allow us to begin again.'

Laura hesitated, studying him. Though he appeared sincere enough, she was certain she'd not been mistaken in reading disdain, rather than preoccupation, in his attitude during their first encounter. Was he offering an olive branch to please his sister?

Whatever his reasons, civility demanded that she respond in kind. 'There's no need for apologies, Mr Rochdale. I'm sure you did not deliberately mean to give offence.'

Though her words were polite enough, she couldn't keep the scepticism from her tone. Susanna appeared not to notice, but Mr Rochdale raised an eyebrow.

Before he could reply to that—if indeed he intended to—Susanna said, 'Shall we have the tea we postponed this morning?'

'I would love some,' Laura replied, able to second that development with genuine enthusiasm. Turning to Mr Rochdale, she said, 'It was kind of you to take a moment from your busy schedule to apologise. Susanna tells me you are most occupied with business affairs, so please don't let me keep you.'

She smiled, expecting him to rise and take his leave. Instead, he said, 'I should like a spot of tea myself.'

Her smile faded, a tiny frown taking its place. He was determined to be sociable, then. Did he genuinely want to redeem himself with her?

His expression was genial enough when she was looking directly at him. But when she gave him a glance from the corner of her eye while her friend poured tea, the welcoming expression was replaced by something quite different, something almost—watchful? She couldn't quite put a name to it. But she also couldn't dispel the feeling that, however pretty his speech might be, Miles Rochdale still regarded her with disfavour.

While she, silly creature that she was, was having a hard time resisting the attraction that made her want to smile at him, converse with him, engage his interest.

A pox on him, she thought, taking a gulp of tea so hot she nearly choked on it. Very well, his handsome person attracted her—nothing unusual about that. Any observant woman would respond to a virile, compelling male. She'd indulge herself by appreciating his masculine beauty for the duration of their tea, then dismiss him and his subtle censure from her mind.

She truly wasn't used to encountering disapproval. Hopefully, enduring it for the time required to take tea would cure her of this unsuitable attraction.

Turning to Susanna, she said, 'As you can see, I've brought some props. I had intended to begin the lesson at once, but we can wait until after our tea.'

'That shouldn't be necessary,' Susanna said, setting down her cup. 'In fact, I've convinced Miles to stay for the lesson too—if his presence wouldn't inconvenience you. As you've seen—' she gave her brother a fond glance '—

Miles tends to be altogether too serious, entirely focused on his work and often impatient with polite conventions. There's a young lady both families expect him to wed, a lovely girl he's known since she was a child. The match hasn't been formalised yet, and I for one believe it might never be unless he can learn to treat her more like a beloved than a second sister! I believe he's in even greater need of lessons in courtship than I am.'

Was Miles Rochdale to join their lessons? Once again caught off-guard, Laura's gaze flew to that gentleman.

His expression carefully neutral, Miles said, 'That assessment is a bit overly dramatic, Susanna. I suppose it wouldn't hurt me to pick up some pointers on how to please a lady.'

If his treatment of her was any indication, he could certainly benefit from some lessons. But she found it hard to believe so driven and business-absorbed a gentleman really wanted them.

Was he participating to encourage his sister?

Trying not to frown, Laura shook her head, unable to decide what Miles Rochdale's motivation might be.

'You wouldn't mind, would you?' Susanna repeated, looking anxious now.

Laura would rather not have Rochdale remain, not wishing to spend any more time than necessary in his disturbing presence. But she couldn't think of a polite way to exclude him.

'Would his presence not…inhibit you?' she asked Susanna, grasping for an excuse.

'Not at all!' Susanna replied. 'It would add to my enjoyment, actually. It will be fun to watch my oh-so-serious brother practise light-hearted flirtation. And I won't feel quite so self-conscious if I am not the only one learning. Besides, I could practise on him.'

'I would like to participate…if it wouldn't *inhibit* you, Lady Laura.'

Laura gave Mr Rochdale a penetrating look. Did she detect an undercurrent of a quite different meaning in his deceptively mild tone? Or was it only the suspicion she was unable to shake that he'd not confessed his true reason for wanting to join their session?

'You fear I may try to turn your sister into a hopeless flirt and wish to prevent it?' she guessed.

The sudden widening of his eyes confirmed that she'd scored a hit. Quickly recovering his countenance, Rochdale said, 'I don't believe Susanna could ever become a hopeless flirt.'

No matter how much you tried to make her one… She heard the unspoken remainder of his sentence.

A laughing Susanna spared her making any reply. 'Lady Laura knows me well enough to realise the best she can hope for is to coax me out of being hopelessly shy.'

Nettled, Laura said, 'I don't know that I could teach you anything you'd find useful, Mr Rochdale, but if you wish to remain I have no objection.'

Since she couldn't get rid of him, she'd focus on Susanna and try to ignore Rochdale's disconcerting presence. Turning to her friend, she said, 'I thought we would begin with the fans.'

'Ah, yes. You mentioned studying the language of the fan.'

'It's quite useful to be able to communicate without having to employ words. It can ease you into interacting with gentlemen, sparing you the worry of what you have to say.'

'And men understand this means of communication?' Rochdale said sceptically.

'*Gentlemen* do,' Laura said, irked into placing a slight emphasis on the word. 'It would hardly be useful as a means of communication if they did not.'

'I suppose not,' Rochdale allowed. 'Although I'm not sure Charlotte has any more knowledge of fan language than my sister does.'

'Perhaps not,' Susanna said. 'But, if I can convince you to accompany me into Society occasionally, it would be useful for you to know what the ladies are trying to communicate to you. After all, they cannot help but admire my handsome brother.'

'An admiration that would be short-lived once they learned who I am—a man without title or pedigree.'

The sudden bitterness that passed swiftly over his countenance belied the light tone of his remark. Had someone in Society disparaged Miles Rochdale, as he had her upon their first meeting? Laura wondered. That might explain the disapproval she sensed.

She searched for something appropriate to reply—for, however harsh the observation, it was essentially true. With her great dowry and genteel manners, his commoner sister was accepted, if not welcomed, by the highest sticklers in Society. But despite the Rochdale wealth, her brother the banker would never be considered a gentleman or an eligible match for any of the gently born maidens on the Marriage Mart. And therefore would likely be snubbed if he approached any of them.

By the stricken look on her face, Susanna belatedly realised that too.

'Do not fret for me, little sister,' Miles said gently. 'If you should tease me into attending some Society event, I shall not attempt to charm the ladies. I'll remain safely with the men of my acquaintance and observe you from afar.'

'Shall we begin?' Laura said, wanting to soothe the troubled look from her friend's face.

'Yes, let's,' Susanna said, her countenance clearing.

'It might be best if you fetched one of your own fans,' Rochdale said. 'So you can practise and become comfortable with the one you'd actually be using.'

'Perhaps you are right,' Susanna said. 'I could ring for Betsy to bring me one, but it's probably faster for me to run up and get one myself. I don't want to waste time, yours or Lady Laura's.'

Turning to Laura, she said, 'I'll have Haines wait just outside the door, so there will be no impropriety in you remaining here with Miles.'

'Knowing Haines is within call will prompt me to contain my ardour,' Rochdale said drily.

Laughing, Susanna batted her brother on the arm. 'As well it should, wretch. Though Lady Laura would inspire any man with ardour.'

Laura was about to reply that she was certain she had no such effect on Mr Rochdale, until she caught him observing her with an unmistakably heated glance before, catching her eye, he looked quickly away.

Shaken, she vaguely heard Susanna chatter something as she hurried away. Maybe Miles Rochdale did feel the current vibrating between them she sensed so strongly. Would he *want* to attempt some impropriety with her?

She felt again the burn of his hands gripping her wrists. What would it feel like to have those strong arms wrapped around her? Those stern lips brushing hers?

A shiver of excitement rippled through her before she

could squelch it. Feeling her face heat, she chastised herself as an idiot. Why should she wish to be embraced by a man who, despite his apology, still disapproved of her?

Of all the attractive men in the world, why did she have to be drawn to Miles Rochdale?

'Hurry back,' Miles was saying to his sister. 'I want to stay for your lesson, but I do need to get back to the bank this afternoon.'

A tense silence fell after Susanna's exit. Avoiding her gaze, Rochdale made no attempt to speak. All too conscious of Rochdale's physical presence, once again Laura found her usual ability to make polite conversation had deserted her.

Finally, Rochdale looked back at her. 'I hope you will not encourage my sister to be too flirtatious.'

Ah, so he did worry about her influence.

'You don't wish her to be turned into a frivolous, empty-headed flirt?' *Like me*, she left unsaid.

The disparaging look he gave her said he was thinking exactly that. 'In a word, yes. Susanna is the soul of sweet gentleness. Any man worthy of her will be captivated by her charm and innocence and appreciate her just as she is. My acquaintance with Society is admittedly limited but, from what I've observed, it could gain from more ladies of genuine character and fewer who try to ensnare every man they meet whether they are interested in him or not. Why would I want her to have lessons that might turn her into someone like that? Besides, men don't like women who chatter and scheme.'

Ensnare every man? Chatter and scheme? Holding on to her temper, she said, 'Mr Rochdale, I don't know much about banking and finance. But if a man is thinking of making an investment, isn't it wise for him to know the terms, understand how the investment works and estimate what his return should be before he invests his capital?'

He gave her a puzzled look, as if baffled by the turn of the conversation. 'Y-yes,' he said slowly. 'It's never wise to throw money into a scheme without fully understanding the terms.'

'It isn't wise for your sister to navigate through an environment *she* doesn't understand. Of course, a man worthy of her will appreciate her just as she is. But the best of the gentlemen will have many young ladies competing for their attention, and sweetness alone may not be enough to catch their eye. For that deserving young man to discover her, she needs to be able to engage him in conversation and attract him in other ways. Unless you are content to have her pursued only for her dowry?'

'That's precisely the sort of attention I don't want her to receive,' he said vehemently.

'Then she needs the skills and confidence to encourage the men she wants—and discourage the fortune hunters she doesn't.'

The sound of Susanna's light step in the hallway put an end to their sharp exchange. Rochdale regarded her thoughtfully—not looking convinced, but no longer quite so dismissive.

'I fetched my favourite fan to bring me luck. Shall we begin?'

Nodding, Laura picked up one of her own fans. 'We'll start with the simplest gestures.' Touching the fan to her right cheek, she continued, 'This is "yes" and this—'she touched the fan to her left cheek '—is "no".'

While Susanna practised, Laura said, 'For instance, if a gentleman suggested everyone in your company get refreshments, then looked at you as if in invitation, you could signal silently whether or not you wished him to escort you. Sparing you the discourtesy, and him the embarrassment, of a verbal offer and refusal.'

'I suppose that could be useful,' Rochdale admitted.

'Even better, if the gentleman truly attracts you—which would be sure to inspire you with excitement and nervousness—you could signal your interest without trying to say something clever, and in your agitation trip over your words.'

'Now that would truly be helpful!' Susanna said.

'Should you see a young man you wish to know better, you can do this,' Laura said, holding the fan in her left hand before her face.

'Which means?' Rochdale said.

'I should like to be acquainted; come talk with me.'

Susanna giggled. 'Very helpful—except I shall not be able to employ that until you have tutored me in what to say!'

'Soon enough,' Laura said, smiling.

Over the next hour, Laura showed Susanna a dozen other fan gestures, signalling everything from "we are being watched" to "forgive me" to "we shall be friends". She had her friend practise the motions, then had her ploy the fan and have her brother interpret what she was trying to convey.

Not at all to Laura's surprise, Mr Rochdale learned the gestures quickly.

'Enough for today,' she said after a thorough practice session. 'I think you have a large enough repertoire to feel more comfortable at Lady Ashdown's soiree. At our next lesson, we'll practise some phrases you can use when you encounter those banes of your existence—

the Society doyennes, top-lofty gentlemen and snobbish young ladies.'

'Do you intend to teach her how to counter discourtesy?' Rochdale asked.

'Knowing how to do so—politely—is just as important as knowing how to treat gentlemen,' Laura said. 'She should be able to hold her own—graciously. Not allowing anyone to intimidate or disparage one without being shrill or unpleasant is a vital skill—for all of us.'

'I'd like that lesson tomorrow, if you can spare the time,' Susanna said. 'I'll need that expertise at Lady Ashdown's ball too.'

'I have a few hours free tomorrow afternoon, if that is convenient for you.'

'I'm supposed to make calls with Mama, but this is more important.' Turning to her brother, she said, 'You won't need this lesson.'

'No, I can't imagine Mr Rochdale ever allowing anyone to intimidate him,' Laura said drily.

He gave her an imperious glance. 'Certainly not.'

'The privilege of the male! A female can't confront such situations directly. She must always act obliquely, with courtesy and deference.'

'You could observe the lesson,' Susanna said. 'Then help me practise. You could play the part of the disdainful one.'

'A part he could play to perfection,' Laura said, unable to help herself.

Susanna giggled. 'Yes, I imagine he could.'

Avoiding Rochdale's eyes after her impertinent remark, Laura said, 'I must be going. Papa is expecting me to serve him afternoon tea.'

She rose, Susanna rising with her to give her a hug.

'How can I ever thank you? I already feel much more assured.'

With a challenging look at Rochdale, Laura said, 'When we're finished, you'll have the confidence you deserve, a self-assurance that matches your looks and charm.'

Rochdale trailed them to stand at the threshold of the parlour. Laura bade him farewell, then walked arm in arm with Susanna to the front door, where Haines returned her pelisse and sent a footman to summon a hackney. After a final goodbye, she walked out...feeling Rochdale's gaze still fixed on her.

Hopefully she'd given him something to think about. If he was fair-minded, he'd recognise her aim was to equip his sister to be better appreciated and less likely to be slighted by Society.

If he recognised that, maybe he'd no longer consider her just a frivolous, empty-headed Society girl.

Chapter Four

Despite her resolve to think no more about Rochdale, Laura realised when the hackney jerked to a halt that she had spent the whole journey to Mount Street brooding over her encounters with the banker's son.

Enough! she chided herself. So Miles Rochdale didn't approve of her and implied she would be a bad influence on his sister. She'd met more handsome—and equally disdainful—men before. She'd simply concentrate on helping Susanna and dismiss the irksome Mr Rochdale from further consideration.

And if her nerves still vibrated with awareness, it was only because she hadn't recently encountered a man who'd stirred her senses as he did. Soon enough, the image of another handsome gentleman would distract her.

She banished the unwelcome observation that, in her year and a half in Society, she had not yet been so distracted. She just needed to be more observant, she concluded.

Dismissing the hackney, she walked up the entry stairs and was ushered inside by their elderly butler.

'Thank goodness you've returned, Lady Laura. It's coming on to rain, and you wouldn't want to catch a chill.'

She smiled at the old man, who had been butler to her mother's family and had doted on Mama when she'd been growing up. After her mother's death from an infection of the lungs following the carriage accident that had gravely injured both her parents, the man had grown particularly protective. 'Thank you for your concern, Ridley. But, as you can see, I'm quite warm and dry. Is Papa in his study?'

'His Lordship is resting in his chamber.'

The ever-present concern reviving, Laura said anxiously, 'How is he?'

The butler patted her shoulder. 'No worse than usual, my lady. He said to tell you not to worry, he was just tired and would be down to join you for dinner. You're to attend the Harrisons' rout tonight, I believe. What time shall I tell Cook to have dinner served so you will be ready when Lady Swanston arrives to collect you?'

She'd forgotten about the Harrisons' rout. Laura knew, the hostess being a high stickler, that Susanna hadn't been invited. Still vaguely out of sorts after the meeting with Rochdale, Laura didn't particularly feel like making herself agreeable to Lady Harrison and her equally discriminating friends.

Knowing her father had been uncomfortable enough to take to his bed that afternoon decided her. 'I'm about to write Lady Swanston a note to tell her I wish to spend the evening with Papa.' Fully aware of her father's condition, Lady Swanston, her chaperon and her late mother's best friend, would understand without needing any further explanation why she'd suddenly cancelled their evening plans.

Ridley needed no further explanation either. Nodding, he said, 'I'll send Jackson up straight away to fetch it. Speaking of notes, one arrived for you this afternoon. I had Gibson take it up to your chamber.'

He'd said 'note', not 'invitation'. Curious about who might be writing to her, Laura said, 'Tell Mrs Arsby we'll dine at the usual time, and have Gibson come up in an hour to help me dress.'

'Very good, Lady Laura,' Ridley said, bowing.

Laura ran lightly up the stairs, then paused outside her father's chamber. Uneasy, she felt urged to check on him. But if he were sleeping, she didn't want to disturb him, and Ridley had said he was doing no worse than usual.

After an irresolute moment, she continued to her own chamber. There wouldn't be much she could do for him anyway, so better to let him rest. She would see him soon enough at dinner.

Once in her chamber, she quickly penned a note to her chaperon, finishing just as the footman rapped on her door. The note handed over, she sat back with a sigh.

Lady Swanston would be disappointed that she'd pulled out of the evening's entertainment, Laura thought guiltily. Fortunately, her chaperon's sunny disposition never remained cast down for long. After a short time at the rout, being entertained by her friends and cronies, that kind lady's spirits would revive, Laura reassured herself.

Much more eager than Papa for Laura to marry, Lady Swanston welcomed every opportunity for her charge to meet eligible gentlemen. Though Laura didn't imagine, with the Season already well begun, that she would have been likely to meet at the rout tonight anyone she'd not already encountered.

And thus far she simply hadn't encountered any gentleman who'd attracted her enough to consider wedlock.

The image of a certain imperious gentleman with dark hair and ice-blue eyes flashed into her mind, sending that frisson of awareness through her again. Firmly, she dismissed it.

If she were to wed, she wanted more than a physical connection. She wanted an intellectual as well as an emotional bond, a spouse who would value the same pursuits she did—and allow her to continue them.

She didn't want to wed even an amiable man if it meant spending the rest of her life looking over the dinner table at a man who could talk of nothing but horses, hounds, cards and clubs. She'd established a possible connection with several political gentlemen but, though she had a lively interest in politics, that preoccupation was not her primary passion. She'd certainly never encountered a man who'd tempted her enough to forgo the realm of mathematical theory that fascinated her.

She was quite content to remain as she was. Her older brother's wife had already produced an heir and spare, providing the grandsons Papa craved and furnishing Laura with nieces and nephews to spoil whenever she wanted to visit their country estate, which her brother now managed. She had ample pin money to buy whatever apparel, theatre or concert tickets and books that appealed to her. There was pride and satisfaction in running their London household, managing the accounts and caring for her father.

If she sometimes felt she was missing *something*, she wasn't sure she truly wanted to find it. Her parents had made a love match and been devoted to each other. Losing her mother after the accident had been more devastating to her father than the injuries that still plagued him. No longer able to ride or drive without pain, he'd withdrawn from life, turning the running of the estates over to his son and remaining secluded in their London townhouse, where he occupied himself with his books and tending the plant collection that was his one remaining passion. Though he was as loving to Laura as ever, she had the sense that he was only partly with her, a vital part of him permanently lost.

If her life now didn't lift her to the heights of passion, neither did it plunge her to the depths of despair. She'd just as soon remain on that even keel.

Nodding in agreement with that resolution, Laura went to her dressing table and picked up the note Gibson had delivered. With a little cry of delight, she recognised her name written in Lady Margaret D'Aubignon's distinctive hand. Eager to read Maggie's news, she hurried to the wing chair before the hearth, breaking the seal as she took her seat.

She hadn't seen her good friend since near the end of the last Season when, after refusing to marry her father's candidate, she'd been banished by the Earl of Comeryn to their Somerset estate. As stubborn as her strong-willed father, Maggie had defied all the earl's efforts to force her to capitulate, bearing her punishment with cheerful determination. Knowing her friend, Laura suspected she would never cave in to her father's demands, even if it meant permanent exile.

Fortunately, much as Maggie loved London, she also loved riding, reading and life in the country and was fiercely devoted to protecting her gentle mother from her father's harshness. Her notes were always filled with amusing and sometimes outrageous observations on life and her activities. And in the last one she'd hinted that exciting developments might be forthcoming.

Hoping this note might illuminate that possibility, Laura unfolded the missive.

My dear Laura,
You will be surprised and I hope pleased to learn that Mama and I are now installed in Portman Square. I can't wait to see you and Eliza and tell you my latest news—and all about the plans I have for both of you!

Please reply by return note and let me know whether you can join us tomorrow morning at ten o'clock for tea. I'm so thrilled that we shall be together again!

Ever your dear friend,
Maggie

Leave it to Maggie to say just enough to leave her agog with curiosity. Going back to her desk, Laura took out paper and composed a quick note accepting the invitation, then rang for a footman to deliver it.

Had the Earl relented and allowed his wayward daughter to return to London? Based on her acquaintance with Comeryn, that seemed unlikely. Had something come up requiring the family to make a quick visit to town?

And what sort of plans was Maggie hatching that would involve Laura and Eliza?

She shook her head. It was well that she intended to read aloud to Papa tonight, else she'd have a hard time doing anything but speculating on what unusual course of action the irrepressible Maggie had embarked on now.

She'd just have to bear herself with patience until tomorrow.

Promptly at ten the following morning, Laura descended from a hackney in front of Comeryn House in Portman Square. About to go up the steps, she turned to see Eliza Hasterling alight from a carriage emblazoned with the arms of Eliza's married sister, Lady Dunbarton.

Smiling, she walked back to greet her friend. 'I'm so pleased to see you!' she exclaimed, giving Eliza a hug. 'I see you are still with your sister. Has Lady Dunbarton's youngest recovered from her putrid cold at last?'

'Not really,' Eliza said, linking her arm with Laura's as they strolled to the entry. 'Maria claimed she could not spare me, but there was no way I was going to refuse Maggie's invitation, especially when she dangled the hint of exciting news. Have you any idea what it might be?'

'None at all. But, as apparently both she and Lady Comeryn have returned to London, I'm hoping perhaps her father is allowing her to re-join Society. You haven't heard anything either?'

Pausing to wait for the butler to answer their knock, Eliza shook her head. 'Not a word since her last letter. I didn't get the least impression from it that she expected to return to town.'

'If she is able to stay, will you allow us to tear you away from your family at last?' Laura wagged a finger at her. 'Your father really shouldn't allow your sisters to impose upon you so.'

Eliza sighed. 'With Mama still preoccupied at home

with the youngest ones and Papa wrapped up in his work in the parish, both Maria and Penelope have only me to call upon when they need extra help.'

Laura raised her eyebrows. 'Lady Dunbarton employs two nursery maids and a nanny, and Mrs Needham has adequate staff as well.'

'I know, but they both say I have such a soothing effect on their children.'

The butler opened the door before Laura could utter a blighting reply—which was probably just as well. 'Lady Laura, Miss Hasterling, so good to see you again,' he said, ushering them in.

'Good to see you too, Viscering,' Laura said, smiling at the old retainer whom they'd grown to know well during their debut Season. As they handed their pelisses to the butler, she said to Eliza, 'If you are ever to have a home and family of your own, you need to spend more time in Society. Surely Lady Dunbarton understands that? She's supposed to be sponsoring you and assisting you to find a husband, not using you to augment her nursery staff.'

'There will be time for that, I suppose.'

Putting her lips together to keep from uttering any further criticism of family she felt took advantage of her gentle friend, Laura took a deep breath. 'Well, shall we see what exciting news Maggie has for us?'

A moment later they entered the morning room. With a beaming smile, Lady Margaret jumped up from the sofa and ran over to give them each a hug. 'Laura, Eliza, so happy to see you! Viscering, bring us tea, please,' she said as she ushered them back to the sofa before the snug fire.

'We're thrilled to see you again too,' Laura said. 'But

surprised. Has your father relented? I have to admit it doesn't seem in character.'

'I am still in awe of you, standing up to him as you did.' Eliza shuddered. 'He's so…disapproving and cold. Whenever he looked at me, I felt like a specimen under a microscope that he'd found particularly distasteful.'

'That sounds like my esteemed parent,' Maggie said drily. 'No, the earl did not relent. However, I managed to circumvent him.'

'I knew it, you clever thing!' Laura exclaimed. 'Tell, tell!'

'All in good time. First, you must both give me your news.'

While they waited for tea, and then as Maggie poured, Eliza related her sojourn with her older sister, whose ever-increasing brood seemed always to include one ill child who required a doting aunt's tender care. In her turn, Laura related meeting and befriending Susanna Rochdale who, she told them with a fond glance at Eliza, strongly reminded her of their friend.

'She's just as sweet and innocent as you, Eliza, and just as likely to let the arrogant of the *ton* intimidate or snub her. I've promised to give her lessons to help equip her with civil but appropriate remarks that, I hope, will lessen or eliminate that abuse.' Laura laughed. 'And to teach her how to flirt.'

'You mastered that art better than either of us last Season,' Eliza said with a smile.

'At least Eliza is gently born,' Maggie said. 'It can only be worse for Miss Rochdale, as the daughter of someone the *ton* would consider a *tradesman*. You may remember that Marcella, my brother Crispin's wife, suffered similar harassment when she was forced into a Society debut. "The Factory King's heiress", they called *her*. I will tell Mama about your Miss Rochdale. We must do what we can to help her.'

It was on the tip of Laura's tongue to tell them about her encounters with Miss Rochdale's handsome but disapproving brother. But though she could frame the account in humorous terms, thinking of Miles Rochdale still unsettled her enough that she feared the observant Maggie would notice.

She wasn't prepared to try to explain to anyone else the odd effect he produced in her. She didn't want to examine it too closely herself.

Better at present to reveal nothing. Accordingly, she said, 'We've been patient long enough, Maggie. Now you must tell us your news! I do hope it will include the announcement that you are able to remain for the rest of the Season.'

Maggie grinned. 'It will indeed.'

'Excellent!' Laura crowed, while Eliza clapped her hands. 'How did this transformation come about?'

'Well,' Maggie said, giving them a conspiratorial smile, 'After we arrived back at Montwell Glen last year, hoping to cheer me, I suppose, Mama reassured me that I should never be indigent, even if I didn't marry. Her aunt, she said, had left me a small bequest, which was on deposit with a London bank and not under my father's control. I'd had no idea, of course—my father certainly never told me and Mama only knew because she'd chanced to overhear the earl grumbling about what a burden I was and how he couldn't even touch that inheritance to offset what he was forced to expend on my maintenance.'

'That's wonderful news! Are you going to use that to fund the rest of this Season?' Laura asked.

'It's better than that. As soon as I learned of the fund's existence, I wrote to Crispin and asked him to investigate. Once he confirmed the amount, I deputised him to invest it for me in the most promising railway venture he could find. As you might expect, given his expertise, the investment flourished, returning several times the original sum.'

Bowing with a flourish, she said, 'You see before you now a woman of independent means. Never again will I have to subject myself to a man's authority, suffering the control of either a father or a husband!'

'The earl must be furious,' Laura said drily.

'Apoplectic,' Maggie confirmed with a grin. 'He tried to forbid my coming to London, refusing to give me transport or to allow me to stay here in Comeryn House.'

'You are here against his wishes?' Eliza said on a gasp. 'How did you dare? This is his property! He could have you cast into the street if he wished!'

'Wouldn't he just love to?' Maggie said. 'But you mustn't worry. I assured the earl that I was perfectly happy to arrange my own transport and would hire a house in London for Mama and me to live in—permanently.' She paused. 'When he failed to stare me down, he knew I meant it.'

'So he let you come?' Eliza breathed.

Maggie shrugged. 'Short of trying to drag me into my chamber and lock the door, he couldn't prevent me. As I'd had the foresight to come to the interview armed with my riding whip, he decided not to attempt the dragging and locking in this time.'

Before an alarmed Laura could ask if he'd done so

before, Eliza said, 'So you are only staying here until you find your own house?'

'No, we shall likely remain at Comeryn House. Once the earl considered the matter, he realised it would cause a minor scandal—and a great deal of speculation in Society—if Mama and I resided anywhere else in London. In the end, he sent me a note, graciously allowing Mama and I to reside here. And so we shall, for the present anyway. Despite his treatment of me, I don't wish to embarrass Comeryn. Or, more importantly, make my mother the focus of gossip and conjecture.'

'So you are truly independent, just as you've always wished to be,' Laura said enviously. 'How lucky for you!'

'Do you never mean to marry?' Eliza asked. 'What of family, children of your own?'

'Marry? Why should I?' Maggie said. 'There will always be Marcella and Crispin's children to dote on— she's increasing, you know. And my sister Elizabeth's brats, if I can stomach being around their mother. If the price of having children would be living under the thumb of someone like Comeryn, then no thank you. I shall luxuriate in my new-found, blessed freedom.'

'Surely you don't believe all men are as…difficult as your father?' Eliza objected. 'What about your brother Crispin?'

'I concede, not all of them are as bad as the earl. But enough are that I do not wish to gamble my future on being lucky enough to end up with an amiable man. Besides, even if my husband were amiable, as a married woman any money or property I own becomes legally his—to fritter away if he choses! My own plans and desires would always be subordinate to his while I run his household, care for his children and follow his dictates, with no recourse even if he beat or abused me. I prefer the freedom I have now. A freedom, by the way, I am eager for you both to experience. Which brings me to The Plan.'

'Ah, yes, the mysterious "plan" you mentioned in your note,' Eliza said with a smile.

'How do you intend us to attain independence?' Laura asked. 'Sadly, neither of us has an obliging relative to leave us money for your brother to invest.'

'Yes, more's the pity. You will have to take the traditional road, at least initially. But even treading that path can lead to independence, if you follow my advice and choose wisely. At the end, you will have attained even more freedom than I possess!'

Freedom to do what she wanted—without marrying? Her initial amusement now sharpened into keen interest, Laura said, 'How?'

'Despite all the restrictions that hem women in, one category of female has quite a bit of liberty—a rich widow! No husband to control her wealth, none of the constraints on her behaviour to which a spinster who wishes to remain respectable must submit. The quickest way to that enviable destination is for each of you to marry a wealthy, obliging elderly gentleman. You might have to act the nursemaid for a few years, but at the end of that you will have funds which you control yourself, can possess property and make transactions on your own account. You may go where you wish, when you wish with whomever you wish, without oversight, interference or censure. As long as you are discreet, there will be very few limitations on your actions.

'Save for the inconvenience of having to suffer through several years of marriage, it provides the perfect outcome! Although you must at all costs avoid wedding a *nobleman*. Pride in their lineage and a status that allows them to do virtually whatever they wish makes almost all of them as arrogant, dictatorial and controlling as my father. Take a congenial commoner for husband and a short marital interlude could be tolerable. Especially when you consider all you will gain once you are finally free!'

Laura waited, expecting any moment for Maggie to burst into laughter, pleased at having taken them in with her joke. But her friend's expression remained earnest.

After exchanging an incredulous glance with Eliza, Laura said slowly, 'You are truly serious about this?'

'Indeed, yes. I would not joke about something as important as the future and happiness of my dearest friends.'

Laura shook her head, wanting to make sure she understood correctly. 'So you are proposing that we look about in Society for elderly widowers to entice into marriage, with the expectation that they will soon expire and leave us wealthy widows?'

Maggie nodded. 'Exactly.'

While Laura blew out a breath, Eliza said, 'I can't believe you would really encourage us to do something so...'

'So what?' Maggie countered. 'The whole purpose of the Marriage Mart is for a young lady to entice some eligible gentleman into marrying her. What's wrong with trying to attract an older, rather than a younger, gentleman?'

When, still shocked, neither could summon a reply, Maggie continued, 'Don't dismiss the idea out of hand. I shall be going about in Society looking for the most suitable candidates. You know I wouldn't press on you

anyone you might find distasteful! Consider the possibility—that's all I ask. And keep in mind the myriad
benefits! Promise me?'

Laura exchanged another dubious glance with Eliza,
who shrugged. 'I suppose we could consider it.'

Maggie reached out to press their hands. 'You must.
I do so want you to be safe, secure and happy!'

'We want that too,' Eliza said with a smile.

Laura smiled too, but her mind was racing. Would
it be so ridiculous to consider Maggie's suggestion? A
short-term husband that led to long-term security and
independence…if she could discover a kindly gentleman
such as the one Maggie had in mind…even if it meant
leaving passion behind?

The sudden vision of a pair of icy-blue eyes in a
strong, handsome face sent a shiver through her.

With resolution, she blotted out the image. Whether
she decided to follow Maggie's advice or not, businessman Miles Rochdale—who in any event was expected
to marry another woman—could never be a candidate
in any of her matrimonial schemes.

Chapter Five

Late the following afternoon, to his bemusement, Miles found himself riding in Hyde Park at the fashionable promenade hour, escorting his sister and her sponsor Lady Bunting in their open carriage. Lady Laura Pomeroy, mounted on a handsome bay mare, trotted close beside his gelding.

He was keenly aware just how close. This circuit of the park, he thought with an inward sigh, was providing an additional period of temptation of the sort he'd hoped to avoid.

Trying to ignore Lady Laura's appeal during his sister's lesson earlier that afternoon had been strain enough for one day. But upon learning that Susanna's sponsor wished to promenade her charge through the park that afternoon, Lady Laura had persuaded his sister not to cancel the event. Riding round Hyde Park, the Marquess's daughter pointed out, would provide an excellent opportunity for Susanna to practise the skills Lady Laura had just taught her in an environment where her interactions would be briefer and less intimidating than those occurring in a ballroom.

Miles hadn't intended to take part in the excursion. Despite his continual efforts to remind himself he disapproved of the friendship, he was still having a difficult time reining in his unfortunate response to a lady he continued to find far too attractive. But accompanied as it had been by a pleading glance from his sister, he'd found himself unable to refuse Susanna's request that he provide moral support by escorting them.

He hadn't been surprised that Lady Laura turned down Susanna's offer to ride with Lady Bunting in their carriage. An aristocrat's daughter would hardly wish to be seen by the *ton* travelling in a vehicle belonging to the plebeian Rochdales. If she deigned to appear at the park with his sister, she would doubtless want them to be driven in the Marquess's crested carriage, Lady Bountiful bestowing her largesse on a grateful charge.

He was surprised, though, when after politely thanking his sister for her offer, Lady Laura went on to say that after being cooped up indoors all day, she couldn't bear to be confined in a carriage. She would accompany them on horseback, even though the crowds at the promenade hour would make it impossible to gallop as she'd prefer.

'Remember, keep your head up and look about with a cordial smile.' Lady Laura's quiet reminder, delivered while Lady Bunting had turned aside to greet someone in a passing carriage, recalled him from his reflections. 'If you recognise an acquaintance and they smile back and greet you, respond in kind. If the person should not acknowledge you, continue to smile sweetly and slowly avert your gaze. On no account must you jerk your head away, blush or appear embarrassed.'

'Good advice, but hard to do,' Susanna murmured.

'Just the thought of being rebuffed makes me uncomfortable,' she admitted, the forbidden blush tinting her face.

'Of course it must—if you let yourself dwell on the slight. What are you to do instead?' Lady Laura prompted.

'Turn my face away slowly, behave as if I had not noticed the person and think of something pleasant,' her pupil responded.

'Exactly. Envisage, for instance, that beautiful green crepe ball gown you just ordered,' Lady Laura said. 'Think how confident you will feel wearing it, knowing you look your best.'

Susanna brightened. 'The gown is lovely, isn't it? And I am excited at being able to wear it tomorrow night.'

Miles noted that his sister's considering how elegant she would look in her new gown had chased the daunted look from her face, replacing it with a lovely, glowing smile. It seemed Lady Laura's suggestions were indeed giving his timid sister more confidence.

In fact, fairness compelled him to admit that he had not yet found anything to object to in the advice Lady Laura had been imparting.

Though they hadn't yet progressed to the 'flirting' part of the curriculum.

'And how do you respond if the person who initially ignored you should belatedly hail you and enquire why you did not greet them?' Lady Laura was asking.

'I look back as if startled, apologise for wool-gathering and tell them I am delighted to see them.'

They continued their slow progress around the park, his sister nodding, smiling and exchanging a few words with many of the people they passed. Susanna even managed to ignore the one or two who did not acknowledge her with only a slight reddening of her cheeks, after which Lady Laura added soft words of approval and encouragement.

Between himself and that lady, however, silence reigned. Occasionally she gave him a quick glance, her lips parting as if she meant to speak. But she then turned quickly away, her fingers seeming to tighten on the reins.

The unwelcome, unspoken connection he felt between them was stronger and more potent than any words they could have exchanged.

Did Lady Laura feel that charged atmosphere? The idea that she might sent a thrill of desire and anticipation through him.

Immediately he squelched it. Aside from that odd tension in her fingers gripping the reins, she gave no outward sign that she was aware of it. Was that tightness of her grip a result of her own disquiet, or did she merely sense his?

Just as well that she did not feel the pull that tugged at him. His position, torn between wanting to end his sister's involvement with Society and honouring his agreement to assist her in the lessons that would make her more comfortable there, was complicated enough if he alone was struggling with an unsuitable attraction. Besides, the episode with Arabella should have taught him how presumptuous it was to imagine a marquess's daughter would find a mere Mr Rochdale attractive.

However, if she did sense his attraction, she'd made no attempt to use it to her advantage, he realised suddenly—either to further entice him or to toy with him.

Once Arabella had become aware of his interest— he'd been so obviously admiring, he recalled with chagrin, it would have been difficult not to notice it—she'd lost no time drawing him completely under her spell. Until, foolish enough to believe her sweet sighs and loving looks indicated she was as bedazzled by him as he was by her, he'd made her that ill-advised—and haughtily refused—offer.

Perhaps, secure in her looks and lineage, Lady Laura felt no need to utilise the power her beauty exerted over men.

Or perhaps she was indifferent to him, viewing him merely as her friend's older brother. He ought to find that possibility encouraging. Paradoxically, he felt a vague annoyance at the prospect that Lady Laura might be immune to the attraction that pulled so strongly at him.

But a swift review of their often sharp exchanges, with its innuendoes he was certain he was not imagining, convinced him she was not indifferent. He ought to be more troubled than relieved by that conclusion.

He was studiously avoiding glancing at Lady Laura when Lady Bunting gave a loud halloo, then instructed the coachman to bring the carriage to a halt. He and Lady Laura pulled up their mounts as Lady Bunting invited the two strolling friends she'd spied to join her in the carriage. Once the newcomers were settled, the carriage set off again, Susanna engaging in the conversation with their visitors.

After riding along for several minutes, so acutely aware of Lady Laura's presence beside him that his skin felt overheated and his neck cloth uncomfortably tight, Miles felt compelled to break the silence.

'Susanna seems to have gained more confidence after practising your techniques.'

Lady Laura turned to him, nodding, the force of her blue-eyed gaze giving another jolt to his senses. 'I think so too. I'm so pleased! I shall recommend that she ride in the park again tomorrow, so she may have one final practice before the ball tomorrow night.'

She looked away, narrowing her gaze as if considering. 'If one calculates an average of six persons in each party she encounters—four in a carriage, two riding beside it—and with her greeting about half the individuals in each group, passing twenty-five or thirty such groups in a typical circuit of the park would give her at least seventy-five to ninety more chances to practise before the ball.'

He'd been listening idly, thinking it a general comment, until he realised with a start that her estimate was mathematically accurate. 'Seventy-five to ninety!' he echoed. 'You are very precise!'

She gave him a look. 'Precise for a female? Just a lucky guess, perhaps.'

Though her tone was dry, he was quite sure her response had not been happenstance—it had been too calculated, he concluded. Lady Laura could not only frame an idea in mathematical terms, but could do so fast and accurately. He'd be willing to bet his sister had never thought of anything mathematical beyond the price of a gown or bonnet.

Before he could sort out his reaction to that curious observation, Lady Laura said, 'I was surprised that you chose to ride, Mr Rochdale. I expected you would accompany the ladies in the carriage.'

'Meaning a mere banker must not be very adept at riding?' he asked, his tone sharper than he'd intended.

Her eyes widened in surprise. 'That wasn't what I meant at all. People of all walks of life are competent horsemen—after all, the beasts provide our main source of transport. It's just that your sister said you have always resided in town, where it would be more convenient to go on foot, in a hackney or your own carriage. You wouldn't have much need to ride.'

Oddly pleased that she'd not meant her remark to be disparaging, he said, 'It's true, we have always lived in London. One hasn't much need to ride here, except for leisure,' he affirmed, gesturing to the riders ambling about the carriage ways. 'But I had a good friend at Oxford who often invited me to spend term breaks at his family's country estate. I became a competent rider so I might accompany him, and in the process found I truly enjoy it. Not enough to bother with keeping my own mount in London, but I do often hire one for an early-morning ride.'

Evidently overhearing this bit of conversation, Susanna looked over to add, 'Miles developed quite a love of the countryside while he was Oxford, didn't you, Miles? He often came home extolling its beauties—so much so that by the time he left university he'd decided that he would one day purchase a property of his own. I'm not much acquainted with the country myself, but he does make it sound so appealing. You favour it too, Lady Laura?'

'It may lack *modistes* who create the latest fashion, the entertainments of opera, the theatre and the active social life of the city, but I am fond of it. Having grown up in small country manor, I certainly recommend the purchase of one by anyone with the means to do so.'

A small country manor? Miles thought, surprised. From all he'd learned, the Marquess of Carmelton's family seat in Warwickshire was a large estate crowned by a palatial residence.

Curious, he hoped Susanna might question the comment. But when her attention was recalled by Lady Bunting, Miles found himself asking, 'I would have thought Warnton Hall would be described as "grand and imposing".'

Too late, he realised that remark might suggest he'd taken the trouble to investigate the background of the woman with whom his sister was spending time—which he had. Evidently reaching that conclusion, Lady Laura said with a lifted eyebrow, 'Were you checking up on the respectability of your sister's new friend?'

Miles was trying to scrabble together a reply that was at once polite and somewhat truthful when Lady Laura laughed. 'No matter. Warnton Hall is indeed grand and imposing. But my father didn't grow up as heir to the Marquessate. His parents being country gentry from a junior branch of the family, he was raised at Haddenly—which is, I assure you, a lovely but very modest manor house.'

Miles frowned. 'A junior branch of the family? How did he come to be the heir?'

'Papa was attending university, training to be a clergyman and engaged to my mother—daughter of another country gentleman—when the heir to the Sixth Marquess died in an accident, leaving no son. After tracing the line back, it was discovered that the next closest heir was the great-grandson of the brother of the Fourth Marquess—who happened to be my father. Still, until the death of the current Marquess, a widower in his prime, it was always possible he might marry again and sire another son. However, at the Marquess's request, Papa did not take up holy orders. After leaving university, he agreed to visit Warnton periodically to become more familiar with the duties he might one day have to assume, but insisted on remaining at Haddenly. We led the usual life of country gentry until the death of the Sixth Marquess, when I was in my adolescence. Not until my father actually inherited the title did my brother and I learn of the change in his circumstances. Papa never told us, he said, because he wanted us to be happy with who we were, not counting on or lusting after some great elevation in status that might not occur.'

Lady Laura shook her head wonderingly. 'I still remember how awed I was at its grandeur when we moved to Warnton Hall! And honestly, if we're not in London, I still prefer modest little Haddenly. So you see, I wasn't raised as a wealthy, titled girl of distinguished lineage.' She laughed. 'My experiences attending a ladies' academy with girls who were probably explains why I have so little appreciation for individuals of great wealth and distinguished lineage.'

Understanding dawned. 'Ah—the techniques you've been teaching my sister. You developed them to deal with disdainful and dismissive high-born girls at school.'

She nodded. 'Boys can always resort to fisticuffs. And my brother did instruct me, but as furious as I sometimes was when one of the girls became too insufferable, I refrained, so as not to embarrass my family. However satisfying it would have been to plant one a facer, it would only have confirmed their haughty disdain at my "inferior" breeding. Verbal sparring was all I could allow myself.'

'That can be as brutal as fisticuffs,' Miles said feelingly, recalling some episodes from his time at university.

'You were at Oxford, Susanna said? As a commoner

surrounded by all those sprigs of gentility—many of them, I imagine, as condescending and arrogant as the girls I had to deal with—I suppose you would know.'

She hadn't been raised a marquess's daughter. She'd been looked down on and ostracised as some of the *ton* were doing to Susanna. Maybe he had misjudged her. Maybe she had taken up his sister not on a whim, or as Lady Bountiful dispensing favours, but out of genuine appreciation for his sister's sweet nature and with the empathy of one who had experienced disparaging treatment herself.

While he remained silent, mulling over this new perspective of her, Lady Laura continued, 'Papa, the would-be clergyman, raised me to believe all God's children are equal before Him, regardless of their birth.' A mischievous sparkle in her eyes, she added, 'I did find some Biblical teaching useful. Whenever I made a gracious reply to someone who'd uttered a snub or a criticism, I would think of Paul's admonition in Romans to bless those who curse you, thereby heaping burning coals on their head.'

Miles had to laugh. 'I doubt your would-be clergyman father would approve of the way you applied that particular verse.'

'Probably not! But it did help me maintain a sweet expression when I would rather have just told them what I thought of them.' Breaking into a chuckle, she added, 'Papa would have approved even less of my conduct at the academy after his unexpected inheritance. Oh, the looks on the faces of the girls who'd lorded it over me, who'd boasted of how—unlike poor me—they would catch rich, titled husbands, when they discovered my father was a marquess and I, Lady Laura, now outranked many of them!'

'Do you intend to catch a rich and titled husband?' Miles asked curiously. To his surprise, something deep within stirred in protest at the thought.

Lady Laura wrinkled her nose in distaste. 'A firm advocate of Papa's teaching, I still don't care much for wealth or titles—a person's character is more important, in my book. In any event, I don't intend to marry at all until I absolutely can't avoid it any longer. My father…isn't well. I care for him and manage the London household, while my older brother has taken over for him running the estate at Warnton. Of course, someone else could tend him and run the London house, but I love him dearly. And selfishly, he allows me much more freedom to pursue my interests than a husband probably would.'

Amused, he meant to ask her what interests she thought a prospective husband might feel compelled to rein in when she rushed on, a glow in her eyes. 'So you were at Oxford. How I wish I might study at university! Although I would choose Cambridge.'

Study at university? It seemed an odd aim for a female, but he didn't know her well enough to tell if she was serious—or somehow mocking him. 'You would truly wish to attend Cambridge? Why?'

'So I might study at Trinity College—Sir Isaac Newton's school. Others have further developed his theories, but he was one of the inventors of calculus. I've always been fascinated by numbers, but at that excuse for a ladies' academy we weren't even permitted to study basic mathematics. What I know of geometry and higher maths, I've taught myself from books. I've just learned that Mr Babbage, Mr Herschel and Mr Peacock published a translation of Monsieur Lacroix's lectures on calculus, which I intend to obtain from Hatchard's—'

She halted abruptly, a blush colouring her cheeks. 'Please excuse me! I don't usually prose on about my studies! I suppose knowing you are a banker and deal with numbers all the time, so presumably enjoy them, I got—carried away. Now you will conclude I'm un-maidenly and definitely a bad influence on your sister.'

Miles hardly knew what to say—or think—about all the unexpected bits of information he'd just learned about Lady Laura. But he could reassure her on one score. 'I'm quite certain that no amount of enthusiasm on your part would persuade my sister to develop a fascination for anything outside the usual female pursuits. She's far too enamoured of fashion, wholly absorbed by home and family and quite detested her short time away at her academy.'

To Miles's regret, as he would have much liked to continue this unexpectedly illuminating private conversation, at that moment Lady Bunting's friends descended from the carriage, allowing Susanna to turn back to them.

'Are you talking about school? Despite everything, I know you enjoyed Oxford, Miles, but I couldn't leave Miss Giddings' Academy fast enough! The instructions in needlework, dancing and deportment were useful, but I had no aptitude at all for French or Italian and I hated being away from home. I never thought to ask you, Lady Laura, if you'd spent time at school.'

'I did, but I too was glad to return home. My father's library contained far more instructive books than the school possessed—and my family was much more congenial company.'

Susanna smiled at Miles. 'As is mine! Papa is often preoccupied by work, but Mama is a sweetheart, and Miles has always been so indulgent of me tagging after him, even though I know he often thought me a nuisance.'

'You are too sweet-tempered ever to be a nuisance,' Miles told her fondly.

'Even when I drag you away from the bank far too often of late?'

'I expect the bank can survive a few afternoons without my eagle-eyed presence.'

'Since you have it running so well. He would never boast about himself, but my father says Miles has a gift for management, for handling clients and for searching out investments.'

Lady Laura raised her eyebrows. 'You must be good with numbers indeed, Mr Rochdale.'

'I am fond of them too, Lady Laura.'

Susanna chuckled. 'The only numbers he isn't fond of is the total of my bills for gowns, bonnets and sundries!'

'You may be occasionally extravagant, but why shouldn't the loveliest girl in London have whatever finery she chooses?' Miles teased. 'We're not at the point of having to outrun the bailiffs yet.'

'Well, after that vote of approval, Lady Laura, I see we must go shopping again,' Susanna said. After a quick glance at her sponsor, who was once again calling a greeting to a friend, she added *sotto voce*, 'With so many more entertainments to be borne until I can retire from the Season, I should be able to indulge myself by purchasing as many pretty gowns and fashionable bonnets as I like!'

'And so you shall,' Lady Laura agreed with a grin.

'Are you about ready to return? I must get Athena back to the stables and tidy up. I've promised to help my father with some of his studies this afternoon.'

'I'm ready to go home,' Susanna said. 'I think I've had a…profitable excursion.'

'Are you feeling more confident?' Lady Laura asked, and at Susanna's nod said, 'Then it has been profitable indeed.'

'Will you have time to tutor me in conversation tomorrow?' Susanna asked, her smile fading to an anxious look. 'As the ball is tomorrow night, I fear I shall have need of more than polite greetings and smiling looks.'

'Yes, I think I can manage a short session,' Lady Laura replied.

'And you, Miles?' Susanna asked. 'You don't need help staring down the discourteous, but I'm sure Charlotte will be pleased to exchange more conversation beyond polite enquiries about her health and that of her family.'

Annoyed, Miles said, 'I'm not as bad as all that.'

'Perhaps, but I've never heard you tease her about anything, or even compliment her gown or her bonnet.'

Miles rolled his eyes. 'If shallow drivel like that is what you consider "pleasant conversation", I don't think I wish to learn it.'

Lady Laura laughed. 'Now, Mr Rochdale, don't be churlish. Learning a few simple phrases to charm a young lady will hardly tax a gentleman of your intellect, and will be so gratifying to the young lady—who, I can assure you, will be doing her utmost to charm you.'

'You see?' Susanna said. 'Charlotte will wish to please *you*, so it's only fair that you sometimes attempt to be pleasing in return. If you want a happy, loyal, devoted wife.'

Charlotte was lovely, pleasant and, his mother assured him, competent in all matters of household management. But for the present, he wasn't eager to take her—or any woman—to wife. 'All in good time. There's no urgency for us to marry yet.'

'I doubt she is so sanguine about waiting,' Susanna observed somewhat sharply. 'You had better consider doing a bit more wooing, brother or, regardless of the plans the families have made, she may tire of waiting and find someone else!'

His immediate reaction—what a relief it would be to be released from that expectation—Miles squelched, castigating himself for disloyalty. He would have to marry some time. He and Charlotte had got along well since they were children. They understood each other, had family and background and history in common.

Perhaps he should dredge up a little enthusiasm for treating his future wife the way his sister insisted a woman wished to be treated.

'I stand corrected. I should honour my future wife by wanting to charm her.'

Though Lady Laura gave him a speculative look, Susanna nodded approvingly. 'Good. Then you'll join us tomorrow afternoon?'

'Another afternoon away from the bank?' he teased.

Susanna made a face at him. 'You've already said you can be spared. And I shan't need too many more lessons—shall I, Lady Laura?'

'Only a few more. Then you will be fully capable of taking on the *ton* on your own.'

Susanna shuddered. 'I doubt that will ever be the case, but I shall at least be better armed against them!'

'Very good! I'll leave you now, and head home,' Lady

Laura said. 'Until tomorrow, then.' Turning to Miles, she added with a grin, 'Prepare to be charming.' Then, giving her horse the office to start, she trotted off.

Miles watched her ride away, more bemused than ever. The only woman at the moment who piqued his interest enough to want to charm her was Lady Laura.

He'd thought her at first a shallow, empty-headed debutante, an assessment he now conceded was wrong. The advice she'd given Susanna thus far had been level-headed, practical and helpful.

Lady Laura, who hadn't been raised a marquess's daughter. Who believed character, rather than title, mattered most. Who, most intriguingly of all, was fascinated by numbers and wanted to study calculus.

Small wonder she was concerned about acquiring a husband. Few gentlemen, himself included, could view as a prime matrimonial candidate a female who preferred immersing herself in mathematical theorems over managing a household and seeing to her husband's concerns.

Intrigued he might be, but he was realistic enough to know there could be no permanent friendship between a banker and a marquess's daughter, even one not born to that status. But, before he went on to settle down with the woman who *would* make him a proper wife, he could steal a little time to get to know this unusual woman better.

Good thing Charlotte appeared in no hurry to marry.

Chapter Six

The next afternoon, a thoughtful Laura embarked in a hackney bound for the Rochdale townhouse. While helping her father with his collections the previous afternoon, then attending a musical evening with Lady Swanston last night, she'd been able to put Susanna's lessons—and Miles Rochdale—from her mind. But ever since she'd opened her eyes this morning, she'd had to push back thoughts and speculations about the banker that kept recurring despite her efforts to resist them.

Now that she was on her way to Susanna's, she would finally allow herself to examine them. She felt a wry smile curve her lips. Miles Rochdale had disapproved of her when he'd thought her a frivolous debutante leading his sister into idle flirtation and expensive purchases. Now that she'd revealed her bent towards mathematics, he was probably even more disapproving.

But...he had seemed more amused than critical. Or maybe just sure enough of his sister's devotion to the usual female role not to be worried that the odd interests of her new friend might persuade her to stray from the expected.

Still, she shouldn't have blathered on so, she thought with a sigh. Why had she? Because a banker who worked with numbers must surely enjoy them? Ah, to be involved with accounts all day, every day, rather than only as necessary to oversee household expenditures. How wonderful to immerse herself in mathematics, even if it were the straightforward totalling of sums—income, expenditure, gains and losses. Even those commonplace calculations were so precise, so elegant.

With regret, she let go of that wistful dream and focused on the task of the moment—teaching Susanna how to converse so as to engage a gentleman's attention. As compellingly lovely as Susanna was, Laura didn't anticipate it would be a difficult task. Susanna would need to master only a modicum of pleasant chat to appear enchanting to gentlemen who preferred a lady to be sweet and innocent.

She was less sure she could teach Susanna's brother how to charm a lady. Besides, his physical presence was already compelling enough. It was probably a disservice to the female gender to burnish that appeal with charm that would make him even more attractive. What woman would be able to resist him?

Alas, she was all too susceptible. She'd been so keenly aware of him riding beside her yesterday that her nerves had been in knots. Her mind so frozen by the necessity to resist the urge to gaze at him, she'd been unable to produce the light conversation that normally came to her so naturally. Not until he'd enquired into her background had she been able to forget his presence enough to find her tongue.

She hoped soon to be finished with the lessons, or at least with Mile Rochdale's participation in them. She'd wanted to show him she wasn't mindless or frivolous, and felt she'd succeeded. Unfortunately, he was harder to resist when he wasn't being disdainful.

Much as she was tempted to learn more about banking and his role in it, it would be wiser to keep her distance. Let space and time dissolve his appeal and the temptation to pursue an attraction that could have no satisfactory resolution.

Thus decided, as the hackney halted at her destination Laura descended, ready to put that conclusion into practice.

Setting her mind to it and getting her senses to cooperate were two different things, she discovered as she sat in Susanna Rochdale's parlour, drinking tea. She didn't need to look at Miles Rochdale to know precisely where he was.

If that wordless communication still hummed between them, at least she was not so disconcerted by it now. More like resigned to the fact that apparently it was not going to disappear. Though 'resigned' wasn't quite right—she might not have wished for the tingling thrill that kept her senses on edge, but she couldn't deny it added a heightened awareness to the mundane process of taking tea, an intensity she'd never before experienced.

If the sensation wasn't going to fade, maybe she should just stop trying to resist and enjoy it. Soon enough, he would be back to his banking, and she would return to her daily routine.

Her calm, even-paced…and slightly dull routine?

'So, how do you intend to make Susanna a brilliant conversationalist?' Mr Rochdale's slightly sardonic comment recalled her attention.

Pulling herself back to the present, she said, 'It's a contradiction. In Society, a lady is the best conversationalist when she speaks the least.'

'That would hardly make her a conversationalist, would it?' Rochdale said.

'Conversation is two or more persons engaged to amuse, entertain or exchange information. As long as that is being done, it is not necessary that each participant contribute an equal amount. A lady's best contribution is to pose questions and allow the gentleman to answer, trying to discover what interests him most, then leading him to talk about it. He will then believe the exchange stimulating, his partner clever and charming and enjoy expounding upon the subjects she's suggested.'

'And ladies do not enjoy speaking about their interests?' Rochdale asked.

'They might, but it is best for them not to, unless they happen to enjoy pursuits beyond the domestic sphere—else the gentleman is likely to become bored rather quickly. Besides, learning what interests a gentleman will also tell her whether or not she wants to pursue the acquaintance. If she abhors dogs, for example, she wouldn't want a husband whose greatest enthusiasm is for hounds. And if the gentleman's interests are pleasing to her, in the interim between meetings she can learn more about them, so she will know how to engage him and what to ask about when she encounters him.'

Susanna frowned. 'Would you demonstrate with Miles?'

Did she really want to know more about Miles Rochdale? She wouldn't want to learn anything that would make him more attractive. But perhaps, she thought, brightening, discovering something further about his interests would make him *less* compelling.

'When you first meet a gentleman, you might ask—' she turned to Rochdale '—Do you prefer London, or do you enjoy time in the countryside?'

'Both have their attractions,' he replied.

'When you venture outside of London, where do you prefer to travel?'

'I'm best acquainted with Kent.'

Exasperated, she said, 'Come, Mr Rochdale, these short answers will not do! If we were attending some social event and I were a young woman you'd *chosen* to speak with, you would be more enthusiastic about answering me, else why seek to make my acquaintance at all?'

Susanna giggled. 'She's right, Miles.'

'Once again, then. You prefer Kent, Mr Rochdale? Have you family there?'

With a resigned look, he said, 'The family of a good friend from Oxford resides there.'

'And what is it about Kent you find particularly attractive?' Laura asked, soldiering on.

With a quirk of a smile, as if giving in, he continued, 'The verdant green of the countryside. The tranquillity and quiet after the constant noise and bustle of London. The rolling hills with long vistas to the sea. The armies of hop pickers at harvest. The fields of crops and meadows of grazing horses. Especially the horses.'

Encouraged that he was at last cooperating, she continued, 'Magnificent beasts, are they not? You keep a stable yourself?'

'Not at the moment. I might one day, however. Perhaps even breed horses.'

He was considering horse-breeding? That was unexpected. To improve bloodlines, or simply continue them? The goal of improving stock would be one he had in common with her father. Genuine interest, rather than a need to demonstrate a technique, prompted her to enquire further.

She caught herself before she framed another question. She didn't need to become more interested in Miles Rochdale. It was bad enough that he attracted her more than any man of her previous acquaintance.

Squelching her curiosity, she turned to Susanna. 'You get the general idea of it? Beginning with broadly based questions about where he prefers to live and how he spends his time will lead you naturally to further questions. If he should be enamoured of the country, you may ask about hounds, horses, carriages, hunting or supervising crops. If he professes a love of the city, enquire about his favourite operas, plays, clubs and entertainments. I'll give you some examples.'

Laura continued, suggesting a sample of questions and having Susanna repeat them back, until her friend declared she felt prepared to carry on a basic conversation on her own.

'We shall cover one more topic, which you must know about if you attend a ball—bouquets.'

'Before we move on, you should give Miles a chance to practise his conversation,' Susanna said.

So he might query *her*? A ripple of anticipation and agitation quivered in her belly. Abstractedly placing a hand there to calm it, Laura knew she didn't want Miles Rochdale to beguile her further by even pretending an interest in her.

'I don't think he needs any practice, as he will generally just answer a lady's questions.'

'He should learn how to ask something that will charm a lady, shouldn't he?' Susanna persisted.

'Very well, let me practise,' Rochdale said. 'Lady Laura, I understand you reside mostly in London?'

Unable to come up with a reasonable way to stave off participating in the exercise she herself had suggested, she answered reluctantly, 'Yes, with my father. It is easier for him to get about in the city. On the few occasions when he does go out.'

'And your brother? I understand he oversees family estate?'

'Yes, Warnton Hall in Warwickshire. He's a countryman born and bred and seldom comes to London.'

Frowning, Susanna broke in, 'Perhaps such enquiries are meant to display a flattering interest, but were they directed towards me, I would consider them more like interrogation than admiration! A lady prefers some sweeter comments—like compliments. Doesn't she, Lady Laura?'

'Compliments are always welcome.' Hadn't she received myriad ones, thinking them just polite chat? Why did she find the idea of *Rochdale* complimenting her so disturbing?

Because he would have to look at her closely to decide on one?

Her mind flashed to the image of his hand touching her face, her hand resting on his arm. Heat flared in her belly and both face and fingers tingled.

No, she'd prefer Rochdale to stick to prosaic questions about home and family. But there was no way she could admit or explain that.

Caught now in a trap of her own making, she could only keep going and get to the end of the session as soon as possible. Hoping the warmth she felt wasn't colouring her face, she said, 'Compliments are acceptable, yes. General ones, such as "how fetching you look today, Miss Rochdale". Or you may comment on how charming the lady's attire is. Only if her appearance merits a compliment, of course, lest observers think you mocking.'

'What if the lady is a harridan in an unbecoming gown?' Miles asked with deceptive innocence.

From the suppressed smile curving the corner of his lips, she suspected he'd sensed her discomfort with the topic—and was enjoying it, the wretch!

Trying to ignore her unease, she said, 'Then make the compliment even more general. "What a lovely rose colour that gown is". Or "feathers trimming a bonnet are so elegant".'

Rochdale choked back a laugh and muttered something that sounded like, 'What rubbish!'

Undeterred, Susanna said, 'Well, Miles? Produce something complimentary, if you please! Lovely as Lady Laura is, that should not be difficult.'

Rochdale focused those blue eyes on her with an intensity that sent a shiver through her. 'What a beautiful shade of blonde your hair is, Lady Laura,' he murmured, his voice low and intimate. 'Like spun gold reflecting moonlight.'

He lifted his fingers, as if imagining pulling them through her unbound tresses. The quivering sensation in her stomach grew stronger.

She forced herself to look away, trying not to blush. 'That was…lovely, but a bit too intimate. Comments about a lady's person are best avoided unless you want her—and anyone who overhears you—to believe you have a very serious interest in the lady. Or have already declared yourself.'

'I should stick to praise of her gown, shoes or bonnet?'

'Yes.'

'I cannot tell her that her eyes are striking, her lips soft and kissable, her figure beguiling?'

Laura felt a tingle as if his fingers, not just his gaze, were brushing her eyebrows, tracing her lips, trailing down her body. Looking up, she noted the laughter in his eyes and the deepening of his smile. He was quite aware of the effect his words were having, the rogue!

Annoyed, she said sharply, 'Definitely not.' *Two could play this game, Mr Rochdale.* 'Just as a lady may not comment on a gentleman's…attributes,' she said, and let her gaze rove over *his* body.

'Ah, but a man might enjoy having a lady compliment his…attributes,' he replied, no longer able to hide his grin.

'If she can find any,' she snapped back, drawing a laugh from Susanna.

'Enough about compliments,' she said, determined to move on. 'Let's discuss one final thing you will need to know—the meaning of flowers.'

Seeing Rochdale roll his eyes, she said tartly, 'You may dismiss it if you wish, Mr Rochdale, but this topic should be pertinent to you—if you actually intend to woo your lady.'

'Are you going to assure me that gentlemen understand this, as they do the language of the fan?' Rochdale asked.

'*Cultivated* gentlemen do,' she said pointedly, still irked with him. Turning to Susanna, she continued, 'As you know, it is customary for any gentleman who dances with you at a ball to send flowers the next day. The blooms chosen can give the bouquet an additional layer of meaning. Gentlemen need to be aware of the meanings as well, as the wrong sort of flowers would convey a message that could be anything from embarrassing to improper.'

'You ought to send Charlotte bouquets as you are so busy, you seldom see her,' Susanna said.

'That's not entirely my fault,' he protested. 'If you will remember, she went to Norfolk last month to stay with her grandmother, who has been ill. It's uncertain when she will return.'

'Arranging to have flowers sent through a Norfolk merchant would be a thoughtful gesture, then,' Laura said.

'What flowers should he send?' Susanna asked.

'White flowers are most appropriate for an unmarried lady; they symbolise innocence and purity. One could add to them ivy, which indicates fidelity, yarrow for everlasting love or rosemary for remembrance. If you do favour other colours, yellow tulips, crocuses or daffodils signal the happiness your association with the lady gives you. But on no account should you send yellow carnations, which indicate disappointment, or yellow hyacinths or roses, which signify jealousy. Bluebells or blue hyacinths signal constancy and devotion, and violets praise your lady's modesty and your devotion to her.'

'I am duly instructed,' Rochdale said drily. Although Laura thought he didn't look very enthusiastic about sending flowers to his almost-betrothed. Did he truly care about the lady?

Not that it was any of her concern whether the two

were sweethearts, or their proposed union merely an alliance of family and business interests, as was often the case with marriages among the *ton*.

Though she couldn't help feeling a little…relieved?… that Rochdale didn't appear to be besotted with his potential bride. Ridiculous as that notion was.

'Now, for those you receive from your dance partners,' she continued, turning to Susanna, 'Be wary. If a gentleman sends you pansies, he's indicating he is fond of you, but not in love. Worse yet would be sweet peas, which thank you for your company but bid you goodbye, or lavender, which signifies distrust. Bachelor buttons, as the name suggests, warn that, though the gentleman may enjoy feminine company, he is not interested in entering the married state.'

'I shall hope for bouquets of white carnations, white roses and violets from those I favour,' Susanna said.

'But never red. The colour signifies passion and is inappropriate to send to an unmarried lady, unless the couple is already engaged or the gentleman intends to propose.'

'Don't worry, little sister. Any man who sends you red flowers will have me to deal with.'

'You could send them to Charlotte, though,' Susanna said. 'Indicating you are ready to court her in earnest.'

'I suppose. They definitely need to be sent to the right lady.'

He'd turned to look at Laura as he said that, and she felt a shock go through her. Was he admitting he had a passion for her? That he felt as intensely as she did the physical tension between them?

She broke her gaze before Susanna noticed them staring at each other. Time to leave Rochdale's too-disturbing company.

'That's enough, don't you think? We both need to rest before the ball tonight and I'm sure Mr Rochdale wishes to visit his bank this afternoon.'

Susanna's expression turned anxious. 'Will you be there tonight?'

'Of course,' Laura said, putting her hand over Susanna's. 'I promise to seek you out as soon as I arrive. My good friends will be there, too. I'm so pleased to be able to introduce you.'

'What friends?' Rochdale asked, frowning.

'No one who will pervert her character, I assure you,' Laura said with some asperity. 'Miss Eliza Hasterling, daughter of a clergyman, whose sweetness you reminded me of upon our first meeting, Susanna. And Lady Margaret D'Aubignon, with her mother, the Countess of Comeryn, who will make a useful ally for you.'

'A countess!' Susanna echoed. 'She sounds…formidable.'

'Not a bit, she's the most engaging lady. All my friends will be prepared to assist you in any way they can.'

Though Laura was excited at the prospect of seeing Maggie and Eliza and attempting a reprise of their debut season's camaraderie, she hoped to spend most of her time supporting Susanna. How much would Maggie try to distract her with her 'quest'? She'd had a note from her enterprising friend, informing her—'warning' might be a better word, she thought with a sigh—that she already had some candidates picked out she wanted her friends to consider.

The prospect of marrying any of them was vaguely disturbing, so Laura pushed it from her mind, as she usually did when the subject of matrimony arose. She had plenty of time to worry about finding a husband later—hopefully much later. For now, she was quite content to remain at home, supporting her father.

She stood, Susanna and brother rising with her, and walked out, Rochdale remaining on the threshold of the salon while Susanna accompanied her to the front door, waiting with her while the butler fetched her pelisse. Nodding a goodbye, Rochdale turned and proceeded down the hallway towards the room Susanna had told her he used as his office when at home.

Laura gazed after him, suppressing a sigh. After the session just ended, she had no doubt that Miles Rochdale was fully aware of how he affected her. She'd had rather firm confirmation that she affected him just as strongly. Which should alarm her. Instead, she felt relieved that she was not suffering these intense and unwanted feelings alone.

In fact, she realised with a trace of excitement, if Rochdale *was* aware of them, he was also just as conscious as she was of the need to resist temptation. A temptation she wouldn't then have to fight on her own.

As long as they both remained on guard against letting something develop of which neither their families nor society would approve, maybe she could indulge her curiosity and learn more about him. Because if she were honest, she had to admit there was still much she would like to know about Mr Rochdale, the city banker with a love for country estates and a passion for horses. Who happened to be temptingly handsome in the bargain.

A guilty sense of anticipation rose in her at the prospect of seeing more of him before they inevitably went their separate ways.

Chapter Seven

Later that night, Laura proceeded into the crowded ballroom at Ashdown House with her sponsor, Lady Swanston, and looked around, trying to locate her friends. She spied Susanna immediately, hovering not far from the entrance as if waiting for her, and made her way speedily to her friend's side.

'Thank goodness you're here,' Susanna murmured as their chaperons exchanged polite greetings. 'I tried to time our arrival to coincide with yours so I'd not have to deal with anyone until I had you nearby to lend me courage.'

'Now, don't go faint-hearted on me, else I shall conclude my lessons gave you no benefit at all.'

'Oh, they did, and I thank you for them! I do know better what to do and what to say, but… I'm still nervous. Not until I entered this room crammed full of members of the *ton* did I realise how much my self-confidence depended on having you and Miles nearby. I wish I could have persuaded him to attend, but he was adamant in his refusal.' Susanna smiled nervously. 'He said you would be here and do me far more good.'

Laura felt a little glow that she'd apparently succeeded in making Rochdale think better of her. But a moment later, when the full import of Susanna's words registered, satisfaction was succeeded by curiosity.

'Was your brother invited?' she said, surprised. Lady Ashdown was not the highest of sticklers, including on her guest list Members of Parliament, many of whom had origins in trade, along with some of the *nouveau riche* who had burnished their pedigrees by purchasing country estates, and bourgeois heiresses like Susanna. But Laura wouldn't have thought that goodwill extended to inviting a man with only a university education to separate him from his merchant class roots.

'Yes,' Susanna was saying. 'You remember I mentioned Miles made a good friend at Oxford who used to invite him home on term breaks—Thomas Ecclesley, offspring of a baron who is related to Lady Ashdown? As a youngest son, he had few prospects and no independent income to maintain himself, so after they left Oxford Miles arranged for him to take a job at the bank of a family friend. He's quickly risen through the ranks, and now that he no longer needs to marry an heiress to support him, he's allowed his relations to persuade him to mingle in Society.'

As Laura nodded, Susanna continued, 'The point of this long story is that Thomas made it a stipulation, if he agreed to attend a relation's social function, that they would have to invite Miles too, as he considers my brother the benefactor whose assistance allowed him to become independent. Thomas has only succeeded once or twice in getting Miles to actually attend a Society event, but he keeps trying.'

Something in Susanna's voice as she talked about

the young man made Laura curious. 'Are you fond of Mr Ecclesley too?'

'I shall always be grateful to him for helping my brother at university. Though Miles never complained about it, I know it wasn't easy for him. Being befriended by a man of birth didn't render him acceptable to everyone, but it certainly allowed him to gain a larger circle of friends.'

Laura gave Susanna a penetrating look. 'Is it just gratitude for his befriending your brother that makes you approve of the young man?'

Blushing, Susanna admitted, 'He is attractive on his own merits.'

'I should like to meet him, if he is here tonight.'

'I'll be happy to introduce you...if you'll not make any attempt to push us together.' Darting a quick look at her sponsor, now in conversation with another matron, she lowered her voice. 'Lady Bunting thinks him an acceptable prospect. Whenever we meet at events, she's always trying to manoeuvre us together for a dance or a chat. It's so embarrassing! It's fortunate that he isn't wealthy or she would be pressing me on him even harder.'

'I can imagine how uncomfortable that must be! It's a wonder the young man doesn't flee when sees you,' Laura teased.

Susanna chuckled. 'No, he is quite good-natured about her manoeuvrings. I asked Miles to extend my apologies and appreciation for his indulgence. Miles only laughed and said Thomas told him, if he couldn't get Miles to attend society events and perform the duty himself, it was up to Thomas to make sure no fortune-hunters or scoundrels bothered Miles's little sister.'

'He sounds delightful. I want to introduce you to the friends I mentioned too, both of whom should be here tonight. Eliza Hasterling and Lady Margaret D'Aubignon.'

Susanna shook head. 'I shall be honoured to meet your friends but…the daughter of an earl sounds rather… daunting.'

'I assure you, she is nothing like Lady Arbuthnot or Miss Wentworth!' Seeing that Susanna still looked doubtful, she said, 'Let me tell you how we became friends—that will reassure you about how approachable she is! During our debut Season last year, after we'd been introduced but didn't yet know each other well, I was chatting with Eliza when a young man asked her to dance. He appeared a bit too much on the go, but gentle soul that she is, she couldn't find the words to refuse him.

'When she didn't return after the dance, I went in search of her—and found her by the doors to the terrace, her inebriated dance partner crowding her towards the exit. Before I could intervene, Maggie stalked over, drove the offender away with a blistering condemnation of his character, then scolded *Eliza*, albeit in gentler tones, for not sending the young man packing. Which led me to take Maggie on, protesting that not every female was as bold about confronting a gentleman, no matter how uncomfortable he made her.'

'Gracious! What a scene! I would have been mortified!'

Laura nodded, smiling. 'As that incident demonstrates, Maggie cares nothing about convention! To continue my story, instead of transferring her displeasure to me, as I expected, Maggie apologised. She explained that having to live with her autocratic father, who tried to exert iron-fisted control over her and harshly cowed her gentle mother, meant she was immediately enraged when she saw a female being harassed by a gentleman, and intervened before she even considered what she was doing. At which point the three of us avowed our mutual admiration and became best friends. So you see, they will both be nothing but helpful and sympathetic!'

At that moment, her face pinking, Susanna murmured, 'I see Mr Ecclesley. Over there, by the columns,' she said, giving a slight wave in that direction.

Laura watched with interest as a tall, fair-haired young man, nudged by his companion, looked up and spotted them. His smile deepening, he murmured something to his friend, then made his way across the ballroom towards them.

Laura noted Susanna's blush deepening as the gentleman approached. 'Thank heavens I shall be able to introduce you, so he won't believe I was just angling for his company.'

'Judging by the warmth of that smile, I would say he's delighted to claim it.'

A moment later, the young man halted beside them, bowing to their curtsies. 'Miss Rochdale, how nice to see you. And your lovely friend, of course.'

'Lady Laura, may I introduce Mr Thomas Ecclesley?'

'Charmed,' Ecclesley said, bowing again. 'Unfortunately, Miss Rochdale, I was unable to persuade your brother to join us tonight.'

'Rather a losing cause, I fear. But I appreciate you making the attempt. I would be grateful for his support. These grand social occasions do make me nervous.'

'You have no need to be,' Ecclesley said. 'May I distract you by claiming the next dance?'

Watching her friend blush, Laura felt certain Susanna was not indifferent to her brother's good friend. 'I'd be happy to,' she replied.

'Shall we take our places? I think the set is forming up.'

As Laura watched the young couple walk off, her friend and sometime-escort, Lord Innesford, strolled over.

'What are you doing here hiding among the chaperons?' he chided, smiling. 'Come, you must dance.'

Borne off by her partner, Laura maintained a desultory conversation during the movements of the dance, frequently glancing back at ballroom entrance, anxious to spot the arrival of Maggie and Eliza.

'I see you are unmoved by my scintillating company tonight,' he said as the music neared its conclusion. 'You are obviously watching for someone. Should I be jealous?'

He was teasing, for as Laura knew well, Innesford was an eligible *parti* of charming manners and large fortune who had no desire to be married—one of the reasons they got along so well.

'I'm not expecting any handsome swain,' she replied. 'My dearest friend, Lady Margaret, is back in town, and tonight's ball is to be the first entertainment she attends.'

'Lady Margaret D'Aubignon? The Earl has allowed her to return to town? Of course, the exact circumstances of her abrupt retirement from Society last Season were hushed up, but rumour claims she refused Randolph and his pots of money. It's said the Earl was so furious, he banished her. Was she finally penitent enough to induce Comeryn to relent?'

Laura laughed. 'You know Lady Margaret. What do you think?'

Innesford smiled. 'I'd guess she got around him some-how. I can't see that firebrand turning meek and obliging.'

Laura laughed. 'No, indeed! But enough of me. How are you? Has your mother recovered from her putrid cold? Is your father embroiled in debates in Parliament?'

'Yes and yes,' he said. Following her own advice, Laura plied Innesford with occasional questions, keeping her partner talking about his current doings for the remainder of the dance.

Just as the music drew to a close, she spotted Eliza and Maggie entering the ballroom. Noting the direction of her gaze, Innesford said, 'Has your friend arrived? Let me escort you over.'

After crossing the floor to meet her friends, and ex-changing bows and curtsies, Innesford said, 'Welcome back to London, Lady Margaret, and good to see you, Miss Hasterling. Another dance later, perhaps, Lady Laura?' After Laura nodded her assent, Innesford walked off.

Inclining her head after the disappearing Innesford, Maggie said, 'As a younger son with money, if Innes-ford were older he might make you a good prospective husband.'

'He's both too young and quite uninterested in mar-riage, so we complement each other perfectly. I hope you don't intend to engage us in any schemes tonight. My protégée, Miss Rochford, is here and I wanted you to meet her.'

'No meeting candidates tonight,' Maggie assured her. 'We've plenty of time left in the Season, so there's no ur-gency to begin. Tonight, we will just enjoy being together again.'

'Excellent,' Laura said. 'Speaking of together, I thought your mother would accompany you tonight.'

'She intended to, but is at present suffering from a trifling headache. I prevailed upon Eliza to bring me.'

'Ah, here comes Susanna!' Laura exclaimed, spotting her friend crossing the dance floor to re-join her.

'What a lovely girl,' Maggie murmured, watching her approach. 'If she's an heiress, she should have no trouble finding a husband.'

Before Laura could say her friend was as uninterested in snagging a title as Maggie was in having either of them do so, Susanna halted before them. Introductions were made, with Ecclesley bowing himself off after asking if he might seek Susanna's hand again later in the evening.

'I had hoped to have you meet Lady Comeryn as well, but she is indisposed this evening,' Laura explained.

Smiling shyly, Susanna said, 'Meeting your two friends is pleasure enough.'

'As it is a pleasure to meet you!' Maggie said. 'Laura has told us of your situation, and we do hope to help. My brother married a railway engineer's daughter—an absolutely darling girl whom we adore. But Marcella found dealing with the *ton* difficult, as I imagine you do. We're prepared to assist you in whatever way we can. Laura, you must bring Miss Rochdale to call on Mama. She knows everyone who is anyone and has corresponded for ever with most of them.'

'Having a countess to support you in Society is enormously useful,' Eliza assured her.

'C-call on her?' Susanna repeated, glancing at Laura with a look of alarm.

'Why don't you and the Countess visit us at Mount

Street instead?' Laura suggested. 'Susanna has already visited us several times and would feel more comfortable there, wouldn't you, Susanna?'

'It's very kind of you to invite me to call, Lady Margaret, but I would feel more at ease at Laura's house. If that is agreeable to you?'

'Certainly,' Maggie said. 'How is your papa doing, Laura?'

She frowned, her friend's question reviving her ever-present worry. 'I want to believe he's improving, but I'm not sure he is. I wish…' Her voice trailed off to a sigh.

'I wish there was something I could do to alleviate his constant pain. He continues his reading and his experiments with plants but… I'm afraid he will never be the same. I sense that I'm losing him, little by little,' she ended softly.

Reviving to toss Maggie a challenging look, she added, 'I want to remain at home and help him, so you ought not to waste your candidates on me.'

Turning to Susanna, who appeared puzzled by the turn of the conversation, Laura quickly explained the essence of Maggie's 'plan'.

'Marry an older widower?' Susanna said doubtfully. 'But what of love?'

'Some are lucky enough to find it,' Laura conceded. But if they were then unlucky to lose it—was that love worth the pain of its loss? She wasn't sure it was. Not for her, anyway.

Eliza was saying, 'My parents were so blessed. I want to make that sort of love match as well—although,' she added hastily, 'I shall certainly consider Lady Margaret's suggestions.'

'A congenial older gentleman could make you a kind and loving spouse,' Maggie argued.

'But what of passion? Romance?' Susanna protested.

Maggie wrinkled her nose. 'Better to find that outside of marriage. Then, if passion fades, one can escape. Once married, one is trapped for ever.'

Noting Susanna's shocked expression, Laura said, 'You mustn't pay Lady Margaret too much heed. Her father is…difficult. He's given her a strong distaste for aristocratic men and the estate of marriage in general.'

As the musicians began tuning for the next set, Thomas Ecclesley returned to offer his hand to Susanna, who accepted readily. As she walked off, the friends, not interested in dancing yet despite Lady Swanston's urging, informed her they would withdraw to the adjacent salon to continue their conversation and return to dance afterwards.

'Mr Ecclesley seems attentive to your friend,' Eliza observed as they entered the refreshment room.

Laura smiled. 'I think there is an inclination there. I've been trying to help her overcome her shyness, which is much easier when she is partnered with Ecclesley. He's a good friend of her brother's from Oxford.'

'Her brother is Oxford educated?' Maggie said. 'That speaks well of him. What does he do? Is he employed in the banking firm with his father?'

'He's taken over for his father, actually. I understand the senior Mr Rochdale may stand for Parliament. His son Miles oversees day-to-day operation of the bank. And is quite exceptionally competent, Susanna tells me.'

Maggie gave her a shrewd look. 'What do you think of him? You've met, I trust?'

'He's an impressive young man,' Laura said carefully, trying to keep her tone neutral.

'Is he handsome?' Eliza prodded with a grin.

'Quite.' Laura laughed. 'Also quite dismissive of Society ladies. He thinks we are all empty-headed and frivolous.'

'You'd be the lady to convince him otherwise,' Maggie said. 'Laura the mathematician. Not that you need to win his favour, of course. A banker's rich *daughter* may find an aristocratic husband, but a banker's *son* would be entirely ineligible as a match for you.'

'How fortunate I am not angling for a husband,' Laura retorted. No matter how appealing she might find the admittedly unsuitable Mr Rochdale.

'Maggie wouldn't approve, even if he *were* eligible,' Eliza said with a grin. 'He's much too young!'

After batting Eliza's arm, Maggie turned back to Laura. 'Speaking of mathematical ladies, how is Ada—Lady King now, isn't she?'

'Yes, she married the baron at the end of last Season. I understand she's soon to be delivered of their first child, but writes that she intends to continue her interest in mathematics. She took me to meet Mr Babbage at his salon last year, you will remember. I'm looking forward eagerly to returning, when he does one of his lectures to discuss his new Difference Engine.'

Maggie waved a hand. 'You may stop now. You know neither of us would comprehend a word.'

Suppressing a tiny sigh, Laura wondered what it would be like to be able to discuss the invention with someone else who was knowledgeable about mathematics. Someone like… Miles Rochdale, who might not be suitable husband material but who was intimately involved in the world of numbers she loved.

Would the concept of the device fascinate him as much as it did her? She would bet he'd at least be able to understand the idea—which, if Babbage were successful in constructing his machine, might be useful to Rochdale and his bank.

She refocused to find Maggie staring at her, looking as if she intended to enquire further. Wanting to avoid any other questions about Mr Rochdale, Laura said quickly, 'So you have candidates for us to consider?'

Fortunately, that question immediately diverted her friend. 'I charged Mama when she paid calls to enquire particularly after any widowers who met my criteria. She discovered several, all reputed to be amiable, all quite wealthy and all in town this Season.'

'All looking for wives?' Eliza asked sceptically.

'Two of them, definitely. I'm sure either of you could change the minds of the others if they are not intentionally in the market at present. If you choose to. Remember, I'm not forcing you to do this.'

'Are you not?' Laura said, raising her eyebrows with smile.

'Of course not. Just offering alternatives that have the greatest potential to leave you safe and independent. Meet any that interest you and then decide if you wish the acquaintance to go any further.'

'And if we don't?' Laura asked.

Maggie grinned. 'I'll look for other candidates.'

'You don't need to be that diligent. I'm not eager to leave Papa yet.'

'I'm not sure I'm ready to give up on finding a handsome, passionate *young* husband,' Eliza said.

Maggie sighed. 'If you are both going to be impossible, I should wash my hands of you. But I can't. I love you too much. I just want you to be happy.'

Laura linked an arm with each friend. 'We want the same for you.'

'Then you should be satisfied, for I am perfectly happy.'

Would Maggie be 'perfectly happy' to live her whole life alone? Laura wasn't so sure. Would *she*, once her father was gone?

But she couldn't lose Papa—not yet. Papa, who was her link to the halcyon days of her youth, when their family had resided at Haddenly and she'd been secure and happy. Pushing away the disturbing thought of his demise, she said, 'Well, I for one shall be happy to dance now. Shall we?'

After the others nodded agreement, they walked back towards the ballroom. As they entered, a tall gentleman looked over and spied them. An expression of surprise followed by delight lit his face as he walked towards them. 'Lady Margaret! I didn't know you'd returned to London. How nice to see you again!'

'I'm pleased to see you too, Atherton,' Maggie said, offering her hand, which he kissed as she curtsied. 'You'll remember my friends, Lady Laura Pomeroy and Miss Hasterling?'

'Of course. I'm charmed to see you again too, ladies.'

'Why don't you escort Lady Margaret to the refreshment room and let her explain the events that led to her return?' Laura suggested.

'An excellent idea. Ladies, will you accompany us?'

'Thank you, but I need to watch out for my protégée,' Laura said.

'I've promised to help her,' Eliza added, giving Laura a conspiratorial wink.

Offering no objection to being sent off with Atherton, Maggie said, 'I'll find you both later,' and took the gentleman's arm.

'Is there an interest there?' Laura murmured to Eliza as they watched the two walk away.

'I always thought there was. On Atherton's part, at least. Or perhaps he was just amusing himself, dancing attendance on her last Season. He has the reputation of being attentive and charming, but stopping short of any commitment. But Maggie is unusual…'

'If he is interested, given her determination never to wed, he's in for disappointment.'

'Probably,' Eliza agreed. 'However, what happens is up to them. Unlike a certain managing person I could name, *we* do not interfere.'

Laura laughed. 'She *is* managing, but only because she loves us and wants us to be happy.'

'I know. And we love her for it.'

'Ah, I see Innesford approaching with Mr Brightling in tow. Are you ready to dance?'

'Absolutely,' Eliza replied as the gentlemen drew near.

'Me too.' Her dear friends were all together again, Maggie wasn't forcing them to try to charm any of her widowers and Susanna was relaxed and enjoying herself. Without Mr Rochdale present to agitate and tempt her, Laura intended to relax and enjoy herself as well.

Chapter Eight

Two afternoons later, Miles once again took time away from the bank to escort his sister. Having been invited to Lady Laura's house for tea to meet the Countess of Comeryn, Susanna had begged her brother to go with her and help shore up her confidence.

Not in favour of such a plan, he'd argued that first, he'd not been invited; second, the Countess could not be at all interested in meeting him; and, third, that she'd have Lady Laura there to support her. But his sister remained so panicky and nervous that at length, he had relented and agreed to escort her.

When he wondered wryly whether Lady Laura's elevated visitors would even deign to receive him, Susanna reminded him that the Countess's son and heir had married a merchant heiress who, according to Lady Margaret herself, had been warmly embraced by the family. Not wishing to argue further, he'd stifled his reply that an heiress might be accepted; a commoner who earned his bread working in a commercial banking establishment was another matter entirely.

Still unconvinced of the wisdom of the journey, as

they descended from the hackney, he steeled himself for the humiliation of being left to cool his heels in an antechamber while his sister was summoned to meet their hostess.

But Susanna proved correct. The butler who answered their knock greeted his sister cordially and didn't raise an eyebrow at the addition to the party. A few minutes later, they halted on the threshold of the salon as the butler announced them. Hearing Susanna's panicky indrawn breath, he squeezed her hand in encouragement.

His sister's faith in Lady Laura again proved justified. She rose as they entered, coming over to embrace Susanna and curtsey to him, then led them to the sofa where an attractive older woman sat beside a younger one who strikingly resembled her. The Countess of Comeryn and her daughter, Lady Margaret, he assumed.

He steeled himself again to be acknowledged with no more than a nod, but as the introductions were made, Lady Comeryn showed herself as cordial as their hostess, greeting them both warmly.

While Lady Margaret studied him.

'Have you met Lord Carmelton?' Lady Margaret asked him.

'I've not had that pleasure,' Miles replied.

'Laura, why don't you take Mr Rochdale to meet your father while Mama and I get acquainted with his sister?' Lady Margaret suggested. As his sister shot him an alarmed glance, Lady Margaret looked up at Susanna with a smile. 'Here, sit beside me, won't you, Miss Rochdale? Don't worry, Mr Rochdale, we shall take very good care of her. Try to convince your father to join us for tea, won't you, Laura?'

While Susanna took a deep breath and settled into

the place indicated, Lady Laura turned to Miles. 'I think we've been dismissed,' she murmured. 'And I should like to present you to my father.'

Noting that his sister appeared reassured by the cordiality of the Countess and the open friendliness of her daughter, he felt comfortable leaving her. 'I'd be honoured,' he said, meaning it, and automatically offered her his arm.

Not until she looked down at it dubiously did Miles recall that it might not be wise for them to touch. But with Lady Margaret watching them, she must have realised it would look odd if she were to rebuff him. A moment later, murmuring her thanks, she laid her fingers on his arm.

He felt the shock of that contact clear through his jacket and shirt sleeve.

She felt it too, for her gaze flashed to his, her eyes widening as she caught her breath. For a long moment, both stood there, immobile, staring at each other.

She recovered first. 'Sh-shall we go?' she asked, stumbling a little over her words.

Beyond speech himself, the attraction he always felt around her intensified as the intoxicating, disturbing feel of her fingers burned through his garments, he merely nodded and led her out.

For a few heady moments he walked her down the hall, too acutely conscious of her enticing proximity to be aware of anything else. When his brain finally engaged again, he came to a sudden halt. 'I have no idea where your father might be. You will have to tell me where to go.'

That admission seemed to break the spell that bound

them. Removing her hand from his sleeve, she said with grin, 'I'll remember that you invited me to do that.'

Chuckling, Miles said, 'I should perhaps modify that permission.'

She nodded, her eyes dancing. 'That would probably be prudent.'

He didn't want to be prudent. Already regretting the loss of her hand on his arm, he was tempted to snatch it back. But he wasn't reckless enough to do that.

Would she slap him for presumption if he did? Or link her fingers with his and squeeze them?

Stifling a groan, he felt body his harden at the thought. Better direct his wayward imagining elsewhere if he meant to get comfortably through this time alone with her. He had no doubt the Marquess would not appreciate so unsuitable a man lusting over his daughter.

Dragging his thoughts to a more appropriate subject, he said, 'You mentioned that your father has been ill. He is better, I trust?'

Sighing, she looked troubled. 'My parents were involved in a serious carriage accident several years ago. My mother…did not long survive it, and Papa was gravely injured.'

From the distress he read in her face, she still felt the tragedy keenly. 'I'm so sorry.'

She nodded absently to acknowledge his condolence. 'Papa broke his hip and several ribs. Gradually, the bones healed, but it's still difficult for him to walk and he's in constant pain. We brought him to London after the accident so he might be treated by the foremost experts, and we have remained here ever since so they may continue his treatment. Which forced him to turn the management of our country properties over to my brother.'

She sighed again. 'He never complains. The only way I know a day is particularly difficult is when he retires to his room, and he only does so when he really can't bear it any more. Easier, more manageable days, he spends in the conservatory he had constructed at the back of the garden. Which is where we'll find him now. If you'll follow me?'

Miles nodded, wishing he dared reclaim her hand. She walked him down the hall, past what appeared to be an informal morning room into a larger room whose fully stocked floor-to-ceiling bookshelves identified it as the library. French doors at its far side led to a bricked walkway, at the end of which he spied a surprisingly large glass house, lush greenery evident on the other side of the mullioned panels.

'Papa developed an interest in botany while at university,' she told him as they walked. 'Later, when he learned he might become the next Marquess of Carmelton, he visited Warnton to meet the tenants and learned that the estate depends on its orchards for most of its income. From his prior studies, he knew the works of Thomas Knight on fruit tree propagation. He joined the Royal Horticultural Society and also participated in seed exchanges with the Chelsea Physic Garden, intent on maximising the yield of the apple crops.

'He was actively involved in managing the orchards, but the riding and extensive walking necessary to tend them became impossible after the accident. He had the glass house constructed here so he might at least continue his experiments with developing new and better varieties. He also enjoys planting seeds of exotic species the Society's plant hunters bring back from all over the world. His current greatest success is with azaleas. Those lovely small shrubs, now blooming, that border the path near the glass house,' she said, pointing.

Miles followed her gesture to a line of small shrubs covered with showy flowers in shades of pink and coral. 'The colours are brilliant.'

'Yes. Lovely, aren't they?'

As they approached the entrance to the glass house, Lady Laura halted, Miles stopping beside her. Gesturing within, she said softly, 'Papa's at his work bench, transferring seedlings from the large tray into small pots. It's difficult for him, keeping his arms raised for more than a few minutes at a time, but he won't let anyone help. The plant roots are too delicate, he says, so he wants to manage the new seedlings himself. I'd rather not interrupt him, but let him complete the process, so he can rest immediately once he's done, if necessary. Shall I show you the rest of the garden while we wait?'

If you'll take my arm again, he wanted to say.

Though that would be unwise. If she took his arm and they strolled down a pathway, hidden from view by the hedges and shrubs, he wouldn't want to let her go. He would want instead to draw her closer. Kiss her.

As he stared down at her, their gazes locked. She ran the tip of her tongue over her lips, as if she knew the direction of his thoughts. As if her thoughts were racing in that same direction. Though they stood several feet apart, not an inch of their bodies touching, his whole body tingled and burned.

He ought to turn and flee back to the house. Instead, he said, 'I'd love to see the rest of garden.'

Please Lord, let me manage it without trying to kiss her.

She jerked her gaze away at last, as if she too were having trouble concentrating on anything beyond the sizzling connection between them. Gesturing to him to follow her, she resumed walking. Did her voice sound strained or was that only his imagination?

He forced himself to concentrate on what she was saying, fixing his attention on the plants towards which she was gesturing rather than on her face, her moving lips, the gentle sway of her lushly curved body…

'Father was first interested only in food crops and trees, but with the limited space of our city garden he turned his attention to herbs and ornamentals. Design fascinates him too—how to arrange plants in the most pleasing order. As in the herb garden.'

She led him to an open square of ground whose centre was planted with a circle of greenery. A low, clipped hedge outlined the area and divided the circle into pie-shaped beds filled with a variety of low-growing plants.

She pointed out blue-leaved rue contrasting with deep-green fringed parsley, tall spiky leaves of onion and garlic, feathery carrot, fennel and coriander, silvery sage and lavender. Bending to trail her fingers through the lavender, she said, 'The purple flowers in summer are lovely, but the scented leaves are marvellous at any time of year.'

He'd initially been too distracted by her proximity to fully take in what she was saying, but as he forced himself to pay attention, his interest grew. 'Your father has a painter's eye for colour and texture,' he observed.

She looked at him, her expression pleased. 'He does, doesn't he? I love the subtle variety of colours and textures. And all the herbal scents.'

She took a deep breath. 'Wonderful, isn't it? There,

against the wall, a line of lilacs will bloom soon. It's the most fragrant walk in the garden before the roses begin. Whenever I'm feeling melancholy, I walk here just to breathe in their scent. It always makes me feel better.'

He studied her face, her serene expression overlaid with a touch of sadness. 'Are you often melancholy?'

'Oh, no. I do worry about Papa, though. I try to help him in his cataloguing work, make sure he rests and doesn't overtax himself. Read to him in the evenings, so he can recline and spare his eyes.'

'Stay at home and read rather than attend parties and dance?' he teased.

'Some things are more important. I've learned not to take for granted the people I love. You never know how long you will have them with you.'

She'd learned that bitter truth at a young age, he thought, compassion filling him. She was a concerned and dutiful daughter, her heart filled with the same kind of care and concern she'd shown his sister.

Hardly the heedless, giddy, shallow debutante he'd first thought her.

Wanting to pull her from sorrowful reflections, he said, 'What do you like to do when you're not tending your father or walking in the garden?'

'I ride most mornings. Update and maintain the household ledgers. Before the accident, I'd begun doing that for the estate books at Warnton and Haddenly, which are much more involved than those for just the town-house. I amuse myself inventing algorithms to predict future expenses based on past expenditures, then comparing the actual figures to the projected ones.'

'You really are a scholar!' he said, impressed.

She waved a self-deprecating hand. 'Not really. Not

like my friend, Lady King. Or her mathematics tutor, Mary Somerville, who has published books on the mathematical working of the solar system! I do like to visit Mrs Somerville and attend the lectures of Mr Babbage. Have you heard of his Difference Engine? He believes it will be able to do calculations faster than a person can think!'

'That would be useful.'

'Yes, I should think anyone who deals with numbers would find it fascinating. Perhaps…perhaps you might like to attend one of the lectures?'

'I think I should like that very much.'

The sparkle of excitement in her eyes gratified him immensely. 'We shall have to arrange a time, then.'

Although his awareness of their physical connection never dimmed, her talk about plants and now numbers helped distract him from its pull. It also made him more curious about her, increasing his urge to know her better.

He pushed away the thought that, attracted to her as he was, getting to know her better wasn't wise. He countered that caution by pointing out to himself that their association would certainly be brief. Once his sister found her husband, probably this Season—and, he hoped, someone from their own social rank—they would have no common acquaintance to bring the two of them together. Moving as they did in different social circles, they would be unlikely to meet again.

He'd indulge himself to spend time with this unusual woman while the opportunity lasted.

Being with her was like…being drawn to solve a mathematical puzzle. Once he had the stimulation of figuring it out, he could return to straightforward accounting.

Though that analogy wasn't quite apt, he thought with a quirk of his lips. He'd never had a simmering desire to kiss a quadratic equation.

She led him back along another path bordered by shrubs planted for their variety of colour and texture, naming and identifying the country of origin for each of them, until they meandered back to the glass house. Peeking inside, she said, 'Good, he's finished transplanting. Shall we go in?'

'After you,' he gestured, curious now to meet the man responsible for the artful arrangement of colour and greenery through which they'd just strolled.

A tall, thin man with greying hair and a face lined by suffering was seated on a padded bench before a table covered by rows of pots filled with small plants. He held a ruler in one hand, measuring the height of the seedlings, then writing in a journal with the other.

He looked up when they walked in, his eyes brightening and his expression warming as he recognised his daughter, who went over to kiss his cheek.

'Don't get up, Papa. Remember I told you my friend Susanna was coming to visit today? She's currently occupied by Lady Maggie and her mother. This is her brother, Mr Miles Rochdale.'

'My lord,' Miles said, bowing.

'Rochdale…' the Marquess repeated, nodding to Miles. 'Your father is a partner in Martin and Rochdale Bank, isn't he?'

'Yes, my lord.'

'About to run for Parliament, I hear.' Miles must have looked as surprised as he felt that a highly placed peer would know much about his family, for the Marquess smiled. 'I don't get out often, but I do keep up with what is going on in the world. Even if my daughter believes I pay no attention to anything beyond my plants.'

'Not at all, Papa,' Lady Laura protested. 'We often debate parliamentary matters. And you read all the daily papers.'

'You've taken over the bank for him, I expect, so he may concentrate on his Parliamentary aspirations?' When Miles nodded, her father continued, 'Yes, the younger generation must take on the duties of your elders in your turn, as my son is doing with Warnton. I understand your bank handles numerous investments.'

'We consider many options to increase our investors' income.'

'Like railway stocks? My banker recently put a large part of his deposits into a new line to be built in the north. I imagine your bank is doing likewise.'

Miles hesitated. The first railway ventures, like the Liverpool and Manchester, had provided their investors with such splendid returns that others had flocked to put their capital into new lines. There was now such a flood of proposed enterprises being approved that the experts Miles consulted had urged caution, as many of the suggested routes paralleled existing ones or were to be constructed through areas that would be expensive, if not impossible, to build on profitably.

His advisor felt there was a good chance many of the recent schemes wouldn't return more than the investors' original sum, and the riskier ones might fail altogether. As a result, despite urging from Martin and some of their bank's other backers, Miles had declined to put any of Martin and Rochdale's money into railway construction.

But he wouldn't be presumptuous enough to caution against the investment policy of the Marquess's bank.

'Railways have been a great investment in the past,' he replied carefully.

The Marquess smiled. 'As long as the returns are enough to fund my plant studies. We need to continue producing superior apples and beautiful shrubs, don't we, my love?' he said to his daughter.

'Your garden is certainly impressive, my lord. As magnificent as anything I've seen in the countryside.'

'Mr Rochdale has a fondness for the country,' Lady Laura said.

'Indeed? I thought you bankers never left your counting houses,' Carmelton said with a smile.

'Now, before you pull Mr Rochdale into a discussion of plant selection, Lady Comeryn is very much hoping you will join us for tea, Papa. Will you?'

The Marquess's smile faded and, for an instant, Miles glimpsed a grimace of pain. 'I'm sorry to disappoint her, but I must admit to feeling rather tired. I don't think I can manage the ritual of tea at present.'

Lady Laura's pleasant expression changed at once to concern. 'Should I call Harris to bring your rolling chair?'

'No need, I'm almost finished here. If you'll walk with me, I think I can make it to my chamber without using the chair.'

'I'm happy to lend my arm, if you'll permit, my lord,' Miles said. He watched with some concern as the Marquess slowly levered himself off the bench, but at a warning glance from Lady Laura he refrained from grabbing the man's elbow to help him up. He did extend his arm, though, which Lord Carmelton took with his right hand, while his daughter put her hand under his left arm. With them bracketing the Marquess, they made their way down the path, slowing their pace even further as the Marquess struggled up the few steps into the library.

Miles watched Lady Laura watching her father, noting with concern the paleness of the man's face, his laboured breathing as he climbed, his hand clutching Miles's arm.

'Are you sure you can manage getting to your room?' Lady Laura voiced the question Miles was wondering.

'I can,' Carmelton said quietly. He gave his daughter a tired smile. 'Don't fuss, my dear.'

Pressing her lips together, Lady Laura remained silent as they helped the Marquess on his slow ascent to his bed chamber on the first floor. He halted by the door, breathing heavily for a moment, before saying, 'Please give my regrets to Maggie and the Countess.'

'I'll see you for dinner?' Lady Laura asked.

Carmelton forced a smile past the whiteness of his lips. 'I shall rally in time, my dear.'

'I'll ring for Harris to attend you.'

This time, the Marquess didn't refuse. But, straightening, he turned to make Miles a bow. 'A pleasure to meet you, young man.'

'The honour is mine, my lord,' Miles said, admiring the man's stoic fortitude in the face of his obvious pain.

Lady Laura's face remained clouded as they walked back down the stairs. 'It must be hard for you to see him in distress,' he said, observing her with sympathy.

She nodded. 'He never complains, no matter how difficult walking becomes. It's…agonising, looking on but not being able to do anything to help.'

'I'm sure just having you near is an immense help.'

She gave him a tremulous smile. 'I hope so. You see

why I'm not interested in snagging a rich title—or any husband. Not when Papa needs me.'

She blew out a breath, her face brightening. 'But we mustn't appear dreary when we return to your sister and Lady Margaret. I don't wish to alarm the Countess, either. She and my father have been friends for many years. She cares about him and has a tender heart. Which she will engage on behalf of your sister.'

'How can she help my sister?'

Lady Laura gave him an exasperated look. 'How can a woman who has for years corresponded with the highest arbiters of London Society help your sister?'

'I'm not that mutton-headed,' he protested. 'Yes, she's a countess, but I understood she hasn't spent much time in London since her marriage. I had no idea how current her connections were.'

'Very well,' she relented. 'The Countess is a lovely, sweet-tempered lady, much beloved of her many friends who did remain in London, sympathised with her…difficult situation and did all they could to support her by corresponding frequently, sending her all the London news and gossip.'

'Her…difficult situation?' Miles said, puzzled. How could a woman as privileged as a countess find her situation 'difficult'?

Lady Laura was silent a moment. 'Her husband, the Earl of Comeryn, is a…demanding individual. Autocratic, dictatorial, ruling with an iron hand. His wife is a gentle creature whom he completely dominated. Their older daughter is as imperious and proud as her father, but their son Crispin and daughter Margaret…'

'Are resistant?'

'Yes. They haven't their father's selfish nature, but

they do have his stubbornness and strong will. Crispin refused to yield to his father's dictates and left home, making financial investments that have left him independent of his father. Maggie defied the earl's command to marry the man he'd selected and was banished to the country. But her brother turned a modest amount given to her by an aunt into a handsome sum that has enabled her to return to London, no longer dependent on her father and able to bring her long-exiled mother back into Society and the city she loves.'

Miles frowned. 'I cannot endorse an abusive husband, but I'm also not sure a lady living independently is a wise practice. Who will protect her?'

Lady Laura laughed shortly. 'Protect? Imagine being subject to the whims of one's father, unable either to earn one's own living or decide what one wished to do with one's life! Being browbeaten into wedding someone one didn't want, or shipped off to be a drudge looking after the children or the elderly of the family, with no hope of escape?'

'It would be hard,' Miles admitted. 'But surely you don't believe all men are as careless of a wife or daughter's well-being as the earl.'

'No. Father certainly isn't.' She sighed. 'It was rather the opposite problem with my parents. They were devoted to each other. When he lost my mother, Papa very nearly lost all interest in living. I was afraid for a while, broken and in pain as he was, he'd not make the effort to go on. I don't think I'd want to be that dependent on anyone for my well-being. In wanting independence, Lady Margaret may have chosen a better way.'

'Probably better for her potential husband as well,' Miles said with a smile. 'If she is as strong-minded as all that, she would probably run roughshod over her poor spouse.'

'Probably,' Lady Laura said with an answering smile. 'She'd lead him a merry dance, in any event. Shall we go in?'

Miles felt an immediate protest at the prospect of ending their private interlude. He wished there was some way to prolong it, to continue to listen to her sweet voice, her unusual perspective on life and interesting observations. But he couldn't think of any socially permissible way to stretch out the time any further.

'I find you fascinating and want to learn more about you' wasn't an acceptable excuse.

'Yes, let's go in,' he said at last. 'I shall watch myself around the strong-minded Lady Margaret.'

'Yes, you'd better. She would not at all be restrained by politeness from taking you to task if she feels you deserve it.' She sighed. 'I only hope I can stave off her little project.'

To his surprise, her face immediately coloured.

'Her project?' he repeated, curious.

'I shouldn't have said anything.' When he raised his eyebrows, she said, 'But, since I did, I suppose I can tell you. She wants us to marry older gentlemen who will leave us rich widows, so we may achieve the independence she has.'

Miles would have laughed, but Lady Laura's expression told him she was entirely serious.

'Are you inclined to follow her advice?' he asked, incredulous.

'No—maybe. Oh, I don't know. I'm not inclined to marry at all, though probably I shall have to some day.

I must admit, the idea of marrying someone who might soon leave me free and independent does have appeal.'

The thought that the physical vitality he sensed in her might be left dormant, untapped by an ailing husband for whom she would be little more than a nursemaid, seemed a sacrilege. 'What of…passion?'

She looked away. 'Your sister asked the same thing.'

Driven by the need to convince her of the folly of such a course, without thinking he took her hand. When she looked up at him, startled, he brought it to his lips and kissed it lingeringly.

He exulted in the scent of her, the softness of her skin under his mouth. He would have preferred to kiss her lips, parted now with surprise, but knew saluting her fingers was audacious enough.

'Do you really want to miss…this?' he whispered.

She stared at him as if mesmerised, those tempting lips still slightly parted. His own breath was coming quickly, heat building up in his body. Damn and blast, how she affected him!

The only thing that made that knowledge tolerable was observing how clearly he affected her, he noted with a fierce surge of gladness.

At last she pulled her fingers away. 'We'd b-better go in,' she stuttered.

He didn't want to let her go. He'd rather have remained in the hall, both of them locked in place by the force of the pull between them. But she was right: they should go in before he was tempted to any further madness.

Such as pulling her into his arms and kissing the lips he burned to touch.

Chapter Nine

Two nights later, during the intermission between acts, Laura strolled with Miles Rochdale through the grand vestibule of Covent Garden theatre, pausing by the Ionic columns flanking the staircase that led to the boxes. Flower girls selling posies and orange vendors offering their fruit mingled with elegantly dressed members of the *ton* who'd descended from the boxes and people in various manners of dress who'd come out from the pit.

Though the area was crowded enough that Laura would have been well justified to take her escort's arm—and crowded enough to forestall any amorous impulses his touch and proximity evoked—after the shock of his touch and those amorous urges she'd had to restrain during their walk in her father's garden, she kept her arms firmly by her side.

Even without touching him, she was still supremely conscious of him walking beside her, she thought with a little sigh. She had hoped that, as she saw him more often and became accustomed to his presence, the potent effect he had on her senses would dissipate. Although, mercifully, it hadn't intensified, neither had it diminished—nor was she less moved by it as she got to know him better and appreciate the individual for himself.

She appreciated him enough to want to continue seeing him, despite the distraction of his physical allure. With a man who understood and enjoyed numbers, who worked with them daily, she wanted to seize the opportunity to learn as much as she could about the fascinating world of banking and accounting before end of Season, or his sister's need for the lessons which had given them an excuse to meet, put paid to the association between them.

It was just as well that association would be brief, else she might grow too fond of someone whose position in life made it virtually impossible for her to keep him as a friend. Or anything more intimate. She could already tell that Miles Rochdale might be someone to whom she could grow attached. She'd seen in her parents' case how devastating a too-strong attachment to another person could be.

But that caution—and the danger of his attractiveness—didn't mean she wasn't determined to make the most of the time they could share.

Though it might be well to avoid unchaperoned walks down leafy garden paths.

He'd wanted to kiss her in the garden, she was almost certain. What was worse, she'd wanted even more to kiss him back. Which would never do. Future meetings must be in crowded venues like this room, a family drawing room or at a lecture given by Mr Babbage.

As they paused to look around, Laura frowned. 'I'm afraid we may have lost Susanna, Mr Rochdale. I cannot see her or Lord Innesford.'

The baron had dropped by their box, and at Susanna's expressed desire for an orange, Innesford had offered to escort her to obtain one. When Rochdale, who'd been chatting with Lady Margaret, had noticed her departure, he'd caught up Laura to accompany him into the milling crowd so they might chaperon his sister.

After gazing this way and that, she looked back to find Rochdale studying her, the intensity of his gaze sending a shock to her nerves.

His face colouring slightly at having been caught staring, he immediately looked away to scan the room, giving her a chance to recover. 'I don't see them either.'

'Don't be too alarmed. They continued downstairs ahead of us while I was admiring the pictures of Shakespearean theatre scenes in the vestibule. Your sister wouldn't allow anyone to lead her off—even if Innesford were rakish enough to suggest such a thing. Most likely, he bought her oranges and a posy and has already escorted her back to the box.'

From his superior height, which gave him a better view, Miles turned and pointed. 'No, I see Innesford over there, haggling with a flower girl.'

The tension she'd noted in him when he'd not been able to locate his sister relaxed. Rochdale might be judgmental and quick to jump to conclusions—she recalled again his disdain at their first meeting—but he truly was a concerned brother. She had to admire his protectiveness and genuine desire to see to sister's welfare. Which evidently stretched far enough to accompany her to the opera, an entertainment he'd already confessed he didn't much enjoy.

'He's just obtained the posy, so they will likely head back upstairs. We can return too, if you'd like.'

'There's some time remaining in the intermission.

You must be glad of the break, since you don't particularly care for opera. Are you fond of any other music?'

'I prefer ensemble music—without singing. Handel, Bach, Beethoven.'

'I'm particularly fond of Beethoven myself,' she said with a stir of enthusiasm at discovering he shared her interest. 'Have you attended the concerts of the Philharmonic Society in Hanover Square?'

'Occasionally.'

'If you insist on nobly dragging yourself out to fulfil your duty of watching over your sister, you must persuade her to attend some concerts there. You might as well make duty more enjoyable.'

He turned from surveying the crowd to look back at her, his thoughtful gaze roving her face to rest on her mouth. She felt the force of it, almost as if the tip of his finger rather than his glance had skimmed over her, leaving her skin tingling. 'I am enjoying it tonight,' he said softly.

'As am I…' she breathed, not sure whether or not she'd murmured the words aloud.

Just then a passer-by jostled him. Startled, he looked away, ending the moment.

Though his gaze had left her, she still felt the shimmering echo of it on her skin. What if his lips, rather than his gaze, had caressed her mouth, as they had her hand two days ago?

She felt suddenly warm, and a swooping sensation fluttered in her belly. Yes, she was enjoying his company. She was tantalised by it, as she'd been in Papa's garden.

What power he exerted over her senses, that he could stimulate them even in this noisy room crowded with people! Shouldn't that be a warning to her to avoid him?

She suddenly realised he'd resumed walking and scrambled to match his pace.

'I don't discount the significance of the Countess of Comeryn adding her good offices to your efforts to smooth my sister's way,' he said. 'I know you mean to help Susanna by introducing them. But I'd rather you not introduce her to any gentleman she might find *too* appealing.'

Laura followed the direction of his gaze, where Susanna was strolling with her escort.

'You needn't worry about Innesford. He loves squiring the ladies, but has no interest whatsoever in getting married. For another decade at least, he tells me.'

'That's reassuring,' Rochdale said drily. 'But it's not just Innesford—any aristocrat. Better that Susanna remain in her own sphere, married to someone of her own rank.'

Laura raised her eyebrows. 'The marriages of those from the same rank of Society being always happy?'

Rochdale frowned. 'Not always, I grant you. But the lower orders are often too preoccupied working to provide the necessities of life for their families to worry about esoteric concepts of romantic love.'

Laura shook her head. 'I think you're wrong. All humans, whatever their station, long for connection with someone, some intimate with whom to share the grief and joys of life. Besides, if Susanna wants to marry an aristocrat—and I'm not saying she does or would—should that not be her own choice?'

Before he could reply, she went on, 'You mustn't think I don't appreciate your concern. I wouldn't want to see her wed to the son of someone like Lady Arbuthnot. But, despite my friend Maggie's assertion, not all aristocrats are puffed up with their own importance. Your friend Mr Ecclesley, for example, whom she seems to like. Surely you would approve of him, were they to make a match of it?'

Rochdale sighed. 'That would be difficult. Thomas is a capital gentleman. But I know his family wants him to make up for his lack of inherited fortune by marrying a girl of sufficient dowry, preferably one with exalted connections. Given his family's aspirations, I'm not sure he could make my sister happy. I still believe in the long run she'd be more content remaining among her own.'

'Isn't it more important that she wed the man *she* thinks will make her happy?'

'Love can blind one to facts that, once the romantic mist dissipates, make for disappointment and disillusion.'

The sudden sharpness of his tone surprised her, its bitterness making her think he must speak from experience. Could some female have injured him? The possibility was so startling she almost didn't catch his next remark, uttered in a more moderate tone.

'A disinterested observer who has one's best interests at heart can see more clearly.'

Leaving aside speculation about his possible heartbreak, Laura said, 'But a disinterested observer doesn't know the claims of the heart or their importance. True, if Susanna's husband were very highly born, his family might not want to entertain your mother or your father's business associates. But, if your father is to become a Member of Parliament, that would make a difference.'

'Perhaps. But what if he does not? I wouldn't want to gamble her happiness on that prospect. But enough about Susanna. She tells me you have some prospective beaux too, to whom Lady Margaret plans to introduce you. Who, I expect, given what you've told me of Lady Margaret's requirements, must be rather elderly gentlemen. How is that calculating scheme working out?'

Laura laughed. 'She hasn't introduced us—yet. And, if she does, why should that scheme be any more calculating than a female trying to attract a rich *young* man? Which is the goal most parents set for their daughters, along with cementing alliances or increasing family status. At the very least, the goal is attracting a suitor who will best be able to support her and their eventual children.'

'I suppose,' he allowed.

'You have to admit, the idea of swiftly becoming a rich widow isn't as outlandish as it might at first seem. As a man, you cannot appreciate how little control women have over their lives. You, who have the freedom to remain with your family or move away, earn your own fortune, pursue whatever vocation you choose.'

'But as you just said, the whole purpose of marriage is for a woman to find a man who can provide for her and her children. Someone who can keep her, and them, safe. A girl's parents won't live for ever. Don't you want for yourself the protection of a husband? And what of children? Do you have no wish for any of your own?'

That was the sticking point. Unlike Maggie, who claimed to be satisfied to have her brother's children to dote on, Laura wasn't so sure she was ready to give up the possibility of holding her own babe in her arms. 'I would like children,' she admitted. 'And as a rich widow, having them would mean being willing to live with more scandal than I would find tolerable. If only children didn't come with a husband attached!'

'Someone like Mr Fullridge of Fullridge Manor in Essex? He's a major investor in a bank directed by a friend of my father. A good, steady man. Mr Garthorpe I don't know, but I assume Lady Margaret wouldn't propose to you anyone who wasn't a true gentleman.'

Laura looked at him in surprise. Susanna must have told him about Maggie's candidates. Was he checking up on her again? Or…did he feel protective towards her, as he did towards his sister? Once upon a time, her father had fulfilled that role, but since the accident she'd had no champion. The thought that Rochdale might be willing to fill that void was warming.

Before she could hit upon a reply, Rochdale said with studied casualness, 'Are you inclined to favour either of them?'

Could he be…jealous? The very idea produced a spark of feminine gratification, quickly snuffed out. More likely he was merely curious, or making polite conversation. As she'd instructed him—to ask about a lady's interests. Every gentleman believed a female's prime interest was her suitors.

Unfortunately, in most cases, that assessment would be correct.

'Both appear to be respectable gentlemen, but as I told you before, I'm not sure I'm inclined to favour Lady Margaret's proposition, much less choose any particular prospect. As I said, for the immediate future, my father's well-being is my greatest concern.'

'It would be a comfort to him to know you were settled, though, I would imagine. Especially if his health is…precarious.'

The prospect of losing him was still so distressing, she pushed it away. 'It's true he suffers chronic pain, but otherwise his health is good. I expect to have him around to dote on for many years.'

'Before wedding that feeble older gentleman who will soon make you a rich widow?'

His slightly mocking tone annoying her, she countered, 'Is that any different from a young man seeking to wed a woman with a substantial dowry to bolster his estate...or his business? Or wishing to forge an alliance of families with similar interests, like yours with Miss Dunnock?'

She regretted the remark the instant the words left her lips. 'Excuse me, I shouldn't have brought your Miss Dunnock into this,' she said quickly, feeling her face colour.

'Such alliances are made, I concede,' he said. But the faint trace of a grin on his lips said he was enjoying her discomfort.

Somehow that annoyed her even more. 'Susanna gave me to understand you are very busy at the bank. I wonder that you are able to get away so often to accompany her,' she said tartly.

His grin widened. 'You are ready to be rid of me?'

She felt her blush heighten. At the moment she'd spoken, she had wished him elsewhere. But now...once again, she resented the strong pull that made her want to appease him, to ensure he thought well of her. 'Or will you only accompany Susanna until you are sure I'm not going to lead her astray?'

'I'm about ready to acquit you of that now,' he said quietly.

Trying not to feel gratified, she mumbled, 'How gracious of you.' Why should she need to prove herself to him? Susanna knew her interest was genuine and helpful, and that should be all that mattered.

'Shall we cry *pax*? I'm willing to concede we both want the best for her.'

It was a handsome admission. This time she felt truly gratified, even if she resented having the feeling, and its effect in magnifying his already too-strong attraction.

'I'm glad you now believe I do want what's best for her. She's a sweet, gentle soul who should be happy.'

'I'll do my best to guarantee that. I insist on meeting any suitors who call, naturally. I'll put the fear of God into them and frighten away any who think to snatch her up for her fortune.'

'I agree with that, but you mustn't scare off all her suitors. Unlike me, Susanna does want to marry.'

'And I want her to as well. Just…'

'Someone suitable,' Laura filled in for him.

The bell rang, signalling the end of the intermission. 'I suppose now we must get back,' Rochdale said with a grimace.

Laura grinned. 'I know how eager you are to hear the soprano aria in the third act.'

He groaned and put a hand to his ear. 'Maybe if I move my chair to the wall and press my head against it, I can block it out.'

Laughing, she let him lead her back up the staircase.

As she walked, Laura marvelled at how much he attracted and intrigued her. But she'd better decide quickly what else she wanted to learn from and about him. With him admitting he no longer thought her a bad influence on his sister, there was no reason for him to continue to attend her lessons. For despite his bland assertion that he needed practice in wooing, Laura was certain he'd only agreed to join them to protect Susanna from her supposedly malign influence.

Once he stopped attending the lessons, it was unlikely that they would meet again.

Before she could regret the fact, she resolutely pushed the thought away.

Chapter Ten

As it happened, at their next lesson two days later, Rochdale was not present. Laura was uncomfortably conscious of a sharp disappointment when her friend informed her a meeting had been called at an associate's bank that her brother thought it necessary to attend.

She enjoyed Susanna's company, and as the lesson went on felt satisfaction at watching her increase in confidence. But much as it perturbed her to admit it, she was honest enough to acknowledge that Rochdale's absence took the spice of excitement out of the session.

The disappointment and missing him was followed by a vague sense of alarm. Now that he'd conceded he no longer believed her a bad influence on his sister, had he abruptly ended their association? An unwelcome dismay rose in her at the possibility she might never see him again.

Torn between asking about him and saying nothing, after Susanna finished her practice, Laura said, 'I believe you probably only need one final lesson—conversation while dancing. As for flirtation, the most effective form is good conversation, along with subtle use of the fan. But there are a few additional techniques we can practise.'

'I would appreciate doing that before my next ball! I cannot always dance with Eccleston, who makes conversation so easy.'

'Conversation is always easier with someone you know well and with whom you feel comfortable. Or with a new, interesting acquaintance about whom you are curious enough that you forget to be self-conscious. It's gentlemen who give you monosyllabic answers and contribute almost nothing to the exchange that make it difficult.'

'Like my brother at that practice session before I scolded him!' Susanna said with a laugh.

Fortunately, as Laura was still unsure whether or not or how to enquire about that gentleman, Susanna added, 'I will make sure Miles attends *this* lesson. Besides, I will need a dance partner to practise with, since you will have to play for me.'

'Very true,' Laura agreed, feeling a wave of guilty relief and an anticipation greater than she should have.

She would see him again at least once, then.

She'd better have all her questions ready, for that session might indeed be the last time they would meet.

She would be sad to have their association ended. Rochdale reminded her of her adored older brother in many ways—his sense of responsibility, his concern for his sister, his dedication to work and family.

Although the attraction that always simmered between them engendered feelings that were far from sisterly. He was, she admitted to herself, a man she might well become attached to. However, even if they might somehow work out the difference in stations, he obviously had no interest in becoming attached to her. Despite the physical attraction she had no doubt he felt as strongly as she did, he had his future mapped out with his intended, Miss Dunnock.

Although he didn't seem much more interested in his supposed intended than he was in her. Certainly she didn't sense in him the eagerness of a lover she would hope for in anyone she herself agreed to marry.

Had he experienced an unhappy love affair that had left him resolved never to risk his emotions again? She recalled his cryptic comment about Society needing fewer ladies who tried to beguile every man they met. Had he been 'beguiled' and deceived?

A question she could never ask him, of course. Too personal, and really none of her business. Especially as they were soon to part ways.

She smothered an automatic protest of that fact by reminding herself she'd known from the start their association would be brief. What good would it do to stretch it out anyway? Strongly as she was drawn to him, more exposure to his tantalising presence might lead her into an indiscretion they would both regret. Knowing and liking him better would only increase the disappointment that they couldn't become permanent friends.

Which they could not…could they?

Brought up short by that tantalising speculation, she was still distracted when Susanna rose to escort her to the door.

'Mama is coming to claim me for a shopping trip,' she said as they entered the hall. 'Are you sure you won't join us?'

'I have a burning desire for a new bonnet, but I cannot. I promised Papa I would stop by Kew Gardens today and bring back some boxes of plants. Mr Foster, the head gardener, wrote to him that cuttings he'd made of some rare varieties from China have taken well and are now large enough for transplanting into pots that Papa can tend.'

'Very well, then. You mustn't disappoint your father.'

After bidding each other goodbye on the doorstep, Laura set off to meet the waiting hackney.

She'd descended the front steps and was about to board the vehicle when Miles Rochdale appeared from round the corner, walking towards the townhouse.

Her heart giving a little leap of gladness, Laura halted. Rochdale stopped too and made her a bow.

'Lady Laura, good day. I'm sorry to have missed your lesson. I imagine it was very informative.'

Did she detect a touch of teasing in his tone? 'I'm sure you could have learned something useful, had you bothered to attend,' she said tartly.

He chuckled. 'I'm sure I could have. I must thank you again, though. Little as I like to see Susanna forced to associate with Society, most of whom look down on her, I can't help but notice how much happier and more confident she has been since you've begun your tutoring.' He smiled. 'I'll thank you even more if you can manage to help her avoid becoming infatuated with any of the aristocrats she chances to meet.'

'Now on that point we will never agree. Should she meet someone worthy of her and fall in love, I cannot promise to discourage her attachment.'

'Very well, we'll agree to disagree. Are you heading home, or off for more shopping? Where is the footman to carry all your purchases?'

'I'm off neither to home nor to shopping. I'm heading to Kew Gardens to collect some rooted cuttings for my father. He could have the gardener just send them, but I would rather inspect them first, to make sure they are of the size and condition he requires. I've assisted him often enough to know his expectations, which one of our footmen or the garden's employees would not.' She laughed. 'Papa also says the footmen are too rough, and the tiny plants need a delicate touch, which I can offer.'

He nodded. 'I remember you telling me he insisted on personally transplanting his seedlings for the same reason. But…' He looked towards the steps. 'You brought no maid with you? Surely you don't intend to traverse London alone?'

'No, I didn't bring her. I could let her walk along the pathways rather than linger, bored, while I converse with the head gardener, but she wouldn't enjoy that either. Yes, I realise convention says I should be accompanied whenever I go beyond the confines of Mayfair, but it's not as if I intend to walk there and back alone. I'll be safe enough in the hackney and within the confines of the gardens. Papa is well acquainted with Mr Foster, the head gardener, whom I've known since I was a little girl. He trusts the Kew staff to watch out for me while I'm on their property and make sure I'm safely embarked home with the boxes afterward.'

Rochdale frowned, her explanation apparently not convincing him. 'Would you consider borrowing one of our maids to accompany you?'

'It's kind of you to be concerned, but I imagine if I were to drag one there she would be just as bored as my Gibson. I'm sure all your maids are busy with work of their own, which doesn't need to be delayed while one is dragooned into accompanying me.'

Still Rochdale hesitated. 'I cannot feel easy at the

idea of you travelling there alone,' he said at last. 'I was more or less on my way back to the bank anyway. Will you let me escort you? If you will walk with me to the livery, we can take the carriage the establishment keeps ready for my family's use. There would be no impropriety in my accompanying you in an open carriage. I could also wait while you collect your father's boxes and then see you home.'

It was a generous offer, leaving Laura torn. She couldn't make herself utter the falsehood that she would prefer not to have his company. 'I wouldn't want to inconvenience you,' she said at last, hitting upon something she could say truthfully.

'It's no inconvenience. I would never forgive myself if I sent Susanna's dear friend off unattended and something untoward happened to her.'

His concern gratified her, but she managed to still her lips before she could impulsively ask if he was only concerned about her on his sister's behalf. 'I wouldn't want to bore you either. Besides, I'm sure you have even more pressing duties awaiting you than any maid I might borrow.'

'I wouldn't be bored,' he countered. 'I found the walk in your father's garden…fascinating. I'd be interested to learn more about rare plants and their care. True, I do have duties awaiting me, but they will still be there in another hour or so.'

She should be polite and refuse…but she couldn't quite make herself. Not when he'd just presented her with a golden opportunity to ask him all the questions she had about banking and finance, a topic which she found fascinating and about which, once their association ended, she would probably never have another chance to learn.

To say nothing of the prospect of riding beside him, savouring the tantalising, illicit thrill of his presence while perched in a place that would prevent her succumbing to impropriety just as effectively as if she'd sat beside him in Lady Maggie's drawing room under the eyes of Lady Comeryn.

'Very well, if you are sure I wouldn't be imposing,' she said at last.

'Not a bit. I would feel myself failing in my duty if I did not look after Susanna's friend.'

His 'sister's friend' again. Was he not just a *bit* concerned about her for his own sake? But, again, she couldn't ask that.

'I know you are quite protective of her. I only hope duty in this case will not prove too onerous.'

The warmth of the smile he gave her as his gaze roamed her face sent little eddies of delight rippling along her nerves. 'In this case, duty will most definitely be pleasure.'

He offered his arm. A little giddy, she laid her hand on it, savouring the zing of contact.

Plants, his proximity and a ride long enough to ask all the questions she could think of. A day which had already proven enjoyable had just become splendid.

They walked on to the livery, Miles all too conscious of Lady Laura beside him, the warmth of her hand that seemed to penetrate through his sleeve, the heady scent of her rose perfume. Desire warred with conscience, a little voice pointing out that sending her with a maid would have served to protect her just as well, while another countered by noting she had already refused that offer. And he couldn't send her off unescorted, could he? He mustn't disregard her safety just because the chance to spend more time alone with her, to learn more about her unusual interests, filled him with a guilty anticipation.

Anticipation that washed away his disappointment at having missed her lesson with his sister. He'd been annoyed when another obligation had taken him away, knowing he would have only a few more opportunities to see her, despite also knowing that limiting his time with her was a good thing.

He already found her too fascinating, her physical presence too alluring. He should have learned his lesson with Arabella that strong physical attraction could blind him to the facts that made any long-term relationship between them impossible. Facts he'd almost forgot in her father's garden, when he'd very nearly succumbed to the desire to kiss her.

It would have been an insult to her and to his honour if he had done so, trifling with her as if she were some Covent Garden light-skirt when there was no possibility of his ever marrying her.

But if he *were* looking to marry her instead of Charlotte…?

He exterminated that tantalising idea before it could fully form. Marrying Lady Laura would never happen—even if he were free of his obligation to Charlotte. Neither she nor her family would consider a union with a commoner like him—a merchant who worked in his own shop, albeit that 'shop' being a bank catering to some of the highest born in the land.

Nor would his own honour allow it. Should his sister marry into the aristocracy, the union would elevate her status. But an aristocratic girl who married a commoner would be diminished, forfeiting the place to which she'd been born, no longer accepted within her Society. It would be a humiliation for her, unconscionable for him.

As for remaining friends… Despite his wistful longing, their vastly different situations would make that impossible as well. True, he might eke out their association a bit longer while his sister participated in the social Season that provided them with an acceptable link, but Susanna would likely marry soon. After that, only if the man Lady Laura eventually wed were a friend of his would it be proper for him to continue to see her.

And the idea of seeing her while visiting her husband felt somehow worse than not seeing her at all. So why not seize this opportunity to do her a service and indulge his desire to be with her, since it would be one of the very few chances he had left? Seize it, cast away all misgivings and just enjoy it.

By the time he'd argued it out in his head, they'd arrived at the livery. Miles arranged for his family's usual carriage, which was quickly led out. The coachman took his place on the box, Miles helped Lady Laura up and took his place beside her.

'It's very kind of you to go to so much trouble,' Lady Laura said as they set off.

'Not at all. Work will still be waiting when I get there. It's an indulgence to give myself a few hours to enjoy gardens—and your lovely company.'

Pinking at his compliment, she said, 'I am sorry to have been the means of taking you away from your work so often.'

'You shouldn't be. The lessons have been…an interesting experience.'

'Learning to woo your Miss Dunnock?'

That wasn't at all what he'd most enjoyed, he thought, drinking in the heady essence of her nearness. Side-stepping the question, he said, 'My sister insists I need to do more of it.'

'She's correct. A lady needs to know she is appreciated…desired.'

At the word, he couldn't help looking over at her. He would have no trouble telling *her* that. How easily he could get tangled up in her, heart and body!

He needed to remind himself again that he couldn't trust his head to rule his thoughts or his actions when he felt a physical attraction as strong as his pull to her. Ignorance of that threat had led him into one disaster, and he didn't need to suffer another.

It was good that sensible, prosaic Charlotte awaited him. There'd be no worries with her of becoming so distracted by desire that he'd be unable to think clearly or govern his responses.

Even if he couldn't quite view that truth with enthusiasm.

'Appreciation is important,' he agreed. 'But I thought you'd told me once that desire is not?'

She looked over at him. Their gazes locked, something heated flashing between them. His heartbeat accelerated and he felt a strong urge to move closer, close enough that the jolting of the carriage would bring their hands and their knees into contact.

Fortunately, before he could act upon the impulse, she looked away. 'One can live without it, I suppose.'

She drew herself up, as if retreating. Miles was torn between being sorry he had caused her to withdraw and relief. He should know by now that the fierce attraction between them would only remain manageable if he ignored it, never openly acknowledging its power. It was beyond foolish to toy with something that could only lead to either disaster or frustration.

'May I ask you some questions, Mr Rochdale?' she said, jolting him from his reflections.

He raised an eyebrow. 'Questions? About what?'

'I should very much like to know more about the process of banking. What you do and how you do it. For someone like me who loves numbers, it seems like it would be a wonderful occupation. Although... I suppose, as the owner's son, you don't have to be involved in the day-to-day operations if you don't wish to. You have employees to handle all that.'

Thankful for a conversational opening that returned them to safer ground, he said, 'We do, but I'm still heavily involved. Father insisted I learn every aspect of the business if I was some day going to manage it. How else would I know whether it was being carried on properly or not? After university, I started as the lowliest of clerks.'

'With your charts and tables, adding columns of figures in ledgers?' she asked with a smile.

'Some of that. Much of the banking business involves not adding and subtracting numbers but writing correspondence.'

'Indeed? How so?'

'You truly wish to know?' he asked, not wanting to bore her with the minutiae of a banker's tasks.

'I do. I always thought I would love working in a counting house. If you want to disabuse me of the notion, I must have convincing details. What were your jobs as a lowly clerk?'

'First, and the one requiring the most time, was correspondence. One opens letters coming from investors and other enquiries, setting aside anything one thinks the partners might be interested in pursuing. One then copies those letters into the correspondence book, the general book of orders, and then onto an individual page devoted to the transactions made with each customer. Once a partner reads the correspondence and indicates what to reply, one writes a detailed response to the client, again copying that letter into the correspondence book and onto the client's individual page, before posting the letter.'

'That does seem like a lot of writing! What of working with numbers? Surely you do some of that?'

'Of course. The clerk counts any funds brought in for deposit, gives the depositor a detailed receipt and then stores the coin in the safe after noting the amounts in the appropriate ledger. It's the same process with any funds dispersed, depending on their type. Account books of all types are totalled at the end of each day, then monthly, twice yearly and yearly.'

She angled her head quizzically. 'There are "types"?'

'The bank does more than store coin for depositors. Much of its work is done in loaning money—most often for mortgages on property, or as a personal loan to a client. A landowner who comes to town for the Season, for instance, may take a loan to fund his stay as an advance on income he'll later receive from rents on his property, a loan he will repay when those funds come in. Each type of loan is recorded and accounted for separately. Then there are discounted bills...' He gave her inquisitive look. 'Are you sure you are interested in this? Susanna's eyes would be glazing over by now.'

'Yes, I am interested! Females—unless they are rich widows—are not allowed to handle finances on their own, their funds always managed by fathers, husbands or trustees. I'd like to know what investment options I will have if I become a rich widow—or, at the least, know what banks are doing with the funds I am not allowed to control.'

'Going to become a trader in your own right, once you become a rich widow?' he asked, amused.

She gave him a determined look. 'Perhaps. If I do, I shall need to understand what those who want to invest my money might do with it. I can trust that you, who are knowledgeable but have no vested interest, would explain it to me truthfully.'

He shouldn't be surprised by her interest, he thought, impressed despite himself. She'd already shown herself to be a most unusual female. Why should she not understand how money was invested?

'Very well. Though I doubt many of our gentleman depositors care much about exactly what the bank does with their money, as long as interest is paid on time— or they get the loans they want when they want them.'

'Perhaps, being a female with more to lose and less opportunity to regain it, I'm more inquisitive. So—discounting bills…?'

'Discounting bills. A business often sells goods to a client on credit, but it doesn't want that money unavailable while it waits for repayment, so it will sell the bill to a bank at a discount. Say the merchandise is worth one thousand pounds: the merchant sells the bill to a bank for nine hundred and seventy-five pounds in cash, a fifteen percent discount, but he gets his money back immediately. The bank takes over the bill, and the customer eventually repays the full one thousand pounds directly to the bank. Discounted bills and other types of investments are each recorded separately.'

'Investments such as railway shares, like those Papa described being purchased by his bank?'

'Yes.' Miles paused, not sure just how much he should elaborate.

But she wants to know—and why shouldn't she, whether or not she ever has a say in the management of her family's funds?

'Railways are one of the more speculative investments,' he began at last. 'Meaning an investor is less sure of getting a return on his money, or indeed getting back the principal at all. Some bonds, like those issued by the South Sea Company or the Africa Company, are also more speculative, whereas stock shares issued by the Bank of England are much safer. Then there is trading on commodities on the stock market or the insurance exchange.'

'Quite a range, then. How do you determine whether an investment is safe enough to commit your bank's funds to it?'

'One examines the history of its returns, choosing by preference companies which have for a long time returned a good profit, like the Bank of England. Which is why railway ventures are less sure. Since each individual line is new, with no record of performance by which one can evaluate it, one must study instead the route, the estimated costs of construction and make a judgement about whether it seems likely to be built and operated at a profit.

'It's the same process with commodities trading: one studies the history of return on goods like corn or wool or India cotton to decide if the listed price per share is likely to increase enough in value to give a good return. Much depends on what's happening elsewhere in the world—a crop disaster, for instance, could increase the price of corn, or an over-abundant harvest in every producing area could drive it down. So one stops by the commodities market, both to see the current rates and to hear the news being sent in from trading partners all over the world, and by Lloyds, to find out the latest about ship cargoes being dispatched and received.'

She shook her head wonderingly. 'And here I thought banking merely the process of taking in and giving out coin!'

'There's a lot of that too.'

'Who is responsible for deciding whether or not to make loans or investments?'

'Most banks have a board that reviews such decisions. But a senior partner can decide on his own, if he has been given that authority by the rest of the partners.'

'So…in your bank, now that your father has given over the operations, *you* make these decisions?'

Miles nodded. 'Many of them. Which is why banking requires long hours and much study. I'm responsible for the careful use of other people's money as well as our own.'

She blew out a breath. 'Susanna said you carried a great weight on your shoulders, but I never imagined! I'm quite impressed.'

Miles couldn't help feeling gratified—especially when he recalled how dismissively he was treated by many of the aristocrats who patronised their business. To them, he was little more than a lowly tradesman, a servant who trotted out funds when they wanted them.

Whereas Laura was not only interested in what he did, she appreciated its importance and complexity.

'I realise I have much to learn if I wish to manage my own funds eventually. Would it be possible for me to visit your bank some time and see where all these transactions take place?'

Once again, he couldn't help being pleased by her interest. 'Although it would be unusual for a woman to visit, I suppose I could give you a tour of the bank. Not the Stock Exchange, where commodities are traded, though—only members are admitted. Nor would I recommend a visit to the Royal Exchange; although originally it housed shops which ladies could patronise, it was long ago taken over by commercial and insurance establishments—Lloyd's Coffee House, as well as Lord Mayor's Court Office, with offices for attorneys.'

'They sound like exciting hubs of commerce.'

'They are. Especially the Stock Exchange, which is usually a tumult of activity. Definitely not a place for a lady, or any outsider for that matter. Intruders will immediately be unceremoniously escorted out. One might even be set upon by a truculent broker who'd suffered too many losses that day.'

'How colourful and fascinating! I can understand why it is not just an occupation for you, but a passion.'

'Speculation can fascinate and fortunes can be made. But one must also remember they can just as easily be lost. I prefer to concentrate on the less risky forms of investments, which will most likely return a profit, to protect the bank's funds and those of our investors. I would never want an individual or his family to be ruined because I was too carried away by the lure of potential profit to analyse carefully enough whether or not an investment was wise.'

By this time, their carriage had crossed the Thames and was approaching the gates of Kew Gardens. As the vehicle turned in, Lady Laura asked, 'Have you visited Kew before?'

'Never. They are royal gardens, aren't they?'

'They are now, and have been for going on a century. Lord Cappel began the plant collections, then Princess Augusta, and later King George III further expanded them under the direction of Sir Joseph Banks. My father became acquainted with Sir Joseph at university, during his early studies of botany, and first came to tour the gardens then. He continued to visit them over the years when he was in London. But he didn't develop a close association with the gardeners until after the accident, when he of necessity turned his attention from cultivation of a vast estate to a study of smaller ornamental plants.'

'And that is what you are collecting for him today?'

'Yes. Rooted cuttings of two shrubs, both brought back by Sir Joseph's plant hunters from the far east. A camelia, a dark-leaved evergreen that blooms in winter, and a hydrangea, which produces large blue flowers in summer. Papa is already planning where he will plant them if they survive to mature size. He likes to incorporate them into the gardens to maximise the contrast in leaf shapes and colour, bloom shapes and sizes.'

'Painting with plants.'

'Yes,' she agreed, smiling. 'You do appreciate his artistry.'

The coach pulled to a halt, the driver turning round to request directions.

Lady Laura gave them, then turned back to Miles. 'There are thousands of exotic varieties planted here. I love to stroll the pathways in the different seasons and admire them.' She chuckled. 'Unlike my maid, I'm never bored. She says one green tree or bush looks much like another. Though, in her defence, fragrant flowering plants like sweet Williams and roses are much easier to appreciate than subtle differences in leaf shapes and shades.'

'You enjoy plants as much as your father,' he observed.

'I do. Though I'm not nearly as knowledgeable.'

Yet another unique thing about her, he thought. His mother and sister loved receiving or fashioning bouquets, and had enough knowledge of herbs to supervise the cooks and oversee menus, but they left the cultivation and care of plants to their gardeners.

'You seem knowledgeable to me.'

The carriage eased to a stop as the planting sheds came into view. Miles helped her alight, then walked with her to the doorway of the nearest shed, where she was met by burly man in heavy boots, gloves and a gardener's smock. 'Lady Laura,' he said, bowing. 'A good day to you.'

'And to you, sir. Mr Rochdale, this is Mr Foster, head gardener at Kew. He's been sharing his expertise with my father for many years now.'

After the two men exchanged greetings, Foster said, 'I have the boxes ready for Lord Carmelton. How does your father?'

Miles wondered if the gardener heard her tiny sigh before she replied, 'Some days better than others.'

'Give him my best and tell him I hope to see him

here soon. We have a newly planted shrub border full of some of Sir Joseph's prizes that I'm eager to show him.'

'I hope he will be able to come soon. If I might inspect the boxes now?'

Miles followed, curious, as the gardener led Lady Laura to a series of flat wooden boxes, each containing six or eight stubby plants that seemed to him little more than a squat stem adorned with several branches of leaves. Lady Laura stroked the leaves and slid a finger along the stems while she quizzed the gardener about their selection and propagation. After approving them all, she stepped away while Foster called for his assistant to load the boxes into the coach.

'Are you sure you don't mind bringing them back?' she asked Miles. 'Mr Foster can summon me a hackney. The plants need to be transported carefully, which in an open carriage will mean travelling very slowly.'

'I'll not abandon you halfway through the journey! If I escort a lady out, I see her safely home.'

'Thank you. I appreciate the concern and...' She looked away, blushing slightly. 'I am enjoying the company.'

'As am I,' he replied. He was enjoying an ever-deepening appreciation for her intellect and admiration for her wide-ranging interests, her concern for others, such as his shy sister and her impaired father, her charm and approachability despite her elevated birth—and that ever-present scintillation of sensual connection.

The boxes loaded, rough burlap tucked over them to protect the plants from wind and dust, and the coachman cautioned to maintain a very slow pace, Miles helped Lady Laura back into the coach.

He felt the few precious moments he had alone with

her drawing to a close, leaving him still with so much more he wanted to know. Determined to make the most of what little time he had left, he said, 'Do you mind if I ask you some questions?'

She looked over at him with an expression of mild surprise. 'Not at all. Though I can't imagine what you might wish to know. I'm afraid there's nothing very interesting about my life.'

That was so patently false, Miles could barely refrain from laughing. 'On the contrary! Many things about you are unique. For instance, I've never met a lady who was interested in numbers for themselves, rather than just as the price of a bonnet or curtains for the salon. How did you come to be?'

She shrugged. 'I've always been interested, I suppose. I was never so disappointed as when I was sent away to the ladies' academy, sure I would finally have the opportunity to learn more about mathematics than the managing of household accounts that was all my governess was capable of teaching, only to discover I would not even study that.'

She wrinkled her nose. 'Deportment and French and painting on china plates and music and dancing! Interesting subjects, and I did enjoy French and music, but the rest was hardly taxing to the intellect. As I think I told you, I took over the household books from Mama, who was amused to indulge me at Haddenly, then again when we moved to Warnton, but I wasn't introduced to more advanced mathematics until I met Ada Byron during her debut season. You may recall her unfortunate background...'

Miles searched his memory before the name registered. 'Was her father the poet?'

'Yes. It was a dreadful marriage, with her parents separating when she was just a baby. All through her growing up, her mother nursed a fanatical hatred for her father. A mathematician herself, she encouraged Ada to pursue academic matters, and maintained strict control over her in order to prevent her from developing "undesirable moral failings" like her father. It was a frustrating and lonely existence, Ada told me, being constantly watched and kept away from association with everyone, but the blessing was she was able to obtain a real education. Her tutor, as I mentioned, was Mary Somerville.'

'Ah, yes. The accomplished Mrs Somerville, who wrote a mathematical explanation of the order of the universe.'

'Yes. Through Ada, I met Mrs Somerville and also Mr Babbage, with whom Ada has maintained a close correspondence, even since her marriage last year to Lord King. I was able to attend several meetings where he discussed his work on the Difference Engine, and Mrs Somerville kindly recommended several texts for me to study. Whenever either of them hosts a salon, I try to attend to learn the latest about their studies and writings.'

She shook her head wonderingly. 'It was such a...*revelation* to meet another female who was as fascinated by numbers as I am! We even devised a code to amuse ourselves if we happened to be marooned together at some hopelessly dull social event. I'd catch her eye, or she'd catch mine, and whoever spoke first would name a prime number. The other would have one minute to name the next prime after that. If the fete was truly dreadful, we could go back and forth for half an hour, amusing ourselves. Although, I suppose if anyone had overheard us, they would have considered *us* mad!'

Smiling, he looked over at her. 'Seventeen.'

Her eyes widening in surprise, she hesitated. A moment later, she smiled back. 'Nineteen.'

'One hundred and thirteen,' he countered.

She thought for a minute, then said, 'One hundred and twenty-seven.'

'Six hundred and forty-one.'

'Six hundred and forty-three.'

By now, they were both chuckling. 'You see how that would enliven a dull social gathering!' she said when she'd controlled her mirth.

'I suppose it would.'

To his regret, the carriage was arriving in Mount Street. He could find no excuse to linger; she needed to get the plants to her father and he was long overdue at the bank. He did manage to eke out the visit long enough to help the footman who ran out to unload the precious boxes, then escort her up the stairs. He savoured his last glimpse of her before the front door closed, cutting her off from view.

Slowly he walked back down the stairs to the waiting coach, bemused once again. Exchanging prime numbers at a dull ball, he thought, shaking his head. A strong interest in managing her own money as a wealthy widow. With her mastery of mathematics, she would do well, able to calculate interest, risk or potential return like the sharpest of brokers.

Never had a broker been so lovely. He was lucky she possessed so sharp and unusual an intellect, something powerful enough to keep distracting him from the allure of her presence and the always simmering desire to kiss her.

He beat down regret before it could form itself into

thought. He'd bemoaned the facts that would separate them too many times already. They were who they were; nothing was going to change that. He'd see her at least once again, at the last lesson. He'd have to be content with that.

And afterwards he'd just have to deal with the sinking feeling that his life would seem drabber, less exciting, a monotone of unvarying hue once she walked out of it for good.

Chapter Eleven

In fact, Miles saw Lady Laura again sooner than expected, and at a different venue. The day after he'd escorted her to Kew Gardens, Susanna surprised him by appearing as he took his breakfast.

'You're up early, Sunshine!' he said, rising to give her a hug.

'I wanted to catch you before you left for the bank.'

'You need to tell me something of such great import it couldn't wait until dinner tonight?' he asked as he poured her some coffee.

'Yes, as matter of fact. We have no social engagement tomorrow night, so Lady Laura suggested going to a concert at the Philharmonic. Which I know is something you would enjoy.' She grinned at him. 'She advised me that, if I wanted to pry you out more often, I needed to offer you entertainment you would find appealing. Balls, alas, I know are a hopeless case. But…would you join me for a concert? It will feature the work of Beethoven.'

A heady excitement began to simmer in him. 'Will it be just you, Mama and Lady Bunting? I know Father wouldn't be interested.'

'Mama is engaged for dinner and a card party with some friends. Lady Bunting will accompany me. But I intend to meet Lady Laura there. She's a great fancier of Beethoven, she told me.'

Lady Laura…and Beethoven? Some of his favourite music, a delightful venue and another chance to safely savour her alluring company?

'How can I refuse?'

'Excellent!' Susanna cried, clapping her hands. 'I knew Beethoven would entice you! If Lady Laura's presence did not,' she added archly.

Miles looked away. Susanna might be an innocent, but she wasn't totally naive. She'd probably noticed the attraction between them. Since denying it would be the same as admitting it, better to say nothing.

'What time is the performance? Will you dine here first?'

'Yes. Make sure you don't stay late at the bank, or I shall send a footman round to fetch you!'

'I'll try not to become immersed.'

'Which seems so easy for you to do! By the way, have you written to Charlotte yet?'

Once again, he looked away from her pointed gaze. 'Not yet. I will soon.'

'Honestly, have the lessons we've been taking taught you nothing?' Susanna shook her head. 'It would serve you right if she jilted you!'

'I will write her a note soon. And send flowers. White ones.'

'Intermixed with violets,' Susanna said, shaking a finger at him.

'I must be off.' After rising and pausing to kiss his sister on the cheek, Miles walked out with a spring in his step. Not only would he see Lady Laura at their final lesson, he'd be able to share an evening with her listening to one of his favourite composers.

His cheer faded as he grimaced at Susanna's pointed reminder. He wasn't sure Charlotte felt the lack of correspondence from him. But probably any lady would welcome flowers.

What would he send Lady Laura, if courting her were his aim? White for purity, certainly. Was there any flower that symbolised complexity? He didn't recall her mentioning one. Perhaps a blossom from one of the new flowering plants her father was nurturing—something rare, exotic, beautiful but unusual. As was she.

If he were honest, he'd need to include some red blossoms. Beyond purity, rarity and beauty, there was a deep, inexhaustible passion.

Good thing he had no excuse to send her flowers. A bouquet of red roses might result in him getting his face slapped. For effrontery, maybe, but surely not surprise?

She might just as well send *him* flowers of a fiery hue. He had no doubt the desire he felt was reciprocated.

Thank heaven for the intellectual, cooling effect of mathematics.

The following evening, having highly anticipated the event all day, Miles escorted his small party into the music room of the Philharmonic Society in Hanover Square. Susanna immediately spied Lady Laura and her chaperon, Lady Swanston, who waved them over. 'I asked Lady Laura to obtain seats for all of us together,' Susanna confided as they made their way through the crowded chamber.

After meeting and greeting their friends, they arranged themselves in their seats, his sister next to Lady Laura and the two chaperons together, with Miles protectively claiming the outside chair next to his sister's friend. He swallowed hard as he took his seat while the shiver of sensation he always felt at drawing near to Lady Laura ran through him. It was a pleasure just to sit beside her, sensing her warmth, breathing in the sweetness of her rose perfume.

Listening to the works of his favourite composer was the final jewel to crown a splendid evening.

The murmurs from the audience faded as the musicians tuned up, the first violinist turned to signal the orchestra to begin and the glorious melody of the Dance Symphony swelled over him.

He angled his head to look at Lady Laura. She sat with her lips slightly parted, gaze locked on the performers, nodding her head in time to the music, on her face an expression of delight. Even one not enamoured of music would have had to enjoy it more, just observing how enraptured she looked.

At the end of the first movement, as the audience applauded, she turned to him with a smile.

'I'm so glad Susanna coaxed you to attend the concert tonight. The Seventh Symphony is splendid, isn't it?'

'Glorious. Beethoven has sublime mastery, hasn't he? The music seemed to sweep you along—you were flexing your fingers, as if to accompany it. Do you play?'

'Of course,' she said with a twinkle. 'Every well-brought-up young lady plays. My performance is adequate, but nothing as accomplished as the performers here tonight. Do you play?'

'I enjoy listening to the pianoforte, but I don't play myself.'

'It isn't necessary to perform in order to appreciate the music's beauty.'

'I do enjoy this a good deal more than opera.' He chuckled. 'Or those ridiculous melodramas Susanna is so fond of. But then, she's a romantic, her emotions always touched by great tragedy.'

'And you are not a romantic, of course.'

'As you may remember, I believe the association between men and women works much better without the drama of high emotion. Since exultation is inevitably followed sooner or later by disappointment.'

'What a cynical view! I cannot imagine where you come by it. Susanna says your parents share a very warm relationship.'

'They do. A warmth—not an excess of passion. Besides, haven't you several times expressed a disinclination for relationships fraught with an excess of passion? Believing the pain too great if that love were lost?'

She sighed. 'I never claimed to be consistent. I am pulled in two directions. Would I want what my parents shared when Mama was alive? That joy and devotion? Of course! But when I see Papa now, lonely and bereft... No, I would not choose that.'

'So you agree with my assessment.'

'Maybe. Though it doesn't matter what I think, as long as your Charlotte agrees.'

'She does,' he said firmly.

Lady Laura angled her head as if to question that claim, but then put a finger to her lips. 'I made a rash prediction before. I'll not do so again. Let us return to the neutral subject of music, upon which we can agree. I knew you must enjoy it, based as it is on such mathematical principles.'

He quirked an eyebrow at her. 'Mathematical—how?'

'Have you not read of the connection between music and mathematics?'

'I'm afraid my study has been more about interest rates and percentages of return,' he said wryly. 'You are arguing for a mathematical basis for music?'

'Pythagoras first codified it, experimenting with the tones produced when strings of different lengths are plucked. Some specific ration of string lengths created pleasing tone combinations, which he termed "harmonies", and some did not. The most basic interval was produced when the string length ratio was two to one—eight tones apart, or our octave. A four-to-three ratio gives us a fourth, five semitones apart; a three-to-two ratio produces a fifth, seven semitones apart. So even our ears are attuned to mathematics!'

'Given your delight in the study, that knowledge must enhance your enjoyment of music even more.'

She nodded. 'Composers I enjoy most—Beethoven, Bach and Mozart—create the most mathematically faithful music.'

'Can something be beautiful in itself, even without mathematics?' *Like you,* he thought.

She tilted her head, as if considering. 'I suppose. Flowers are beautiful, although the symmetry that makes them so pleasing is also mathematically based. But colour is valued for itself.' She smiled. 'Understanding the mathematical underpinnings just makes any subject more complex and interesting.'

As her presence made the music she was explaining in mathematical terms more beautiful. He'd never hear another chord without considering its proportions.

'The musicians are about to begin again. Shall we

forget about figures and just let ourselves be lost in the music?'

As long as he could both fill his ears with its beauty and his eyes with hers… 'Willingly.'

Her enjoyment of the music made his keener. He wished he dared press her fingers, let her know how much her presence and her novel insights touched him on an intellectual level that now energised him even as her nearness deepened that ever-present sensual connection. As the waves of melody wrapped their mathematically proportioned harmonies around them, he felt as happy and content to live in the moment as he'd ever felt in his life.

He'd been telling himself what drew him to her was mostly that strong physical attraction, a man's natural animal desire that distracted the mind from sober reflection. But after tonight, listening to her expound on mathematical ratios in musical harmony, he had to concede the shining brilliance of her mind exerted an almost equal appeal.

What would it be like to have such a bright, shining spirit opening new insights to him every day?

He suppressed the voice saying it would never be possible anyway by noting that, if he were able to see and hear her every day, the interaction would inevitably lose its magic.

Stop analysing, he told himself. *Abandon yourself to the music, the moment and the thrill of her nearness.*

Like the silvery notes of the music that soared and then vanished, her company was something to enjoy and savour before their association ended. He was no more able to prolong it than he was able to keep sound from fading.

* * *

As the Carmelton carriage was brought up, Laura bid goodnight to Susanna, Lady Bunting and Rochdale. Humming a favourite melody from the Seventh Symphony's third movement, she walked over to let a footman hand her in.

What a wonderful night! The music had been brilliantly performed, and with Rochdale beside her, she'd had someone else who could appreciate not just the melodies, but their complex underpinnings. Only with Ada Byron had she ever before found someone who comprehended and valued the esoteric numerical concepts she found so fascinating.

He'd even joined in the prime numbers game she and Ada had devised! She'd been shocked and a bit taken aback when he'd first named one and looked at her to give him the next—that exchange had been like a secret language, something special to be shared just with her dear friend. Until, in the next moment, she'd realised that having Rochdale not only understand but wish to participate in the exercise meant he must think like she and Ada did. How extraordinary to have found another individual with whom she could share what truly excited her!

The idea had filled her with warmth and an odd sense of coming home. Indulging in more mathematical chat tonight had been stimulating—as stimulating as his physical nearness.

Stimulating and disturbing. Flushing a little, she recalled how pedantic she must have sounded, expounding on harmonic theory. But, acutely conscious of him seated at her elbow, her nerves had been so on edge, her stomach so fluttery that she'd initially grasped at mathematics to calm herself, else she would have remained too distracted to enjoy the music.

The tactic had worked well. The tingling heat and melting arousal at the core of her had never entirely disappeared, but had become a burnished glow in the background, enhancing rather than detracting from her enjoyment.

Hearing Beethoven's Seventh, its masterful performance shared with a kindred spirit... It had been the most wonderful concert she'd ever attended.

She would absolutely not analyse her soaring sense of euphoria any further, or remind herself how rare and probably unrepeatable an episode it had been. For tonight, while the glow lasted, she would just savour it.

Settling into the carriage, she turned to Lady Swanston whom, she thought guiltily, she had neglected over the course of the evening. 'Did you enjoy the concert? I thought the performers wonderful!'

'Yes, the music was very nice.'

Her chaperon's words were unexceptional, but Laura caught a note of constraint in her voice. 'What is it? Is something wrong?'

Lady Swanston sighed. 'I hesitate even to mention it, but I feel I'd be failing in my duty if I did not bring it to your attention.'

A cold nugget of foreboding forming in her belly, Laura said, 'What do you feel necessary to bring to my attention?'

The lady hesitated again before finally saying, 'Lady Harrison stopped by yesterday. We had our usual good gossip but then, just as she was leaving, she mentioned casually that she'd seen you travelling in an open carriage with a young gentleman she didn't recognise. It was quite proper, she assured me. A coachman on the box, a groom riding up behind. I saw her again in the lobby tonight during the intermission and she told me she now knew who the young man was—the brother of your protégée, Miss Rochdale. She asked me in that sly way she has if you were taking up with the banker's son as well as the banker's daughter.'

Pressing her lips together, Laura strove to hold on to her temper. 'And what did you tell her?'

'I gave her what I hope was a look of hauteur and said that Miss Rochdale's brother, naturally seeing himself as her protector, often accompanies her on her evenings out. That he would consider protecting her friend as his duty too, so might well escort her home after she'd called on his sister. All said in a tone which I hoped conveyed my disdain for any attempt to spread rumours.'

Probably the best she could hope for, Laura thought. 'Thank you for that, at least.'

'You're welcome. I hope I may have defused that situation—but you can be sure that, if Lady Harrison mentioned it to me, she has gossiped about the encounter to all of her friends as well. I'm the first to declare that Mr Rochdale is a very amiable, respectable young man, but he's *not* a gentleman. You do see that you must take care in your dealings with him? And why were you in Rochdale's company without his sister being present? Surely you know how…odd such a thing would appear!'

Annoyed to be taken to task, her judgement about propriety questioned, Laura said stiffly, 'I had visited Susanna and intended to go afterwards to Kew Gardens to pick up some plants for Papa, as I'd promised him. Mr Rochdale, as you told Lady Harrison, objected to my travelling across London without anyone to attend me and felt obligated to give me his protection. Thereby giving up some of his valuable time and even summoning an open carriage, rather than engaging a hackney, to make the journey entirely proper.'

Lady Swanston nodded. 'It was gracious of him, and entirely proper, I'll allow. But for you to be seen alone in his company by all and sundry—as if he were gentry-born? Your championship of his sister is considered by the *ton* to be odd, but permissible. However, it will raise eyebrows and cause no end of gossip if you are seen associating alone with Mr Rochdale. Who, no matter how handsome and courteous he may be, even you must admit is not eligible.'

'What difference does it make whether or not he is "eligible"?' Laura burst out. 'He was doing me a favour—not angling to court me! Nor was I encouraging him to do so.'

'Laura, you are an unmarried young lady of birth. Any single man you allow yourself to be seen with will be viewed as a potential suitor, your relationship with him becoming a matter of interest and conjecture. I don't think a single such…incident will too adversely affect your reputation, for it was quite open and above board. Still, some of the highest sticklers may well question your judgement, and it might give some potential suitors some pause if they begin to feel you are…less discerning than you should be about the company you keep.'

'Any gentleman so discriminating as to object to my being seen in the company of my friend's brother, in circumstances that even the highest stickler must proclaim were entirely innocent, would be far too particular about things about which I don't give a jot for me to have any interest in *him*,' she said hotly.

'Perhaps not, but if some gentlemen should decide you…play fast and loose about whom you allow to accompany you, it could end up affecting your reputation, even among gentlemen who are not so "discriminating". And even though I'm sure you could charm any of them out of any misgivings *they* might have about your character, I assure you, their mothers and female relations will be much less accommodating!'

'So you would have me snub the brother of my friend so as to avoid offending some starched-up matron and her fussy son with too high a view of his consequence?'

Lady Swanston sighed again. 'I see I have made you angry. You are so…egalitarian in your outlook, doubtless the influence of your father, but others have different expectations for the behaviour of a marquess's daughter. I just wanted to remind you of that. You are so dear to me, I want you to have every opportunity to marry the best man of your choice. Not to have your options narrowed because of an unfortunate misperception about your character.'

Laura tried to rein in her temper. If she were honest, she hadn't given a thought to who might see her riding across London in an open carriage with Miles Rochdale. Or how that action might be perceived if someone did see them.

'You have made great efforts on my behalf to find me an eligible *parti*—and you mustn't think I am not grateful for that, even though I often offer you little encouragement. But neither do I intend to insult my friends by avoiding them in public because acknowledging them may lower me in the eyes of some of the highest sticklers. I could never marry a man who would view my behaviour in that way, nor marry into a family that would pressure him to hold such a view. But I do promise to be…more mindful of the impression my behaviour may give. I don't wish to embarrass you.'

Lady Swanston patted her hand, looking relieved. 'Thank you, my dear. That is all I wanted to accomplish—just to give you a warning. You are clever, discerning and compassionate. You will do what you know is best.'

While Lady Swanston settled back, obviously relieved to have completed her thankless mission, Laura remained angry and disgruntled. She wasn't sure what annoyed her most: that the reprimand had spoiled the rosy afterglow of the concert, that snobbish society members were criticising her behaviour—or that Lady Swanston's observations, much as she might resent them, were unfortunately correct.

A young lady who associated with persons not acceptable to the *ton* would soon find herself, if not cut, certainly with her social options limited.

But, as she'd claimed to Lady Swanston, would she really care? Maggie and Eliza would stand by her regardless, and the Countess, with her commoner daughter-in-law, would support her too.

In any event, with only a handful of opportunities left to spend time with Mr Rochdale, she did not intend to let the possible condemnation of a bunch of Society beldams whose approval she neither sought nor valued prevent her from enjoying the company of one of the few individuals she'd ever known who knew about, and cared about, the world of numbers that she loved. An individual who thought more like her than all the eligible gentlemen she'd met her in all her time mingling with the *ton*.

If following through on that intention decreased her supply of potential suitors, she thought, still fuming, she wasn't interested in wedding them anyway.

Chapter Twelve

Two afternoons later, Miles Rochdale looked up from the text on harmonic patterns he'd been reading as his sister hurried into his office. 'No time to keep your nose buried in a book now, Miles! Lady Laura will be arriving any minute! Come to the music room. You must help select what she should play for the dancing lesson.'

Giving an elaborate sigh to disguise the leap of anticipation in his pulse, he closed the tome and rose from his chair. 'Very well, if you insist.'

'I do,' his sister said, ushering him with a shooing motion out of his office and up the stairs towards the music room.

He should have made an excuse to avoid this lesson. His sister might insist on his dancing with Lady Laura—which was probably not wise. But, knowing this session might well be last time he ever saw her, he couldn't make himself stay away.

'No reason to be in such a flutter,' he teased as he walked beside Susanna. *As much of a flutter as he was.* 'You'll only be dancing with me, not some handsome beau.'

'You will still have to do your part to uphold the conversation,' she admonished, then giggled. 'It would seem odd to try to practise flirting with you, though.'

'I think you can safely leave out that part of the lesson,' he said drily.

But, if he were dancing with Lady Laura, practising flirtation might not be so objectionable.

That thought was succeeded by a shock of alarm. Did his sister fully realise just how attractive he found her friend? That would never do!

Before he could protest that he himself had no need of instruction in flirting, Susanna said, 'You really should practise yourself. Surely you wouldn't find flirting difficult with Lady Laura as stand-in for Miss Dunnock? After Charlotte's long absence, you must be at your most charming when she finally returns to London. Do you know when that will be?'

Miles didn't feel it necessary to mention that, as he hadn't yet written to his prospective fiancée, nor she to him, he no idea when that event might transpire. Instead, he said, 'As far as I know, she hasn't determined that yet.'

As they entered the music room, his sister tut-tutted, waving a reproving finger at him. 'You'd better send flowers again with your next note, to make sure she doesn't forget you! Charlotte is a very pretty girl with a substantial dowry. Ours isn't the only banking family who might wish to make an alliance with hers. If you're not careful, someone may try to steal her out from under your nose.'

'Surely not, handsome and charming as I am?'

About to open the bench to inspect the selection of sheet music, she turned to bat his arm. 'Handsome perhaps, but I've yet to see you exert much charm in her direction!'

He made no reply, for her observation was only too true. Any time the subject of wooing Charlotte came up, some…resistance stirred within that kept him taking any steps in that direction.

It was just a lingering distaste over the debacle with Arabella, he told himself. Given more time, once that sorry episode faded completely, he could face the task of wooing his suitable bride with more enthusiasm.

He reminded himself again that it was wise to make a sober, sensible alliance with a woman who understood him, who wouldn't expect flowery speeches and slavish devotion, but respect, protection, financial support and security. Which provided a much firmer basis for long-term contentment than will-o'-the-wisp fantasies of passionate love.

'It may be difficult for *me* to think of flirting when I'm dancing with you,' said Susanna. 'But for Charlotte's sake you must practise your technique when you dance with Lady Laura. Promise me!'

Holding Lady Laura close in the movements of a dance would provide temptation enough. And if he were to allow himself some flirtation? Worse yet than the dancing on which his sister was insisting!

But a little imp of enthusiasm whispered encouragement. What harm would there be in flirting a little, with his sister looking on a guarantee that nothing would get out of hand? Why not indulge, this once, the ever-present desire to hold her close instead of always having to suppress it?

Especially since this might well be his last opportunity.

'Very well, I promise,' he said, guiltily aware that, while he pitched his voice to convey resignation, a suppressed excitement expanded and tightened in his chest at the idea of Lady Laura in his arms, smiling up at him...

'What do you think of these?' Susanna's question dispelled that pleasing vision as she held up music for him to inspect.

'A country dance?' he asked, looking at the score.

'Yes. I thought we'd practise that, then a pattern dance. Of course, it's hard to replicate the experience with only one couple rather than a full set to advance through the steps, but we shall make do. Then for last, a waltz.'

Miles had a sudden vision of waltzing with Lady Laura, her hand in his, his arm clasping her round the waist. A wave of arousal washed through him. How could he possibly mask that reaction to her in the intimate posture of the dance? He could manage squiring her through some country dances, but he'd better avoid a waltz.

He heard a murmur of voices, followed by footsteps coming up the stairs.

'That will be Lady Laura. Put the music on the pianoforte stand, won't you, Miles, while I go and meet her?'

While his sister hurried out, Miles stood for a few minutes immobile, the recurring image of Lady Laura in his arms making his mouth dry and his heartbeat accelerate before he shook his head to free himself of the spell.

He needed to be very careful of the physical response she triggered. Trying to ignore it hadn't been effective. Reminding himself that their association was soon to end and nothing could come of it hadn't succeeded in lessening her appeal either. The only prudent course was to acknowledge its power, keeping uppermost in his mind the fact that he would not be able to think clearly while under its spell, and so must be vigilant about resisting any impulse her nearness generated.

In short, exercise the strong restraint over his emotions and behaviour that he'd failed to employ when he'd been swept away by the deceptive charm of Arabella Theakson.

He brushed aside the little whisper that said, while it was true he'd been powerfully attracted to Miss Theakson, he hadn't also had to resist the allure of her intellect or the appeal of her unusual interests, as he was struggling to do with Lady Laura.

Then the lady herself walked in, filling the room with her grace, the warmth of her smile, her subtle rose scent. She was fetchingly arrayed in a deep-blue gown that brought out the summer-sky hue of her eyes and made the tangle of blonde curls glow even more golden. He could feel his lips curving automatically into a smile as gladness swelled his chest.

'Lady Laura,' he murmured, bowing as she curtseyed. He closed his eyes briefly as that strong, constant, invisible connection hummed between them. When he opened them, she was gazing at him silently, an answering awareness in her eyes.

'Mr Rochdale,' she said at last. 'Are you ready to partner your sister?'

'Yes. Though I'm not so sure I approve of your instructing her to be a scintillating conversationalist while dancing. As she's already so graceful and lovely, you may make her wholly irresistible.'

'Making her irresistible is the goal, Mr Rochdale. It's always the lady's prerogative to respond to or reject a gentleman's admiration. But better to inspire many gentlemen to it, the more from whom she can choose.'

'I'd counsel rejecting them all,' he replied.

'I imagine you would,' she said drily. 'But that should always be the lady's choice—should it not, Susanna?'

'I agree,' his sister said tartly. 'As you see, I selected music for several types of dance,' Susanna said, holding the sheets out to Lady Laura, who scanned them and nodded.

'A good choice. Before we add music, I'll have you simply walk through the figures, repeating the practice as often as necessary until it feels automatic and natural to both dance and converse.'

'Good. For it seems anything but natural now to do both,' Susanna confessed.

'Preparation is key,' Lady Laura said. 'If you are well acquainted with your partner, as he leads you onto the floor, use your knowledge of his family and interests to come up with questions you might ask him. For a country dance in which partners change frequently, all that is needed are a few general questions to which he can give short answers when the figures bring you back together. For those dances in which you remain with your partner for a longer time, the questions can be more involved. And naturally, for a waltz in which you will be with your partner for the entire dance, having ideas to support an extended conversation will be quite helpful, since you will face the added complication of having your partner holding you rather closely. Which can be quite distracting, especially if you find the gentleman appealing!'

'It all sounds rather complicated,' Miles objected, a glance at his sister telling him she was thinking the same. 'Can one not just simply dance?'

'Of course, but I wouldn't recommend remaining silent.'

'Why not?' Susanna asked. 'Would my partner not just believe I am concentrating on my steps?'

'Perhaps, but you wouldn't really want him to think that. Only young ladies just out of the schoolroom would be forgiven for having difficulty managing both the steps and a conversation. You wouldn't want to give the impression that you were awkward or slow-witted! Besides, silence can be open to many interpretations, most of them unfortunate. For instance, your partner might conclude that you are too proud and puffed up with your own consequence to deign to converse with him. That you find him disagreeable or lacking in some way. Or that you are too incoherent to be able to express yourself.'

'Or perhaps conclude that you have been pressed by family or friends to dance when you don't wish to?' Miles inserted.

'That's possible, but it wouldn't be desirable to convey any of those impressions. Even if you'd rather not dance with that particular partner, if he feels he's been treated disdainfully, he will surely complain of your behaviour to his friends and relations, which could result in other partners with whom you would like to dance deciding not to approach you. It's best to smile and be agreeable to them all. If you truly don't want to dance with someone, better to refuse him at the outset.'

'That I have never managed to do,' Susanna admitted ruefully. 'How does one do that without giving offence?'

'Any of several replies will suffice. You are fatigued and wish to rest for a bit. Your chaperon requires your presence for some reason. You are promised to someone else who is about to escort you to take some refreshment. If all else fails, say you must visit the ladies' withdrawing room to fix a loose pin or a torn hem. Naturally, if you refuse to dance with one man, you can't accept another supplicant for the same set.'

'Except the gentleman who is supposedly escorting you for refreshments?' Miles suggested.

Lady Laura smiled. 'You could whisper that amendment to your favoured beau if you've used that excuse to wait for him. Now, for a gentleman whom you don't know, have general questions ready—but please, not just a comment on the weather! Something about the theatre or a concert you've recently attended will do. Or an observation about some upcoming event in Society or a happening reported in the newspapers. With any luck, the gentleman will do his part, replying with questions of his own to keep conversation flowing.'

Susanna sighed. 'It still sounds complicated.'

'It's truly much easier than it may sound. Now, think of some topics you might introduce for someone you don't know.'

As Lady Laura waited, Susanna said after moment, 'I recently attended a concert of the Philharmonic Society which featured a performance of Beethoven's music. Do you enjoy orchestral music?'

'Very good,' Lady Laura nodded. 'What if you were asked to dance by Mr Ecclesley?'

'I'd ask after his family and how the crops are progressing at their estate in Kent,' she said, her eyes brightening. 'Perhaps it isn't so complicated after all.'

'Not when you are well prepared. Now, let's choose a dance and have you walk through the motions with Mr Rochdale, asking your questions when the steps bring you back together.'

Though Miles initially thought the exercise rather silly, touched by how serious and attentive his sister was, he stifled the impulse to reply to her questions with teasing or inappropriate answers. Lady Laura had his sister repeat the practice through the movements of several different country dances, then through the course of a waltz—although both he and Susanna ended up laughing at the absurdity of her questioning him before they finished that one.

After giving them a smiling reproof, Lady Laura pronounced Susanna ready to practise with music and took her place behind the piano.

Their accompanist played several more selections, stopping occasionally to ask Susanna if she was feeling more at ease. Finally, his sister pronounced herself able to ask her questions without having to concentrate so fiercely, saying she was now able to relax and just enjoy the dance.

'Excellent, that's just the result we wanted,' Lady Laura announced. Rising from the piano bench, she walked over to them. 'Now that you are comfortable with dance and conversation, we can move on to our last topic—the little looks and gestures you save to employ only with gentlemen you want to encourage.'

'Are you truly going to encourage her to flirt?' Miles asked, alarmed.

'You speak as if flirting were something terrible!' Lady Laura said. 'Whereas most consider it an amusing pastime, equally enjoyable for gentlemen and ladies.'

'It's not enjoyable if one party deceives another into believing they desire an attachment, when it was only a test of their power to entice,' Miles said grimly.

Tilting her head, Lady Laura studied him, then said quietly, 'No, you are right. It would not be enjoyable to believe a light flirtation serious, and then discover you were wrong.'

'How embarrassing!' Susanna exclaimed.

'Embarrassing and hurtful,' Lady Laura said, giving Miles a thoughtful look.

He sucked in his breath, already regretting the statement, which had skirted far too close to the truth. Had Lady Laura been able to discern something in his expression or tone? The idea that someone might discover his foolish obsession with Arabella was detestable. The only thing that made the interlude bearable was knowing only he and that duplicitous lady had been aware of his infatuation.

'One cannot always be sure, especially if the other person is not truthful or honourable,' Lady Laura said quietly. 'It would be shameful for a lady or gentleman to flirt in such a way as to lead another to believe genuine feelings exist when there are none. Or to entice only for sport. Although I'm sure you would never do that, Susanna,' she added, turning to his sister.

'Certainly not!' Susanna confirmed. 'That would be…cruel.'

'Cruel indeed. I imagine it would be hard to recover from having one's feelings trampled on and abused in such a way.'

Miles turned away from the concerned expression on Lady Laura's face, his heartbeat quickening. She spoke as if she did know, or at least suspected, he'd been done an injury. He couldn't decide whether to welcome or resent that possibility.

Meanwhile, in a lighter tone, Lady Laura continued, 'But when flirting is done in good fun—or with one special person, with purposeful intent—there are little signs one can give.'

Susanna clapped her hands. 'The heart of the lesson at last! Little things like…?'

'Keep your eyes focused on your partner's face, your whole concentration fixed on him, demonstrating that what he is saying is of great importance to you. Let your fingers linger on his when takes he takes your hand or releases it during the movements of the dance. Allow your arm to brush his sleeve and, if he looks at you enquiringly, give him an intimate smile, as if he were the only person in the room. While dancing, lower your eyes and look up at him through your lashes with a wondering gaze, as if you consider it a privilege to be held in his arms.'

Focusing on Susanna, Lady Laura demonstrated as she talked. Miles found his stomach tightening as he watched, just imaging those looks, smiles and touches given to him. Imagining how easily they could go to his head and prompt him to respond.

She's just play acting, he reminded himself. Demonstrating how to carry on a pleasant pastime between a man and woman, as she'd said. Despite the strength of the pull between them, that was all it could be. He'd not let himself be fooled this time into believing it to be something more.

While he stood looking on silently, Lady Laura had Susanna repeat the advice, then practise the looks. 'Do you think you will feel comfortable using these?'

'I think so,' his sister replied with a giggle. 'Now I'm eager to put them into practice!'

'I won't make you try flirting with your brother,' Lady Laura said with a smile.

'That's wise. I'd probably burst out laughing before we danced ten steps.'

'I certainly would,' Miles retorted, making a face at her that did set her giggling.

'You will have plenty of opportunity to practise at the ball tonight. If you are feeling confident and eager, my work is done. Perhaps we can share a quick cup of tea before I go?'

'You mustn't go yet! We haven't given Miles a chance to practise.'

Lady Laura's eyes widened, her expression turning apprehensive. 'It's usually the lady's responsibility to carry on the conversation. I don't think he needs to practise.'

'But a gentleman must do his part, replying and asking questions of own, mustn't he?'

'That's probably not necessary with a lady he knows well, and I understand he's known Miss Dunnock since they were both children.'

'True, but I doubt he has danced with her often, though. Have you, Miles?'

Truth be told, he'd never danced with Charlotte. He scrambled to produce an off-putting answer, but lies didn't come to him easily.

Besides, if he admitted the truth, Susanna would insist on having him dance with Lady Laura. He'd be able to take her hand, twirl her in his arms, doubtless the only opportunity he'd ever have to bring her close…

Heat, desire and a bittersweet longing flooded him. Which was reason enough to heed the alarm bells flashing in his brain.

Somehow he couldn't get his lips to form a refusal.

While he floundered, Susanna walked over to seat

herself on the bench and arranged the music on piano-forte stand. 'I'm not as skilled a musician as you, Lady Laura, but think I can manage these pieces. Miles, since you are already acquainted with Charlotte, we can skip the instruction on conversation with a stranger. Just prac-tise asking questions of a person you know well.' Nod-ding her head at them impatiently, she added, 'Well, take your places, both of you! I'm anxious for my tea!'

They started with a country dance where the patterns moved them apart frequently. Despite the brevity of their reunions, it required all of Miles's powers of concentra-tion to formulate a question when, each time his hand met hers or clasped it to turn her, he felt the force of the touch sizzle up his arm.

'How did your father like his cuttings?' he managed, trying to dredge up a topic that would distract them both.

'V-very pleased with them,' she replied, sounding as stilted as he felt.

'Does he think they will be ready for planting in the garden soon?'

'They will need several more months in pots.'

After another few such attempts, he gave it up as a lost cause, switched off his struggling brain and let him-self simply enjoy touching her and being wrapped in her rose scent each time the dance brought them back to-gether. She seemed willing to do the same, making no attempt to revive the conversation either.

When his sister ended the piece, he congratulated himself on managing it fairly well, though he felt light-headed and his heart thudded far harder than the move-ments of the dance should have provoked.

'Just one more and we'll take our tea,' Susanna an-nounced. 'A waltz.'

'Is that really necessary?' Lady Laura asked faintly, her eyes widening with an alarm he shared.

Alarm, yes, but also a surge of anticipation so sharp, a need so keen, that Miles knew he wouldn't be able to refrain unless she refused him outright.

'Of course,' his sister answered. 'I'll bet he's never *waltzed* with Charlotte.' She giggled. 'Holding her that closely might ruffle even your famous composure, brother. So you must practise.'

He looked over at Lady Laura, who avoided his gaze.

But she didn't protest further. Might she be as eager to be in his arms as he was to have her there?

Miles couldn't tell whether she'd stopped objecting so not to offend him by refusing, or was held captive by the same desire that infused him—a desire mingled with a knowledge of the dangers the intimacy of the dance might produce.

She remained immobile, neither drawing away nor looking up in invitation. Too reckless with need now to heed the voice of prudence, Miles offered her his arm.

Chapter Thirteen

Laura should have laughed, brushed off Susanna's suggestion with a humorous rejoinder and moved away from her dance partner. Out of range of temptation, beyond his dangerous proximity.

She'd been unable to force herself to do so.

A little voice whispered it would be the only time she would ever get to waltz with him, to feel the warmth of his body so close to hers, virtually embracing her. Allowing that would be madness. But she found she couldn't refuse the opportunity to be held by him, something she'd longed for since that day he'd first caught her as she'd stumbled on the doorstep of his salon.

Swallowing hard, with an awkward stiffness so unlike her usual graceful self, Laura put a hand on Rochdale's shoulder and let him clasp the other. Little darts of sensation needling up and down her arm, she was hardly able to feel her feet and her head was woozy. She clutched him tighter, not wishing to humiliate herself by tripping as Susanna began to play and he led her into the first whirling turn.

She didn't even try to converse, knowing she'd be unable to produce a word. Rochdale seem equally content simply to hold her and dance. A good thing she was so familiar with the movements that she was able to follow him instinctively, else in her inability to do anything but savour his closeness she might have stepped all over his feet.

She dared an upward glance, to find him staring down at her. Rational thought had been swept away with the first chords of the music, leaving her floating on a mesmerising tide of wonder. She had a nearly irresistible urge to lean closer, to rest her head on his shoulder and pull herself even more tightly against him.

If she didn't break the hold of that compulsion, she was going to embarrass him and shock his sister by succumbing to it.

She forced herself to look away, clearing her throat and dragging her absent mind back from its floating abyss. *Mathematics*, the desperate thought finally broke through. Focusing on something requiring pure intellect would pull her free from sensuality's grip.

Rochdale must have reached the same conclusion, for suddenly she heard him say, 'H-harmonics. I'm intrigued by…by the proportional relationship of harmonic sound you told me about.'

'Harmonic sound?' she repeated.

'You discussed it at the Philharmonic concert. The mathematical relationship of pitch in different chords? I found a study that discussed it. The intervals Pythagoras discovered in his experiments with string.'

'Ah, y-yes,' she said shakily, making herself concentrate. 'The two-to-one octave, four-to-three fourth and three-to-two fifths?'

The need to draw closer hadn't lessened, but the discussion was helping her resist the overwhelming lure of his closeness, she thought, her desperate grip on his arm easing a bit.

'Just as interesting, the use of the tempered scale employed by Bach. You've read of it?'

She dredged up the memory through the molasses-thick slowness of her distracted mind. 'That two adjacent notes on the keyboard be separated in ratio by the twelfth root of two?'

'Yes. Mozart used mathematical ratios as well. Amazing, how he was able to hear those melodies in his ear without having to calculate them. How he could write out every interlacing part for every instrument without ever making a mistake or needing to revise.'

Laura was concentrating so hard on hearing every word, it took her a moment to realise the music had abruptly ended. Vaguely, as if from a vast distance, she heard Susanna say, 'I hear Mama calling me. Excuse me, I'll be back right away.'

Light footsteps hurried away, leaving them in silence.

The music might have ended. But still Rochdale held her.

She looked up again at his face. She could see the faint trace of whiskers left after his morning shave, inhale the subtle fragrance of soap and compelling male. Studied up close, the startling blue of his eyes was even more mesmerising. And his mouth...

The heat of his gaze sent a shiver of anticipation through her. She felt a sigh whisper from her lips as her eyes fluttered closed and she lifted her face to him.

Then he leaned down and kissed her.

An explosion of sensation rocketed through her body at the first brush of his mouth against hers. Dizzy, giddy, her heart beating so hard she felt she might faint, she wrapped her arms around his neck, pulling herself closer. A moment later, the shock of his hot, wet tongue traced her lips, teasing them open.

She parted them, clutching him so she wouldn't fall as he slipped his tongue inside and sought out hers, stroking it, dancing with it as his body had danced with hers in the waltz.

She melted against him, wanting only more, deeper, harder. Until suddenly he pushed her away, gently but forcefully, to stagger to the window where he stood, his back to her as he faced out into the garden.

Laura stood where he'd left her, putting a hand to her burning lips, her heartbeat throbbing in her ears, her whole body buzzing with sensation, her skin tingling and a melting feeling flooding the core of her.

The sound of Susanna's returning footsteps broke the spell. Hoping her cheeks and lips weren't so tell-tale red her friend would know immediately what had happened, Laura turned slightly away, hoping to mask her face until she regained some modicum of composure.

'Sorry!' Susanna said as she bustled into the room. 'Mama thought we were in salon, and was searching for me, needing to discover when I'd be ready to accompany her to visit a friend.' Evidently noting her brother's stance facing the window, she added, 'Bored already, Miles? I take it you've had enough practice?'

'Yes,' Laura answered quickly for them both. 'Is your Mama ready for you now? Just as well—I find I won't have time for tea after all. In fact, I should depart this very moment, or I shall be late to meet Papa when I promised.'

She needed to leave before she had to face Rochdale.

Bad enough she'd have to face herself and try to work out what had happened. What she'd just allowed to happen.

What to do going forward, after having practically begged for his kiss.

And then having responded to it with blatant encouragement, like the veriest lightskirt, encouraging the kisses of a man as good as promised to another woman.

Remorse and embarrassment threatened to overcome her. Resolutely she pushed them aside, all her concentration on escaping before she embarrassed herself any further.

Pacing rapidly to Susanna, she linked an arm with her. 'Will you walk me out?' Giving Rochdale an oblique glance over her shoulder, she added, 'Good day, Mr Rochdale. Thank you for your…assistance.'

She didn't dare look at him long enough to see his response. 'Good day, Lady Laura,' came his quiet reply. Almost toneless, giving her no clue as to what he might be thinking.

What had *she* been thinking?

That she'd wanted to kiss him almost from the first time they'd met. That her fierce delight at seizing her chance was greater than both remorse and embarrassment.

Good thing this had been Susanna's last lesson. They'd both be spared the awkwardness of any future meetings.

Why, then, did she feel more bereft than relieved?

Only half-aware of the conventional phrases flowing automatically from her lips, she found herself by the door, the butler retrieving her pelisse.

'I apologise for Miles becoming so distracted,' Susanna was saying. 'As soon as the music stopped, he probably started thinking of some problem at the bank. I do feel guilty for pulling him away so often lately.'

After Laura mumbled an incoherent agreement, Susanna continued, 'I recall you suggesting once that I should reward him by asking him to accompany me to venues he would truly enjoy. Now that our lessons are at an end, I'd like us to meet with him one more time at the place you once mentioned—Weeks's Mechanical Museum, I believe it is called?—the place full of fascinating automatons. I understand, with the owner's death two years ago, the whole collection is soon to be sold at auction, so this might be our last chance to see it. I've no knowledge at all of the workings of such things, so I shall prevail upon you to accompany us. You're much better able to explain and appreciate them than I!'

A panicky feeling in her gut, Laura said, 'I'd not want to intrude upon private time you could spend with your brother.'

'You'd not be intruding. I'd love your company there! I know he would too! Maybe you could even tease him to practise flirting, for he certainly needs it. He's always so sober! Besides, I know he likes and respects you. Unless I can convince him to attend a ball or two, he'll not be able to see you again and I know he will miss your company.'

Would he? Laura thought sceptically as she frantically searched for some excuse to avoid the meeting without offending Susanna. Or, worse, having her friend suspect something had occurred between the two of them.

As she fumbled, Susanna turned to face her. 'You will help me reward him, won't you? I'm so grateful to you too, for all your help. I'm confident now I shall be able to finish out the rest of the Season without becoming embarrassed, tongue-tied or snubbed. Something I could never have managed without your tutoring!'

In the face of her warmth, friendship and gratitude, how could Laura find a convincing excuse to refuse her request?

She couldn't. Facing the inevitable, she forced a smile. 'Of course I shall accompany you, if you truly desire it. I think you will find the museum entertaining too.'

'I'm sure my brother will love it. Especially with you accompanying us.'

Laura wasn't so sure of that, either. Her behaviour this afternoon might have given Rochdale such a distaste of her, he'd be hard pressed not to act so cold and dismissive when they met again that his sister would be certain to realise something *had* occurred between them.

But then, he would be no more eager than she for his sister to suspect that. Meeting her again amicably might require his best acting abilities. As it might hers. But one way or another, she would have to endure with composure whatever he said or did.

'Shall I ask him which day he might be free, then see if you can join us then?'

'Of course. Send me a note. Now, I must go. Will I see you at Haversham's ball tonight?'

'Yes.' Chuckling, Susanna added, 'Thanks to you, I'm ready to dance, converse and be irresistible!'

'Minx,' Laura said, amused despite her agitation. After slipping into the pelisse the butler held out for her, she said, 'Good day to you.'

'And to you, my dear friend! I shall never forget all I owe you.'

Despite the possible trial of meeting Rochdale again, Laura thought as she walked down the stairs to the waiting hackney, she would never forget that kiss. Already, she was anxious to be alone…not to blot out the memory but to relive it.

If she were to accept Maggie's advice and settle on becoming a rich widow, that kiss might be the only taste of passion she ever experienced. Having experienced it, could she give up passion for ever? she wondered as she settled into the vehicle for the drive home.

But she also couldn't envisage experiencing it with another man.

Not wanting to examine too closely the implications of that gut-deep feeling, she leaned into the squabs and resolutely focused her mind on the planting she would be helping Papa with once she arrived.

By the time Laura stood waiting for the hackney her butler had summoned to convey her to Weeks's Museum to meet Susanna and Rochdale three days later, she had rehearsed in her mind what she would say and do if she had the opportunity to speak with him in private.

She'd also indulged herself far too many times, reliving that kiss and the doubts and questions it had raised in her.

Such as whether she truly wanted to give up passion. If she did not, whether she was willing now to risk her heart and the possible devastation of losing the one she loved, as her father had. If she couldn't bring herself to risk it, whether she would be content to live with Papa until his health improved—she wouldn't let herself think of the alternative—then make a conventional marriage with a partner she respected.

As Rochdale intended to do.

Or should she move ahead now to encourage one

of Maggie's prospects she found most acceptable, such as Mr Fullridge, with whom she'd danced twice at the Haversham ball and who seemed ready to be quite attentive. Should she wed with the goal of becoming that rich widow who controlled her own destiny—and might later take a young lover to recapture the possibility of experiencing the passion she'd foresworn?

A titillating possibility, but unwise. For one, it would be far too dangerous to take up with a lover when she might end up finding herself with child. She couldn't imagine giving up her own babe. She couldn't imagine either subjecting a child she loved to the scandal of being born out of wedlock.

Besides, when she thought of a young man who might appeal as a lover, only one image came to mind. She couldn't imagine tempting an honourable man such as Miles Rochdale into an illicit affair that would make him betray his principles, if he could indeed be enticed into one.

But now, when she thought of passion or desire, only one man tempted her enough even to consider all she might risk.

She might meet another such man some day, she told herself. Just because she hadn't encountered one in her two Seasons didn't mean she might never do so.

Or she might find herself more amenable to a congenial partnership once the immediacy of that thrilling taste of passion had faded.

'The jarvey is here, Lady Laura,' Ridley said.

Startled out of her thoughts, she pushed away the endless circular arguments. She'd arrive at her destination in just a few minutes. As the vehicle made its progress through the streets, she should concentrate on rehearsing what she would say to Mr Rochdale if she managed to exchange a few private words with him—an apology and a frank avowal of her deplorable lack of restraint, ending with a probably forlorn wish that he not think too badly of her for her lapse.

She tried to loosen the nerves that had her stomach tied in knots at the prospect of seeing him again—torn between anticipation and dread at how he might respond.

All too soon, the vehicle arrived at Tichborne Street in Haymarket. Taking a deep, steadying breath, Laura walked to the entrance and paid her fee, then gritted her teeth against the jump in her nerves when she spied Susanna and Rochdale just inside the long, grand room, its walls covered in deep-blue satin, against which were displayed its remarkable collection of automata, clocks and curiosities.

Waving, Susanna hurried over to greet her, followed by her brother—whose eye Laura couldn't yet meet.

'It's just as marvellous as you claimed!' Susanna said, waving a hand to indicate the room. 'The clock of that strange animal is remarkable—what did you say it was, Miles?'

'A rhinoceros, said to have been inspired by an animal imported and displayed by a Mr Pidcock, who kept a menagerie in Exeter,' Rochdale said. 'Or so the guide has been telling me.'

'Shall we look around? The moving animals are so clever!' Susanna said. 'Perhaps you can explain how they function?' she asked Laura.

'I'm sure your brother understands their workings,' she said, still avoiding Rochdale's gaze.

'Clockwork motion,' Rochdale told his sister. 'The same cogs and wheels that make timepieces move are

crafted to animate these creations, even to make sounds.'
He gestured towards a large cuckoo clock mounted on
the wall. 'But you'd probably rather inspect this one.'

Conscious of him near her, Laura followed the gesture, keeping just out of range of the arm he appeared
to offer her, then withdrew.

If he felt he could offer an arm, he must not be too
disgusted by her, she thought, feeling a bit of relief.

Unless he thought her a wanton who could not resist
touching a man. Surely she hadn't ruined her reputation with him that badly? she thought forlornly, feeling
her face redden.

'This is one of the prime exhibits, the guide said.' Rochdale ushered them over to life-size figure of a swan
made of gleaming silver, floating on a stream of glass
rods. 'I'm told it contains over two thousand moving
parts.' He nodded to an attendant, who started the mechanism.

Even Laura, who had visited the museum before, felt
swept up in wonder as the mechanical bird preened its
feathers, searched in the 'water' for fish, then caught
and swallowed its meal.

'Marvellous!' Susanna breathed, clapping her hands.

They moved on to view other mechanical birds that
sang, chirped or flew, miniature squeaking mice, a variety of musical clocks and several life-size musicians.

'One of the other marvels, the guide told me,' Rochdale continued, 'is displayed at the end of the room—
so it may be avoided by any lady visitors likely to be
alarmed by its lifelike movements.'

'The tarantula?' Laura said.

'Exactly,' Rochdale said drily. 'A giant spider, my
dear,' he informed his sister.

Susanna shuddered. 'I certainly don't wish to see that!'

'Why don't you inspect the clocks over there while I go and take a look? Lady Laura—are you more intrepid?'

Did he want to get her alone? If he wished to chastise her out of his sister's hearing, she probably should let him. Besides, it would give her the opportunity she'd been hoping for to apologise.

'Having seen it several times before, I'm more fascinated by its workings than repulsed. Yes, I'd like to see it again.'

'After you,' he said, gesturing towards the corner of the room.

Taking a shuddering breath, Laura walked with him towards the waiting exhibit.

Grateful with relief, Miles thanked a merciful God who had inspired Lady Laura to give him the opportunity to speak to her privately. As soon as they reached the end of the room, he drew to one side away from several fascinated visitors exclaiming over the mechanism's clever workings and said, 'Thank you for allowing me to talk with you.'

'Before you do,' she started, 'you must allow me to apologise for my scandalous behaviour.'

It took a moment for her words to register. She'd rushed away so precipitously after their stolen kiss, he was certain she'd been shocked and appalled by his presumption. Though his senses insisted she had welcomed his embrace, had even responded to it—mad, dangerous and ill-advised as it had been.

But now *she* wanted to apologise to *him*?

'I can only hope,' she continued, her voice dropping

to a whisper, 'that I haven't given you a permanent disgust of me.'

Astounded she might think that, Miles found his voice. 'A disgust of *you*? I was about to abjectly apologise for taking advantage, hoping I'd not given you permanent disgust of *me*! I moved away so quickly afterwards, I robbed you of the chance to slap my face before Susanna returned and put an end to the opportunity.'

She exhaled a shaky breath. 'Surely you could tell from my…intemperate response I was not at all repulsed? You will think me completely shameless and unmaidenly, but to be honest, I invited you to kiss me. Inexcusable, knowing you are all but promised to wed another.'

'A circumstance which makes it more unforgiveable that I seized the opportunity to kiss you, knowing I have…a prior commitment.'

'So are we both confessing to lamentable judgement and complete lack of self-control?'

He was so relieved that she wasn't furious with him he almost felt himself floating on air. After agonising for days about whether to keep his distance and say nothing, or press for a chance to beg her forgiveness, he couldn't stop the smile that sprang to his lips.

'I might as well make a clean breast of it and confess I'd wanted you to kiss me practically from the moment I first knocked into you,' Lady Laura admitted. 'I know you've become conscious of an attraction between us too, though you certainly did not seem to feel it from the first.'

'No? Then you must not recall how long it took me to release your arms after I kept you from falling.'

She laughed shakily. 'It's such a relief to finally admit

it out loud! Rather than trying to ignore and deny how…
drawn I've felt to you from the first. Which doesn't
change the fact that it was wrong to succumb to the desire, and for that I do apologise.'

'It is a relief to acknowledge it. Perhaps it helps to
know we were similarly struck from the very first. With
us both aware, we can guard against a repetition.'

'Much as I might want it,' she said with a little smile
that sent a bolt of fire to his loins. Ah, he wanted to repeat that kiss too. Repeat it and explore even further her
sweet mouth and glorious body…

'But it can't be repeated. We are both destined to…
other things,' she said with a touch of sadness. 'I am
sorry that our association will be ending. Unless…' She
looked up, her eyes widening. 'Unless we might continue
as friends? After all, those who love numbers must appreciate each other. Would you be interested in attending one of Mrs Somerville or Mr Babbage's lectures?'

'I would love it,' Miles agreed at once, exulting in the
possibility of being able to continue their relationship.
Even if it could not be as close as he might wish. Yes,
he desired her, but he was equally impressed with her
mind. He'd never met a woman—or anyone—like her.
The few days when he'd thought he'd lost not only her
company but also whatever esteem she might once have
felt for him had been filled with bitter self-reproach.
Knowing he had not ruined her good opinion warmed
him like coming into the heat of a brilliant midsummer
sun after emerging from the depths of an icy stream.
'Shall we salvage a friendship for that?'

'Excellent,' she said, giving him a brilliant smile that
told him she was as excited at the prospect of continuing their association as he was. 'And…thank you—for

understanding. Many gentlemen would disdain me as much for my honesty as for my inappropriate behaviour. It's a blessing to know that with you I don't have to dissemble, hide my intellect or play the part expected of a well-bred maiden.'

'I want you only to be who you are. One of most exceptional individuals I've ever met.'

Her cheeks pinked at the compliment. 'Well, we'd better re-join your sister. She won't believe I wish to gaze for long on the workings of a giant spider!'

He nodded. As she turned to go, he whispered, 'Four hundred and nine.'

She looked back at him, her smile once again brilliant. 'Four hundred and nineteen.'

As she walked ahead of him to re-join Susanna, Miles felt a vast euphoria fill him. After the anguish of believing he'd destroyed the rapport between them, he now had reassurance—not just that he hadn't done so, but that their association would continue.

Their meetings might be infrequent and encompass much less than he would desire, but that prospect was still much better than the dismaying alternative of never seeing her again.

Chapter Fourteen

In the afternoon a few days later, Laura sat at her desk in the library, reading a note with a smile of delight. Ada, Lady King, had written to let her know about Mr Babbage's upcoming salon. Though, as she was at Ockham Park recovering from the birth of her first son, she herself would not be able to attend, Ada urged Laura to go, then write to her with a full description of everything that happened.

The salon was set for the middle of the following week. Excitement filling her, she took out paper and penned an invitation to Mr Rochdale to meet her there. Only one week—and she might see him again.

It did seem rather a delay, after these last few weeks when she'd met him every few days. But, given that she'd feared the end of lessons for Susanna would mean never seeing him at all, waiting a week was a small annoyance.

Absently she ran a finger over her lips, a tingling warmth filling her. Close her eyes, and she could still feel the brush of his mouth against hers, the shocking, luxurious plush of his stroking tongue.

Thrilling as his embrace had been, there could be

no more of that, of course. Though she herself was un-attached, it was not honourable to try to tempt a principled man who, though he might not harbour romantic feelings for the woman his family wished him to wed, nonetheless meant to do his duty by them and her. She could only admire his loyalty and dedication.

She'd been lucky enough to salvage a meeting of minds, where at the salons they could share mathematical theory—and perhaps exchange a few prime numbers, continuing a secret, private language that they could share indefinitely, she thought with a smile. Whenever she caught herself longing for more, she reminded herself that continuing friendship was more than she'd ever expected.

How exceptional Rochdale was! Not just in his expertise with numbers, though that was striking enough. But she appreciated even more that he accepted her, even seemed to value her, despite her having fully revealed her character. Without thinking her wanton, immodest or unwomanly. As, she was only too aware, most gentlemen would, especially after her unrestrained response to that kiss.

Granted, as she was indifferent to marriage she hadn't expended a great deal of effort trying to squeeze herself into the mould of a conventional young lady, a box into which she fitted so ill. Not for her to profess a false delight in domestic tasks or a fascination with jewels and finery while masking her intellect and interests in order to attract potential suitors. But though not precisely hiding her intelligence and true passions, before meeting Rochdale she hadn't openly exhibited them either, not as clearly as she had to Susanna's brother. Gentlemen sought her company because she possessed sufficient beauty, wit, charm, suitable breeding and an adequate dowry.

How liberating it was to be not just accepted, but admired for who she really was!

If she were truly honest, she had to repress a wistful longing that Rochdale might become more than a platonic friend. To have a husband whom she not only desired but who desired her and shared her interests—the prospect was so appealing, she couldn't let herself dwell on it. With Rochdale—the only man she'd ever met who might fulfil that criterion—not a candidate for the position, it would probably never happen.

Before Rochdale, that realisation had been easier to accept. One could not regret missing out on something one didn't believe existed. It would be harder now to resign herself, if she did marry, to living with a man she respected and admired but who would never value her true self.

Well, enough repining. At the ball tonight, she'd be meeting Susanna, Eliza and Maggie—who was applying more pressure for her to pay serious attention to her candidates, especially Fullridge, whose positive qualities her friend kept reminding her about, encouraged by Laura's tepid interest in that gentleman. She should be at least polite and attentive to all Maggie's suggested suitors in appreciation for her friend's efforts, though neither she nor Eliza were yet convinced any of them would make an acceptable match.

She'd take tea with Papa, then read the comments about the Difference Engine Ada had included with her note.

She was about to ring the bell pull when Ridley rushed in, stopping abruptly to catch his breath. 'Lady Laura, I'm so glad I found you.'

Surprised to see the butler move at anything faster than his usual stately pace, she was immediately alarmed. 'What is it? Has something happened? Not Papa—?'

'No, no, Lord Carmelton is not suffering an attack. But he has received some distressing news. He implored me to find you and bring you to join him in his sitting room at once.'

Fear punching a cold fist into her chest, Laura abandoned the note she'd been about to dispatch and hurried to follow the butler.

She took a deep breath on the threshold of her father's sitting room. As the area adjoined his bed chamber, allowing the Marquess to access it without the need to go up and down stairs, he used it as a sort of substitute library to house the books and papers he was currently using and had all his correspondence delivered there.

She must appear calm so as not to upset him any further. His doctor had impressed on her that agitation was not good for his health and exacerbated his pain.

After tapping lightly on the door, she walked in and crossed to the small desk where the Marquess sat, staring at a letter he held in trembling fingers.

'What is it, Papa?' she asked, keeping her voice level and quiet. 'Ridley said you'd received bad news.' A quick glimpse of the note he clutched reassuring her it did not bear the Carmelton crest, she added, 'Not about Michael or his family, I trust?'

He looked up at her, distress clear on his face. 'No, praise God. The news is bad enough, but not that.'

'If our family is safe, then together we can weather anything else.' Asking Ridley to bring tea, Laura took the chair beside the desk and grasped her father's hand. 'So, tell me.'

Dropping the letter, he shook his head. 'It's my fault—mine entirely! I've failed you in so many ways. I thought to redeem myself somewhat, but I've only precipitated disaster. Oh, my dear, I'm so sorry!'

'Of course you haven't failed me!' Laura assured him, her alarm deepening. She hadn't seen her father look this distraught since the aftermath of his accident, when he'd been given the news that his beloved wife hadn't survived. 'You mustn't upset yourself! You said all our dear ones are well, didn't you? Nothing short of their grave illness or death could be bad enough to be termed a disaster. '

He shook his head rapidly. 'You've made my life so comfortable since the accident, overseeing everything and leaving me to my plants! I've been self-indulgent, content to linger here and keep you with me, not pressing you to make the most of your time in Society. Lady Swanston warned me against it, and how I wish I had paid her more heed! If so, by now you would be married and safe!'

'Safe from what?' She offered him the handkerchief he fumbled for to wipe his glistening forehead, her concern sharpening. His breathing was rapid and shallow and she didn't like the pallor of his face. 'Start at the beginning and tell me calmly.'

'It's so like you to excuse me, but I know since we lost your mama I've not been…myself. It was all right and proper to turn Warnton over to Michael; he would have taken it over sooner or later anyway. Excusable even to allow myself to retreat here with my studies. But I shouldn't have neglected making sure you were settled with a good husband to support and protect you. Now… if the marriage you desire cannot be achieved, it is all my fault and I shall never be able to make it up to you.'

'I'm in no hurry to marry. Why this unusual interest? I'm not at my last prayers, you know.' She smiled, trying to tease him out of his distress.

Carmelton sighed deeply. 'Not being physically able to go about with you, I delegated your care to Lady Swanston. A few months ago I hit upon a way to make up for some of that neglect by insuring, when you at last found the man you wished to marry, the allure of your sterling qualities and fine pedigree would be burnished by the possession of an excellent dowry.'

'And indeed I have a fine one, or at least that is my understanding from Lady Swanston.'

'Your dowry was…adequate. Not large enough to tempt a fortune hunter, or a family who desired its son to marry wealth as well as birth. I thought to guarantee you a wider choice of suitors by investing the amount your mother left you to augment its value. My banker assured me returns on similar investments have been outstanding and, with him highly recommending it, I gave him leave to invest the whole. I should have been more cautious. In truth, with Mansfield so enthused about the venture, I didn't investigate it at all.'

Railway investment is more speculative… She heard the echo of Rochdale's voice and felt a niggle of foreboding. 'The investment has not prospered?'

Carmelton shook his head, misery in his eyes. 'No, it has not prospered. In fact, it failed utterly. I just received this note from Mansfield, who arranged the investment.' Looking down at the letter, he read "I regret to inform you that Grand National Railway Enterprises, the company building the railway line, has gone bankrupt. There will be no return on the investment. In fact, I am extremely sorry to tell you that the whole of the capital has been lost as well." And it wasn't just the dowry funds. So excited was he about the prospects for large gains, I took a loan against this year's rents to add to the sum. That is lost too.'

'Oh, Papa!' she said, pressing his hand. 'No wonder you are distressed. I'm so sorry.'

'It's not you who should be sorry, my dear. He goes on to tell me he will negotiate another loan to cover the year's expenses, which will perhaps even require the mortgaging of some of our un-entailed property. With severe retrenchment in spending, we should manage to get through the year and, with good harvests, recover enough to pay down that loan. But the dowry funds are lost for good. It would take years of good harvests and increase in rents to replace even a tenth of it—and though you are hardly at your last prayers, you are now in your prime. You don't have ten years to wait to marry.'

Her father threw down the letter. 'If only I pressed you to marry last Season! Innesford or Brightling or Maxted—all the gentlemen who pursued you have fine estates, a good income. Any one of them would have made you a suitable husband, would have taken you with the dowry you had then. Now…now I fear you will be on Marriage Mart with only your birth and loveliness to recommend you, competing with too many other ladies of birth and breeding who also possess great dowries. If my selfishness in keeping you with me means you will not be able to marry the man of your choosing…better I should have died in that accident with your dear mama.'

'Papa, never say that!' Laura cried, horrified at the

direction of his thoughts. 'Keeping me here wasn't self-ishly thwarting my wishes—I haven't been seriously pursuing marriage either. Nor have I yet found a man who tempts me to give up my studies and my independence to take up domesticity! If that's an error, it's one we both made. You mustn't try to shoulder that blame alone.'

Ridley appeared with their tea. Laura poured for her father and continued trying to soothe him, assuring him the reversal of fortune wasn't the disaster he thought it, that a man who really loved her would not quibble over a lack of dowry.

'A noble premise,' her father said, putting down his cup. 'But we both know the reality is different. Dowry does matter. I'll ask Lady Swanston to redouble her efforts, for now it's necessary for you to marry with all speed. We…we shall have to give up this house as soon as possible; we can no longer afford to maintain a second residence.'

Shocked, Laura gasped. 'Is it truly as bad as that?'

'I'm afraid so. I shall have to let this house and return to Warnton. And you, my dear, must marry before that happens. You'll never find an eligible *parti* buried in rural Warwickshire. And I'll never forgive myself if you are forced to remain at Warnton, never having a household or children of your own, condemned to becoming just a maiden aunt to Michael's children.'

She murmured a denial, continuing to make soothing noises as the full implications of her father's news slowly penetrated. Despite her protests, it was quite true that her sudden loss of dowry would affect her chances of making a good match. All things being equal, few families would encourage a son to wed a girl with no dowry when there were many well-dowered others of equal birth and beauty. And if she returned to Warnton unwed and unable to afford to return to London for another Season, her chances of marrying at all, as her father pointed out, would dwindle to nothing.

It was one thing to not wish to marry any time soon. Quite another to be forced by penury to live in the country on the charity of her brother for the rest of her life.

She pushed the disturbing thoughts away and finished her tea. Insisting her father rest, she got him settled him in bed and told him she'd see him at dinner, when matters would look brighter after he'd had a chance to think them through.

As she had to do.

Suddenly the idea of becoming a rich widow was no longer so amusing.

Should she pursue Maggie's scheme after all? she thought as she wandered back to her own chamber. Would any of those candidates still want her, a marquess's daughter but no longer supplied with the requisite dowry?

She'd hoped by the time she arrived at Lady Richardson's ball to have absorbed the full impact of Papa's news, worked out how to respond to it and been able to continue on calmly. But as she urged her chaperon—to whom she hadn't yet had the heart to divulge the truth—off to gossip with her peers, telling her she wanted a quick coze with her friends before the dancing started, she was if anything more distraught than she'd been hours ago, after getting the first inkling of what her change in fortune would mean.

She'd deliberately chosen to arrive well after the ball

began to ensure Eliza and Maggie would already be present. Both spotted her immediately and came over to join her.

'Did you get caught up in mathematical equations?' Maggie teased as she linked an arm with Laura's. 'It's not like you to be late.'

But her smile faded as her friend studied Laura's face. 'Something's wrong,' Maggie said flatly.

'Not your papa!' Eliza gasped.

'No, Papa is fine. Or as well as can be expected,' she added grimly.

After a quick look around, Maggie said, 'Come, we can't talk here. There's a small salon on the other side of the refreshment room. We can be private there.'

Eliza linking her other arm, her two friends marched Laura round the receiving line, down the hallway past the room set aside for refreshments and into an adjoining parlour, deserted and bare of chairs and tables that had been moved to accommodate the food and beverages set out in the adjacent space. Walking her to the far side, where windows overlooked the garden and the music from the ballroom faded to a soft hum, Maggie said, 'Tell us.'

Quickly Laura related the bare facts of her father's investment, not only of her dowry but of most of the estate's available cash, into the railway project his banker had enthusiastically recommended and the venture's unexpected bankruptcy—which meant her dowry was lost, impossible to be restored without several years of careful saving, the overall cash loss significant enough that her father needed to close up the London house and return to Warnton as soon as possible.

'What hurts most is how severely he's been cast down

by it all, feeling he's failed in his responsibility to see me settled. I tried to raise his spirits, but he was too agitated even to leave his chamber for dinner. The only thing, he keeps insisting, that will make amends for his lack of foresight and selfishness would be for me to wed immediately, before the end of Season, so he will know that I am taken care of and protected.'

Stunned silence fell after she'd finished as her friends absorbed the implications of the financial reverses she'd just revealed. 'Oh, Laura,' Eliza whispered, giving her a hug.

She clung to her friend for a moment, then her pushed away. 'Well, there you have it. I should probably go out and dance the night way, as this will be my last chance to be feted as a marquess's eligible daughter. I expect by tomorrow the news will begin flying around the *ton*, as such juicy gossip inevitably does.' She gave Maggie a grim smile. 'Once it's known I'm virtually penniless, I expect even your candidates will no longer be interested.'

'We don't know that!' Maggie protested. 'All are wealthy enough to have no need of a bride's dowry.'

Laura's smile turned bitter. 'I've never known a gentleman who wasn't interested in adding money to his coffers, but perhaps you are right.'

'You mustn't worry,' Maggie urged. 'We'll work something out. I'll speak with Mama, do some more investigation and determine which candidates would be indifferent on the matter of dowry.'

'Just how pressing is the financial situation?' Eliza asked quietly.

'I don't know. I haven't had the particulars. Papa was already so upset, I couldn't press him for any. I'm not even sure whether or not he knows them all, or would share them if he does. He's too devastated by what he feels was his failure to do duty by me. He'd probably view telling me any more as an attempt to cravenly share with me a burden he alone should shoulder. If he doesn't tell me, I will try to find out from our solicitor, but like as not he wouldn't reveal anything either.'

'Men!' Maggie burst out. 'They think they know what's best for us, won't let us have any say in what happens to us or our funds and believe *we* are incapable of managing such things! We're forced to depend on them for everything, yet if something goes wrong… who pays the price?'

Turning to Laura, she said, 'Surely now you'll look more kindly on the idea of marrying a rich older man who will leave you independent—'

'—Not now, Maggie,' Eliza interrupted. Turning back to Laura, she said, 'You know we will support you, whatever you decide.'

Looking somewhat chastened, Maggie said, 'You do know if your father feels it necessary to vacate the house immediately, you are welcome to come and stay with us for the rest of Season while you…get settled. Mama would love to have you!'

There were already tears in Eliza eyes. Laura found her own begin and brushed them away impatiently.

Did she want to 'get settled'? she wondered dismally. Not until Maggie's offer had it truly struck home that, once the house in Mount Street was rented out, she would have no choice but to live on her brother's charity for the rest of her days if she didn't beguile some man into marrying her…as soon as possible. Before the end of the Season at the very latest.

Of all the men she'd ever halfway considered wedding, Innesford came closest to being the one she might choose. But she knew he was nowhere near ready to hop into the parson's mousetrap.

Only one came to mind who would really tempt her to take that leap. A hollow, empty feeling filled her when she recalled the warmth of Rochford's smile, the heady excitement of sharing mathematical ideas, the blazing passion of his kiss…though he'd never given her any indication he felt more for her than passion.

But that couldn't be true. He must *like* her as well. Hadn't he expressed sincere admiration for her intellect and interests?

He might like her as an unusual acquaintance…but not as a wife. He'd already demonstrated his preference for an amicable bond with a conventional woman—and had one lined up.

There'd be no help there.

She came back from that dismal reverie to find both friends studying her face anxiously. 'Enough bleatings of self-pity. I don't mean to spoil the rest of your evening. Let's return to the ballroom before our chaperons come looking for us.'

'We cannot accomplish anything further tonight,' Maggie agreed.

'I intend to dance my shoes off, just as I told you. Before the gossip begins and I find myself *persona non grata*.'

'You'll never be that,' Eliza declared, giving her hand a squeeze.

'Most definitely not,' Maggie said stoutly. 'We must consider all the options carefully—not make any hasty decisions. Promise you won't leave London until we all sit down together and talk this through?'

'It may not be up to me.' Laura voiced that doleful fact.

'Nonsense,' Maggie said bracingly. 'If your papa determines to leave the house precipitously, you will simply come to us—and no argument about it! Mama would insist, and you know it.'

She felt tears prick her eyelids again. 'Thank you. I hope it won't come to that.'

'Don't worry. We shall find a golden rainbow somewhere after this storm!' Maggie declared. 'Now, let us cast away all care and go and dance!'

Laura gave her friends her bravest smile, though she still felt dead and hollow inside. How in the space of a single afternoon had her life spiralled so completely out of control? She couldn't help feeling the truth of Maggie's bitter assertion about the complete and disastrous control men exercised over a woman's life.

Maybe becoming a rich widow *was* her best option. If she could still entice one of Maggie's candidates into marrying her.

As soon as they returned to the ballroom, Lord Atherton spotted them and came over to sweep Maggie into the next dance. One of Eliza's beaux came to claim her, and a moment later Innesford bowed over Laura's hand. Giving him a brilliant smile, she let him lead her out, determined to put everything about the disaster out of mind and dance as if it was last party she would ever attend.

Because it might be.

So determinedly did she follow that resolve, it wasn't until almost the end of the ball that she found herself without a partner at the same time as Susanna Rochdale, who waved and made her way to Laura's side.

'You've been merry this evening! I've seen you dancing and flirting ever since I arrived. With you demonstrating your own advice, I've been inspired to follow suit.'

That description of her mood was so at odds with the bleakness within, Laura's smile slipped. Trying to summon it back, she said, 'Am I inspiring you? I hope so!'

But her friend's keen eye caught the hesitation. Looking closer, she must have seen the strain in Laura's face. 'Something's wrong, isn't it?'

She pressed her lips together to keep the tears from welling up. Another dismal aspect she hadn't realised until this moment—having other friends and acquaintances find out about her reverses, be distressed about them or, worse, *pitying*.

Before she could muster speech, Susanna said, 'Something is definitely wrong. Please, assure me your father is not ill!'

Laura shook her head. 'I wouldn't be here tonight if Papa were ill.'

'Of course not. But…something is distressing you.'

Glancing aside, they both saw Mr Ecclesley heading towards them, smiling. 'We cannot talk now,' Susanna said. 'May I call on you tomorrow? Whatever is wrong, know I will do whatever I can to help.'

Laura hated having to confess her humiliating reversal of fortunes to Susanna. But she had been a good friend and deserved to hear the news from Laura herself, not as town gossip.

'Yes, call tomorrow morning,' Laura told her.

She watched as Ecclesley swept Susanna away. There was definite interest in that quarter, she thought, watching the young man's face as he smiled down at her friend. It would be a good match, regardless of her brother's reservations.

Rochford. Her depression deepened. There would be no more chats, no meetings at the salons of Mr Babbage or Mrs Somerville. She'd either be buried, penniless, in the country or married off to some elderly man, if she could persuade one to have her.

And if she chose that option, despite Maggie's cavalier description of marrying a man just to wait until age carried him off, honour demanded she respect her husband, care for him and be the best wife she could.

Before that prospect could send her running off screaming into the night, she seized a glass of wine from a nearby servant and downed it. Then she smiled with determined gaiety at the young man approaching her, intent on dancing for the rest of the ball until she was too footsore and exhausted to think.

Chapter Fifteen

Despite being exhausted and footsore, Laura slept little that night, her available options going round and round in her head.

She could encourage one of Maggie's candidates, if any would still have her, marry quickly to end Papa's distress over her perilous situation and make the best of life with a man she could at most respect. Possible.

Or discover somewhere among the *ton* the hitherto unknown young man she could fall in love with who would be willing to take a wife with no dowry. Unlikely.

Or return with Papa to Warnton and resign herself to living as a hanger-on in her brother's household until the finances of the estate recovered enough that she might be able to return with Papa to London where she could continue her studies. By then, she'd probably be too long in the tooth to marry, even if she found someone compatible. Palatable, if unexciting.

Or hire herself out as a governess or companion, which would at least preserve her independence. But Papa would never forgive himself for her loss of status, so that was probably off the list.

With all the options so unappealing, little wonder she tossed and turned.

Giving up the attempt at sleep, she rose early, washed and dressed. Fortunately, as she didn't think she'd yet be able to summon any optimistic words, her father did not come down to breakfast. She forced herself to eat a little and drink some coffee.

She should enjoy this food and accommodation while she could, she told herself. Her pampered life of luxury as the daughter of a wealthy man, the only existence she'd ever known and had taken for granted, was soon to end.

Too restless to read or study, she went out to pace the garden. Even that place, which could normally lift her from the darkest of moods, didn't cheer her when all that came to mind was the hope that whoever rented the house would appreciate the work her father had done, or at least keep a gardener who could maintain the plantings. How desolated he would be to return in two years, four or six to find the gardens ravaged, nothing left but walkways and a few of the hardiest shrubs.

She knew she needed to embrace a more positive outlook, but her spirits were too low. Before she made herself buck up and face the uncertain future, determined to make the best of it however she could, perhaps she would allow herself one day to mourn the loss of life as she'd known it.

She was still pacing when a footman came out to inform her Miss Rochdale had called and was awaiting her in the salon. A sick dread filling her, she didn't think she could bear being cooped up in a drawing room. As the day was reasonably warm and fair, she told the footman to ask her visitor to join her in the garden and bring tea to the glass house in half an hour.

She could at least offer Susanna refreshments to go with the sympathy she was sure to express.

A few minutes later, Laura heard Susanna's quick step on the garden path. Steeling herself for the interview to come, she pasted a smile on her face and turned to meet her friend.

'It's such a lovely day, I thought you might enjoy a stroll through the garden. I can point out some of my father's prizes.'

From a collection he will no longer be able to add to. What will he do at Warnton?

He could always work with seedlings and look for new apple varieties, just as he'd done when he'd run the estate, she answered herself. Propagate and improve the exotic plants he already had. She needed to encourage him in that, not whine over her own misfortune, which he already felt too keenly.

She could tell by her friend's concerned expression that she was anxious to know what was troubling her. But with the good manners bred into her, Susanna followed Laura up and down the pathways, asking no questions, making suitable compliments on the array of greenery and exclaiming with genuine appreciation over the beds of flowering bulbs and blooming shrub borders.

Once they came to the glass house and Laura saw Ridley bringing out the tea tray, she knew she could put it off no longer.

Still, she dragged out the ritual of fixing cups and took her own first sip before finally blowing out a breath of resignation. 'You've been exceptionally patient, not once succumbing to the impulse to ask me again what has gone wrong. Much as it pains me to reveal it, you've been such a good friend, I feel I must tell you.'

'Please do, and let me know how I can help! Surely it cannot be something so terrible?'

Laura gave a short, mirthless laugh. 'It's terrible enough'.

Your brother would understand just how terrible, she thought.

'Like most gentlemen, my father made investments. Carried away by the enthusiasm his banker had for railway ventures, he invested a substantial sum in a recently approved new line. Unfortunately, the company constructing the line failed and has gone bankrupt. The line won't be completed and all the money the investors put in has been lost.'

'What a terrible blow! Is there no chance of recouping it?'

'Apparently not.' She paused, gathering courage for the final, most pertinent revelation. 'It wasn't just funds from the estate that Papa put into the project. He invested the whole of my dowry too.'

She waited while the significance of that fact registered. Putting down her cup, Susanna frowned. 'You mean to say—you no longer have a dowry?'

Laura nodded. 'Nothing. I'm effectively a pauper.'

'Oh, Laura, I'm so sorry! But—you're still the daughter of a marquess! Surely your prospects won't be affected too severely?'

Laura gave her friend an exasperated look. 'Susanna, you of all people understand how much it will. Families may wish to marry their daughters to a man of title. But no man is interested in claiming a titled wife who does not also possess at least a modicum of a dowry.'

'That cannot always be the case! Surely a gentleman of wealth would overlook a lack of funds to claim a lady of your beauty, intelligence, character and breeding?'

'One can hope. In any event, matters are apparently dire enough that my father feels we must quit London as soon as possible. Before we leave, my friend Lady Margaret will press me to seriously consider one of her candidates.'

'You did seem rather fond of Mr Fullridge. Would he not be a possibility?'

Laura sighed. 'I shall have to carefully consider any man who would still be willing to take me. The question is whether I prefer to bind myself for a lifetime to a man who will allow me to keep my place in society... or retire to the country to become a poor relation in my brother's household.'

'I'm sure your brother would be happy to support you. But it would be a travesty for you to live out your life as an old maid, buried in the country!'

'I'm not sure how I will end up. I just know...everything has changed.'

'You will still go out in Society now, won't you? Evaluate your choices? Maybe meet someone new who inspires you with a greater desire to marry?'

'I will. For a bit, anyway. And see how I'm received.' She gave a rueful smile. 'I may receive more cuts direct and sidelong glances by people who avoid my gaze than ever you were subjected to.'

'Surely not?'

She shrugged. 'I suppose we shall find out. You know the way of the world for women. Family connections and dowry mean everything in the business of marriage. Without both, we females have a very poor hand to play. But now, let's finish our tea and I'll walk you out.

I promised Lady Margaret to call on her and her mother later. Though I don't think there is much anyone can do to affect my options, she is eager to discuss them and I'm willing to listen. I must revive my spirits before I see my father so I can cheer him. He is distressing himself and placing his precarious health at risk, blaming himself for the situation.'

'Yes, I can imagine he is.' As they rose and walked out, Susanna said, 'I know we have not been close friends for as long you and Lady Margaret, but I do care deeply about you. Will you let me know…how events transpire? Of course, if there is anything, anything at all, I can do to help, you will call on me, won't you?'

Laura nodded, determined not to give in to tears. 'I don't know yet what I shall do, but I will hit upon something. I don't intend to weep and moan about lost opportunities for the rest of my life, whatever it may hold. I shall hold my head high, meet circumstances head on and make the best of what is offered.'

'I know you will.' As they reached the French doors leading inside, Susanna impulsively seized Laura in a fierce hug. 'You will come about somehow, I'm sure of it. Keep up your spirits! It will all work out for the best.'

Laura smiled reassuringly, though she was not at all so sure. But, as she told Susanna, wherever she ended up, be it living at Warnton or going out as a governess—a path more likely, despite Maggie's encouragement, than steeling herself to marry a man she didn't love—once she committed herself to it, she would embrace it and make the most of it.

An hour later, Miles was at his bank with his head clerk, in the middle of tallying the percentage gains on the month's supply of discounted bills, when one of the Rochdale footmen trotted up to him. 'A message from Miss Rochdale, sir,' the man told him. 'She said it was urgent.'

Frowning, Miles wondered what could be so important that Susanna would send someone to inform him in the middle of the day. Advising the clerk he'd check back about the figures later, he took the missive and went into his office. Breaking the seal, he read it quickly, frowning again.

He was no more enlightened as to the cause of his sister's urgency, but in a hasty scrawl blotched with what looked like the residue of tears, she told him something dreadful had happened and asked him to return home as soon as possible. A quick postscript assured him all in the family were well, but repeated the plea that he come as quickly he as could.

A mental review of the other tasks that must be completed that day assured him nothing was so urgent that it couldn't wait until later. Telling the head clerk he was needed at home and might or might not return, he summoned a hackney and set off.

Susanna must have been pacing the front parlour, watching for him, for as soon as he arrived and the front door opened, she rushed out to grab his arm. 'Miles! I'm so glad you came quickly. Haines, bring us tea, please?'

Tugging on Miles's sleeve, she led him into the parlour.

'What's wrong, Sunshine?' he asked with concern. There were definite traces of tears on her cheeks, and she looked frantic. 'What can I do to fix it?'

'It's not about me' she said, leading him to a seat beside her on the sofa. 'It's Lady Laura.'

Miles felt as if he'd been punched in the stomach. 'Something happened to her? Is she injured? Ill?'

'Not ill. Injured, yes, but not physically. I'm sure I don't understand the particulars, but you will.' In a rush of breath, she told him what her friend had confided about the bankruptcy of the company in which her father had invested not only estate funds, but her whole dowry.

After a short pause while the butler returned with their tea and his sister poured, Susanna said, 'You're an expert in investments. Isn't there something that can be done? Some way to recoup the funds?'

Miles paused, considering. 'I don't know the details of this particular venture, but for funds invested in railway shares there is normally no insurance to protect the capital, nor any guarantee of any sort that the investors will receive a profit, or even the return of their capital. If the company has declared bankruptcy, there may be a way to regain a portion of the principal, but only if there is anything remaining after all the company's other debts are paid.'

'Which is to say, there is little chance her father will recover any of his money?'

'I'm afraid it's unlikely. Which is why I've been advising our clients against putting their capital in the various railway ventures now going forward.'

'But it's so unfair!' Susanna burst out, jumping up to pace the room. 'You know what it will mean if Lady Laura has no dowry.' When he looked at her blankly, his mind still considering investment returns, she said impatiently, 'She likely won't be able to marry the gentleman she truly wishes! Her choices will be narrowed to only those who are willing to wed her for her birth and beauty alone. You know how calculating families are, even ours, when deciding with whom they wish to make alliances! It makes me furious to think that she might be forced to give her hand to some old gentleman who only wants a wife to manage his household or take care of him in his doddering old age!'

'One of Lady Margaret's "candidates"?' he said.

'You know of them too?' she asked in surprise. 'No matter! Yes, that's exactly what I mean. She feels she may be forced to marry one of them, for the situation is apparently dire enough that her father needs them to let the house and leave London as soon as possible. If she leaves unwed with no chance of returning for another Season, she will probably never find a husband.'

Miles listened to Susanna's recitation in growing dismay, a welter of conflicting emotions tangling in his chest. That bright, engaging spirit forced to wed an old man for security, or risk becoming an indigent relation in the household of a family member? The idea was detestable.

'Has she no younger prospects?'

'She believes a younger man's family would press him to marry a girl with a dowry. Unless he was besotted with her and insisted on his choice, but she has no such suitors at present. And, with the financial situation so grave, she has little time to entice one.'

She stopped in her pacing to turn to him. 'Can't something be done? Shouldn't the banker who convinced her father to make the investment be liable to replace some of the lost funds? Laura said the Marquess has been forced to obtain another loan immediately, just to cover their basic expenses until this year's crop is harvested.'

'I doubt the banker has any personal liability to his investors. He probably lost money in the scheme himself.'

'It's still unconscionable! Those funds should have been *her* money, set aside and consecrated to securing her future! Now that future is at risk, through no fault of her own. Oh, I cannot bear the thought!'

Sobbing, Susanna threw herself into Miles's arms.

He held her, making soothing noises, but as the gravity of the situation had become apparent, he'd become nearly as distressed as his sister.

He didn't want to raise Susanna's hopes, so said nothing about any possible remedies. In any event, he wouldn't know for sure the full extent of the losses and whether there was any way out of the tangle until he learned exactly what had happened.

After he soothed his sister and sent her to her room to recover, he would go back to the City. It would be easy enough to discover the identity of the Marquess of Carmelton's banker, and a business failure as spectacular as what Susanna had described would be the talk of the Exchange. He'd find out the truth—and see what, if anything, could be done.

Hours later, Miles returned home to sit at his desk, pondering soberly.

The situation was as grim as Susanna had feared. The railway construction company had gone bankrupt, with so few remaining assets that its investors' funds were indeed lost with nothing recoverable. Carmelton had poured in not only the cash of his daughter's dowry, but all the coin he had banked from the profits previously generated by his estate, as well as more obtained from a loan he'd taken against the current year's rents.

Miles shook his head, anger simmering deep in his belly. He felt as strongly as his sister that the banker who had pressed on the Marquess a strategy as ill-advised as investing all his capital in one single enterprise ought to be strung up by his heels.

But fury against the advisor would not help Carmelton or his daughter.

Lord willing, if Carmelton's estate had a good year with an excellent harvest, high crop prices and all rents paid in full, he might be able to pay off the loan he'd just secured and perhaps part of the one taken out to invest in the railway company. But it would require a decade or more of careful management for the estate to repay the balance owed on everything. Unless the family possessed other funds of which Miles was not aware, there was no possibility of having enough cash to fund Lady Laura's dowry for years to come.

He experienced a brief thrill of excitement when he considered solving her dilemma by marrying her himself. After savouring that tantalising possibility for a moment, he extinguished his fiery enthusiasm with an icy douse of facts.

For one, he had already all but promised his hand to Charlotte Dunnock. And even if he were free of entanglements, nothing about his status had changed since the situation with Arabella.

He could still hear her voice, laced with scorn as she'd refused his fevered declaration.

'The presumption of it! How could you possibly think I would lower myself to marry you—a counting house clerk? A marriage that would have my friends snickering, see my acquaintances cut me dead and leave none save my immediate family—and maybe not even them— willing to acknowledge my existence for making such a terrible misalliance? You should be grateful I allowed you to flirt with me. I wouldn't have dreamed of permit-

ting it if I'd known it was going to give you aspirations so far above your station. Marry you? I might just as well marry Father's valet.'

Laura wasn't Arabella. She would never treat him with such humiliating derision. But the truth of Arabella's evaluation of his potential suit would be just as accurate if applied to Lady Laura.

Did that mean he would abandon her to be married off to a man she did not love? Nausea rolled in his stomach at the prospect. It was little better to think of her becoming an unappreciated drudge in some relative's household.

There had to be a better solution. He would find it. But first, he needed to know for sure just how much her loss of dowry would affect her prospects.

Chapter Sixteen

Which was why, three evenings later, Miles found himself at a place he normally strictly avoided—about to enter Lady Tallaford's ballroom at the elbow of his friend Thomas Ecclesley.

When Susanna noticed him, which he hoped would be later rather than sooner, she would undoubtedly chide him for attending the entertainment without first informing her of his intentions or offering his escort. He'd prepared the excuse of having been talked into it by Ecclesley at the last minute, which might or might not serve.

But he wanted to be able to watch the activity, and specifically to observe, undetected for as long as possible, how Lady Laura was being treated now that, as Susanna had informed him sadly, news of her change in fortune had become general knowledge among the *ton*.

If it made no discernible difference in her reception or in the number of gentlemen seeking her company, he need do nothing. But if the loss affected her prospects as drastically as Susanna feared it would, he would have to put some plans in motion.

Of necessity he had needed to take Ecclesley at least

partially into his confidence. His old friend knew he wanted to arrive at the ball early, while it was still thin of company, then observe the festivities while attracting as little notice as possible. He'd accepted with good grace that Miles preferred not to tell him precisely why he wanted to do this. Miles suspected his friend thought he wanted to judge how his *sister* was being treated and was content to let him believe that.

That supposition was reinforced when, after greeting their hostess and entering the ballroom, Ecclesley said, 'I understand your concern, but I think tonight will relieve your anxieties. Susanna may not be approached by gentlemen of highest rank, but her beauty and charm are valued by almost all the other gentlemen. She's really blossomed since she began spending time with Lady Laura and has gathered quite a following among the younger bucks. Of course, you may rest assured I keep watch to see that none goes over the line.' He laughed. 'I rather preferred it before she became so popular, when I got more time with her for myself.'

Miles gave his friend a critical glance. It seemed Thomas might well be developing a tendre for his sister and, while he couldn't blame him—how could any man not be charmed by his darling sister?—he was still not sure how viewed it. That Ecclesley would not marry Susanna unless he was ready to devote himself to her happiness was sure, but could he count upon the willing support of his family? Or would they always make his sister feel like the outsider she was?

Sighing, he put those worries aside. Tonight his only concern was Lady Laura.

'Are you sure you want to hide away?' Ecclesley's question interrupted his thoughts.

'Yes. Susanna will launch an attack as soon as she discovers me, after which my ability to silently observe will be at an end. I want to eke out that period of invisibility for as long as possible.'

'As I said, among the entertainments on offer in the next week or so, this ball provides the best opportunity for someone to remain incognito. Using the next large group that enters as a screen, we'll cross the ballroom to the far side. There's a terrace outside that runs almost the full length of the ballroom, with a double door at the centre opening onto it. As you can see, pillars run from the central door to the sides of the room, supporting arches that create curtained alcoves between them. Slip behind one of the pillars and you will be almost completely shadowed by the curtains while still having a good view of room.'

'That should be perfect. Thank you again for your accurate memory of the layout of the *ton*'s most popular ballrooms.'

'Always willing to help a friend. Might as well get some good out of all the boring evenings I've spent in them.' Ecclesley shook head. 'I could have just reassured you, but I understand a protective brother's need to see for himself. Once again, you have nothing to worry about—but you'll soon be able to verify that with your own eyes. Ah, there's a group entering now large enough to serve our purpose.'

Tapping Miles on the shoulder, Ecclesley motioned him to follow as he slipped behind the clutch of people entering ballroom. With the new arrivals shielding them from the view of those already present, Ecclesley walked Miles to the alcove nearest the central door to the terrace. From this vantage point, his view of the proceedings would be good, but as his friend predicted, the overhanging drapery created enough shadow that he was unlikely to be noticed unless someone made a lengthy study of the area.

'Shall I smuggle you some champagne to fuel your observations?' Ecclesley asked.

'I'd appreciate it. Then, please go and enjoy your evening, with my thanks.'

'Will you need me to help you slip out later?'

Miles smiled wryly. 'In the highly unlikely event that my sister fails to discover my presence? No, if that should by chance happen, I'll find my own way out, once I've seen all I need to.'

Ecclesley shrugged. 'You'd probably see what you are looking for just as easily if you mingled with the guests and—dare I suggest—even danced with some of the charming ladies present. But it was a singular enough feat to get you to attend. I won't dare suggest the sacrilege of having you actually participate and enjoy yourself.'

'Not my milieu, as well you know.'

'It could be if you chose to make it so,' Ecclesley countered. 'Our hostess greeted you cordially, you will notice.'

'Only because she had no idea who I was,' he retorted, pushing back a swift, unpleasant memory of his days at Oxford, when he'd been seldom accepted, often snubbed and excluded. 'I appreciate the sanguine nature that has you making that cheery prediction, but most of the attendees here would never accept me—unless I was knighted or elected to Parliament.'

'Both of which are quite possible,' Ecclesley said with smile.

Miles shook his head. 'I'll leave Parliament to my

father and stick with banking, thank you very much. Now, off with you.'

Ecclesley disappeared for a few minutes, sneaking back to present him with a full glass. 'Sustenance for your vigil.'

'Go and enjoy yourself. I'll be fine.'

After his friend crept off, Miles took a sip and settled in to wait. Most attendees should arrive in the next half hour or so—his sister among them, so he'd have to keep well back in the shadows. He reckoned he would need to remain another hour beyond that to make an accurate evaluation. Then he'd slip away—unless he was trapped by Susanna. In which case, his sister would almost certainly force him to dance several times before he'd be able to escape.

He'd rather avoid the notice that would create—and especially avoid having Lady Laura realise he was present, although that would be almost impossible if Susanna discovered him. In that case, he'd just have to get away as soon as he could afterwards.

But it would be worth the possible awkwardness and inconvenience of spending an evening in a place he had no desire to be to learn what he needed to know.

Half an hour later, Laura entered Lady Tallaford's ballroom, a grim edge to her smile as she walked away from the receiving line. She didn't think she was being over-sensitive in believing her hostess had greeted her politely but without the warmth with which she'd been welcomed at the rout Her Ladyship had given just two weeks ago.

A week had passed since her father had revealed the loss of their funds. Over that time, she'd attended another ball and two routs. By the evening of the second entertainment, it had become clear that, through whatever mysterious and anonymous way it worked, the news of her changed fortunes had rippled through the *ton*.

She'd noticed a steady, marked decline in the number of gentlemen approaching her to chat or ask her to dance. Even two of Maggie's candidates, to her friend's chagrin, had ceased to seek her out. She now had to endure the unhappy experience of seeing heads turn and voices murmur as other members of Society watched her when she entered a room. She'd had to endure falsely sweet sympathy about her diminished prospects expressed by several debutantes who'd considered her a rival for the attentions of the most sought-after single gentlemen, even though Laura had never made any attempt to attract them.

She had seriously considered not attending tonight's ball, but when she told her friends and her chaperon she didn't wish to go, all had urged her to reconsider. Susanna had argued that she must keep forging ahead in hope, for who knew when the right gentleman might appear to rescue her? Her gentle friend's belief that a knight on a white charger must certainly arrive to save the maiden in distress might have made make Laura smile, if her situation weren't so dire.

Maggie had told her tartly that failure to appear would allow all who'd been envious of her or those who were just mean-spirited to whisper she was afraid to face the *ton*, or had simply given up.

But she might have refused anyway and taken at least this one night to lick her wounds and re-gather her strength, had Lady Swanston not made the most convincing appeal. She must continue to attend every social event to which she was invited, her chaperon had argued, if she had any hope of making a match before the end of the Season. Although Laura was still debating whether it was preferable to live out her life unwed at Warnton or hire herself out as companion or governess, she knew unless she married, her father would until his dying day blame himself for failing her.

He'd already weathered the heavy blow of her mother's loss, his diminished physical capacity and the constant pain which forced him to prematurely cede control over the running of Warnton. Could she stomach marrying whoever turned out to be her best prospect to spare him that final, greatest guilt?

It was the hope of easing her father's anguish that made her straighten her backbone, grit her teeth and determine to brazen out these appearances in the *ton*, at least through the entertainments whose invitations she'd already accepted. As Maggie had urged, she should never let herself appear cowed or craven, nor give the gleeful whisperers and gossips with their pointing fingers reason to declare she looked afraid or defeated.

As she walked into the ballroom with Lady Swanston, the set was forming for first the dance. One of the previously mentioned envious debutantes, passing by on the arm of a young man who'd been notably attentive to Laura over the past month—and notably absent from her side over the last week—jerked her escort to a halt long enough to murmur greetings and commiserate that Lady Laura was as yet unclaimed. The young man, his face reddening as well it should, said nothing and refused to meet her eye.

Laura continued to the side of the ballroom where chaperons stood with charges unlucky enough not to find partners, still fuming. If she'd been as uncharitable as Miss Reading, she might have congratulated the girl on the fact that the ballroom was now full enough of guests that even *she* was sure to find a partner.

She scanned the room, but didn't see any of her friends present, and wished she had delayed her arrival rather than give in to Lady Swanston's plea that they arrive early, so she might have a better chance to attract eligible *parti* while the company was still thin. She must take every opportunity to remind young men she was still lovely, charming and well-bred, Lady Swanston had encouraged her. And must remember not all suitors were dependent on marrying a fortune.

Laura had refrained from pointing out the obvious fact that, although a young man might not be dependent on it, both he and his family would prefer him to marry one if at all possible. It was early enough in the Season that there were still a number of as yet unattached and equally well-born maidens who were possessed of both looks and dowry.

She stood, a pleasant smile pasted on her lips, as she ran over in her mind again the various options, always ending with the question she was not yet able to answer: *could* she marry one of Maggie's candidates, if one came up to scratch?

A week ago, her answer would have been a definite negative.

But in the last few days she'd had reason to think more seriously about her future. When the estate had been operating with a more than adequate income, the idea of remaining unmarried had not been altogether troubling. She could have continued to care for Papa, convincing him she did not wish to leave him unless she found a gentleman who could sweep her away. Having been swept away himself by Mama, he would have accepted that, especially when he'd known there were adequate funds to take care of her after he was gone, enough to allow her to remain in London, taking part in Society if she chose, where there was always a chance some man might tempt her into matrimony.

That path was no longer open, or at least wouldn't be until the estate's financial health recovered, which wasn't likely for years.

It wasn't fair to remain a burden on her brother, much as she loved him and adored her nieces and nephews, nor did she wish to be. But, even more, she couldn't bear her father to remain in such a state of distress as he had been since the news of the bankruptcy. She'd already noted that he seemed to be suffering more pain, and his mental anguish might well cause his physical health to deteriorate.

She knew if she married, if he could pass caring for her on to a husband who could support and protect her, the guilt that tormented him would be eased or erased. If she was able to project at least the appearance of being happy, and could give him more grandchildren to spoil, it would do much to add contentment to the remaining years of his life.

Ever since her parents' accident, after which she had shied away from the idea of falling in love with a man whose loss could devastate her, she'd at least considered the possibility of settling for an amicable marriage with an honourable man she could respect, even if he were not a confidante with whom she shared her innermost thoughts and deepest interests as her parents had done. Might it not be time to accept that option and set herself to making it happen? Doing so would settle a future turned suddenly uncertain and relieve the anxiety of the father she loved.

Especially since the one man she'd met who might have become that friend and confidante, someone she might even have fallen in love with, hadn't indicated any such inclination for her—and was in any event already spoken for.

While she pondered, Lady Swanston had been making conversation with the other chaperons as the set finally ended. Since she wasn't sure how long she'd be able to keep a pleasant expression pasted on her face while her nerves were rubbed raw by the subtle glances of scorn, curiosity, pity and triumph tossed her way, Laura was relieved to see Innesford approaching.

'Lady Laura!' he said, sweeping her a bow. 'Would the loveliest lady in the room honour me with the next dance?'

As he had uttered that request in a carrying voice designed to reach everyone in the vicinity, his gallantry made her eyes prickle with tears. To stave them off, she answered tartly, 'I'd be delighted to accept the hand of the biggest flirt in the room, since to claim me he had to pass up two or three ladies whom any impartial observer would pronounce definitely more beautiful!'

'Beauty is in the eye of the beholder,' he said with a smile, giving Lady Swanston a bow. 'But,' he added, lowering his voice, 'There's surely no other lady here braver or more steadfast.'

She swallowed hard again as he led her into the dance, which turned out to be a waltz. 'Thank you for your confidence,' she murmured. 'I'm afraid my bravery is becoming rather tattered and my steadfastness is slipping. You've heard the news, of course.'

He clasped her hand and placed his arm at her waist, his smile fading as he gazed at her with concern. Absently she noted that though his touch was…pleasant… it didn't engender the ricocheting explosion of sensation she'd experienced when a certain other gentleman had swept her into a waltz…

'I did hear the news,' Innesford was confirming. 'I can't tell you how sorry I am. I suppose the vicious old beldams are making the most of the gossip? Harridans. It's a shame they haven't anything better to do with their time.'

'Better than tittering over the sudden loss of prospects by a marquess's daughter? You must know that's far too juicy a morsel not be chewed over thoroughly.'

'As I recall, you weren't all that concerned about marrying any time soon. Do you think to wait awhile, let the estate recover?'

'I'm not sure. From what I can piece together—naturally, no one has considered it necessary to inform me precisely how bad the damage is,' she inserted, unable to keep the bitterness from her voice. 'Recovery will likely take more years than I'd still be considered marriageable.'

'What do you intend to do, then? Surely you don't mean to hire yourself out as a governess?' He grinned. 'Somehow I can't see you meekly taking orders from some arrogant matron who thinks herself above you or chasing around a pack of ill-mannered brats.'

'They wouldn't be ill-mannered if I had the managing of them,' she retorted. 'I've been independent so long, it would be hard to follow anyone's orders. But I hate the idea of hanging on my brother's sleeve. And though I've not felt much more enthusiasm for wedlock than you have, it will be a great blow to my father if I don't marry.'

Innesford was silent a moment, then said, 'He feels responsible for your loss of dowry.'

'Yes. And would see my failure to marry as a constant reproach.'

'I can see how he might. Well, I suppose you must start considering the unthinkable. Any candidates who stand out?'

Laura laughed. 'Maggie is pressing Mr Fullridge on me.'

Innesford wrinkled his nose. 'He'd be fortunate to win you but—could you truly consider marrying a man who's probably older than your father? It seems rather appalling to me. In fact, I might feel honour compels me to fall on my sword and offer for you myself. After all, what are friends for?'

She bit her lip, truly near tears now. 'That's an impossibly generous offer, but I would not ruin your life just because mine has been. I know very well you have absolutely no desire to marry now. How could you give up all your ladies? And I'd take a very dim view of my husband seducing every willing widow in town.'

'Giving them up would be a sacrifice,' he said soberly. 'But not as great a one as having you marry a man you can at best only respect. Promise me, if it looks like it may come to that, you'll consider my offer? As you may have noticed, I am a rather charming fellow. I think we could rub along well together. And you are a beauty. I wouldn't be at all averse to taking up a husband's duties.' He wiggled his eyebrows suggestively.

Laura laughed, as she knew he meant her to. 'You are

a dear friend! I promise, if things become truly dire, I will consider your offer. But I hope it won't come to that.'

As the music ended, Innesford walked her back to her chaperon. 'Keep it in mind, won't you? I think I'd look rather dashing as a knight in shining armour.' He bowed gallantly and kissed her hand.

Once again she felt the prickle of tears. 'Your shield is gleaming in the sun as we speak.'

'I'm engaged for the next few sets, but I'll be back to check on you. Chin up, my dear,' he said, tapping her there.

'Always,' she promised.

A few minutes later, Laura noticed Maggie, Eliza and Lady Comeryn standing at the other side of the room. Spotting her, the party swiftly made its way to her side.

'I see you already had a waltz with Innesford,' Maggie said, linking one arm with Laura's while Eliza took the other.

'Yes. Don't breathe it to a soul, but he even made me an offer.'

Eliza gasped. 'Are you going to accept it?'

'Of course not! Though he was a dear to have made it.'

'He probably only did so because he was certain you would refuse,' Maggie said with grin. 'But I have no doubt he'll not be the only one who asks you.' She paused, sobering as she studied Laura. 'Do you think you could accept Fullridge? I'm reasonably sure, if you give him any encouragement, he *will* ask you. He's wealthy enough not to need a bride with a big dowry.'

'I have to say, I've been impressed by how courteous and kind he is,' Eliza said earnestly.

Laura bit back the retort that perhaps then *Eliza* ought to marry him—an uncharitable remark that would never had occurred to her, had she not been weary and uncertain, her nerves strained to the breaking point.

'Yes, he is courteous and charming,' she said instead. 'I can envisage being able to honour and respect him, treat him with fondness, perhaps even eventually love him in a way. I… I'm just not sure whether I can take that step—yet.'

'Despite your circumstances, you don't need to rush to a decision,' Lady Comeryn said softly, pressing her hand. 'As I've assured you several times, you are more than welcome to come and stay with us if your father feels it necessary to close up Carmelton House. We'd be delighted to host both of you for the rest of the Season, or for as long as you'd wish to stay with us.' She glanced fondly at her daughter. 'Maggie and I intend to remain in London permanently, and we would love your company.'

'You are both wonderfully kind, and I will certainly keep your invitation in mind.'

'Do that,' Maggie ordered.

The musicians began tuning up for the next set. While Lord Atherton came to claim Maggie, to Laura's surprise the rather elderly Lord Markham walked over to make Eliza a bow, asking if she would do him the honour. Blushing, her friend curtseyed and went off on the viscount's arm.

Eyebrows raised, Laura gazed after them speculatively. Markham was wealthy enough to make Maggie's list, but as a viscount too highly titled to qualify. She had a vague memory of her friend dancing with His Lordship on several other occasions. Eliza had never mentioned an interest in Markham…but knowing Maggie would certainly disapprove, she likely wouldn't have spoken of him even if she'd been interested.

Laura had plenty of time to speculate about Eliza's possible preferences in suitors. Fullridge did not appear at the ball and Innesford was occupied by other partners, as was Susanna, who came by to embrace her as soon as she arrived with Lady Bunting before Ecclesley led her off. As dance succeeded dance, Laura remained with the chaperons, her hand unsought and, except when her friends re-joined her between dances, without anyone inviting her to converse.

She was wondering how much longer she needed to endure before she could take her leave when, from the direction of the curtained alcove near the door that gave on to the terrace, a familiar but unexpected voice shocked her.

'Good evening, Lady Laura. Are you free for the next dance?'

She turned, astounded to discover the voice did in fact belong to Miles Rochford, who appeared to be emerging from the drapery. Blinking rapidly, not sure his appearance wasn't a mirage dreamt up by a fevered imagination too badly strained by this awful evening, she gasped, 'Mr Rochdale! Wh-what are you doing here? Susanna said you never come to balls!'

'Dance with me, and I'll tell you.'

Stupefied, disbelieving—and so relieved to see his dear face she could barely refrain from throwing herself into his arms—she said, 'I'd be delighted,' before realising that the next dance…was a waltz.

Chapter Seventeen

Having somehow eluded detection by his sister after her arrival, and having observed—his jaw clenching ever tighter as the evening went on—more than enough about how Lady Laura was being treated, Miles should have slipped quietly from his hiding place and left the ball.

But after watching her be the subject of whispers and pointed fingers, hearing one maiden disparage her to her face and a number of others out of her hearing, and then watching her neglected as far less favoured ladies were led out to dance, he was so furious he couldn't bear it any longer.

Not until he stalked over to ask for her hand did he realise the dance for which he'd asked her to stand up was a waltz.

A mistake—but maybe not. Maybe, if he could recapture some of the magic from when they'd waltzed in the music room, he could blot out for her what could only have been an evening of trial and humiliation.

Could he at least bring a genuine smile back to her face?

'So, why are you here, Mr Rochdale?' she asked as he led her out.

'My sister and my friend Ecclesley have been pressing me to attend one of these to-dos for weeks. I thought if I gave in this once, they might stop importuning me.'

'You are attending, but I've not seen you dancing. Nor did Susanna say a word to me about you being present.'

'I confess, I came with Ecclesley and have been avoiding my sister. She would urge me to dance, while the prime reason for a man in my position to come to a function like this is to mingle with the gentlemen, greeting acquaintances and refreshing ties.'

She nodded. 'Making business connections. Like would-be parliamentarians at a political dinner. Yet you are dancing with me.'

He paused, debating how to answer, then burst out, 'I could not help myself! Aside from the pleasure of dancing with you for its own sake, I could no longer bear watching you be snubbed—you, the daughter of a marquess! If I had ever been indifferent about my sister marrying into Society, tonight's spectacle would have convinced me to urge her to avoid it at all costs. How a lovely, intelligent, charming girl whom I know from Susanna's accounts is usually sought-after could suddenly become virtually ignored is inexcusable. I would like to call out the lot of them.'

She gave him a strained smile. 'I'm not sure I appreciate being the object of pity.'

'It's not that and you know it,' he snapped back.

'I hope not. But you shouldn't be too surprised. It's the way of world, isn't it? Not just among the *ton*, but at all levels of society. If her family suddenly had financial reverses, lost their good business reputation and Miss Dunnock her dowry, your family would no longer be so anxious for you to make a liaison with her, would they?'

'Probably not,' he conceded. 'Businesses can succeed or fail. But your father is a marquess! Nothing save treason can strip away his title.'

'He is a marquess now, but you may remember he was not born to become one. My family stems from a junior branch. We don't have generations of intermarriage and close connections with the highest in the land. If Papa hadn't come into an elevated title, we would be considered just minor gentry. And, without important connections, a dowry is a female's most important attribute. As I no longer have that, the value of my stock as a commodity on the Marriage Mart has…substantially diminished.' She laughed without humour. 'It's a good thing it's known, or soon will be, that I am a friend of your sister, else by dancing with a wealthy young man I might be thought a fortune hunter too.'

'I probably should apologise for having asked you. It will further devalue that commodity rating if all the gossiping hens discover the stranger with whom you are dancing is the mere son of a banker.'

'I'm so weary of it all! I just want to *leave*!' she spat out.

The tears welling in her eyes made him want to smash something. He must be distraught, for this was the only time he'd ever been close to her when the physical connection linking them hadn't threatened to overcome every other thought. Now what he felt most strongly was an overwhelming desire to help her, to somehow banish the anguish he saw in her eyes.

Then she was pulling him from the dance floor to the side of room, where she dropped his hands and darted away. Quickly, he realised she was heading for the terrace.

He couldn't blame her for wanting to escape censorious attention, but neither could he let her flee into the darkness alone. There might be gentlemen out there smoking, their judgement impaired by drink. He couldn't leave her unattended.

Following her out onto the fortunately deserted terrace, he found her at the farthest dark corner, her hands clutching the rail, her face swallowed in shadow. In the faint light emitted by the flickering glow of the torches beside the entry, he saw on her cheeks the crystal glitter of tears.

'It's been a miserable evening, I have no doubt,' he murmured as he reached her. 'Come, compose yourself. It's not safe out here alone. Let me take you back in, then go to the ladies' withdrawing room. I'll find Lady Swanston and tell her you need to go home.'

She remained where he'd found her. From the slight trembling of her body in the darkness, he realised she was weeping. Feeling like a knife was slashing open his chest, he muttered an oath and pulled her into his arms, wishing he could take all her pain into himself.

As she clung to him, he rubbed his cheek against her hair, making incoherent murmurs as he would if he were trying to soothe his sister. But he was all too aware it wasn't his sister he held in his arms.

Despite her distress and his concern, his body hardened and he had to grit his teeth to keep from pulling her closer so he might revel in the touch and scent of her. All she wanted or needed from him, he reminded himself, was simple human comfort.

He held her until, with a shuddering sob, she pushed away. Still in the circle of his arms, she turned her tear-glazed face up to him. Then, before he had any idea of her intent, she wrapped her arms around his neck, pulled his face down and kissed him.

What she lacked in finesse she made up for in fervency. For a shocked instant when she pressed her mouth against his, moulded body against his, he remained frozen. Then his exulting senses broke the hold of his conscience and he was kissing her back just as fervently.

Eagerly she assisted as he explored her mouth, her tongue at first tentative, then bolder, while her little sighs inflamed him further. He held her tighter, his hands caressing her back. Not until he realised he was reaching down to cup her bottom and pull her more tightly against his erection did sanity return, allowing him to break off the kiss.

Gently he disengaged from her while she stared up at him, her eyes stormy and her breath, like his, coming in gasps.

'Sorry,' she said after moment when her breathing steadied. 'But while I was dancing with you, one realisation struck me from this awful night. If I must marry to relieve my father's concern and live the rest of my life without passion, I wanted to share it once more with the only man to ever inspire it—you. Once again, my behaviour has been immodest and unmaidenly, and for that I apologise. I'll go now. And I won't tempt you again.'

When she made as if to dart away, he caught her hand, brought it to his lips and kissed it. 'Thank you—for a precious memory of a brave and passionate lady. I'll escort you back inside, then let you slip away. With luck, no one saw us come out here.'

She gave him a wry smile. 'Not that it matters. I haven't much reason to protect my reputation any longer.'

'You have every reason to protect it,' he said fiercely.

'You will need it. Your time as a *ton* diamond is not over, I promise you.'

She shook her head. 'It's kind of you to try to make me feel better. But as you could see for yourself tonight that time *is* over. Nothing can change that now.'

'Your idle aristocratic admirers may be unwilling or unable to change anything, but I can. And I will. But for now, find your friends and your chaperon. Go home, rest and try your best to forget the ugliness you encountered tonight.'

Sweeping a glance inside, Miles confirmed no one was near the doorway and the attention of those standing by the pillars was focused on the dance floor. 'Go now,' he said, easing the door open for her. 'I've spotted Susanna and will seek her out when the dance ends. She will find Lady Swanston and bring her to you.'

She nodded, then looked up to study his face…as if memorising it. 'Thank you again,' she murmured at last. 'And goodbye. May you have a happy life with your Miss Dunnock.'

Then she was gone, slipping into the darkness of the curtained alcoves, heading in the direction of the withdrawing room.

Miles walked in several paces behind her. By the sound of the music, he knew he had a few more minutes before the dance would end—a respite he was glad to have while he sorted out a confusing kaleidoscope of emotions.

Fierce joy and immense pleasure at her kiss which, like the one stolen before, he would savour and never regret. Continued fury at the way she'd been treated by cynical Society. Icy determination to do what he could to resolve her situation, now that he had confirmed the gravity of it.

Even though in so doing he would likely remove her from his orbit permanently.

The next day, Miles went to the bank early. He was reasonably sure he remembered where his personal finances stood, but wanted to consult the ledger to confirm the latest figures. He blessed his father's preoccupation with his plans for Parliament, which removed the possibility that he might be forced to consult him before he did this.

Once he had the rest of the details in hand, he would call on Carmelton's banker and arrange things as quickly as possible, before the situation grew any worse. Then, after all was arranged and the Marquess had been informed, he must go to Norfolk and call on Charlotte.

The interview would probably be unpleasant. Miles regretted the necessity of doing it, but that too needed to be done as soon as possible.

At least he was reasonably sure that, though Charlotte might be disappointed, as there had never been any illusion of a grand romance between them, breaking off their agreement wouldn't cause tear-filled hysterics.

Even if it did, there was no alternative. He might have denied his feelings before last night, trying to convince himself the strong pull he felt to Lady Laura was three parts lust combined with one part admiration for her intellect. But as he'd held her weeping in his arms, anguished by her distress and knowing he would do anything in his power to assuage it, he realised with stark clarity that he didn't just admire or desire her.

He loved her, absolutely and completely. What he had

felt for Arabella seemed a hollow imitation compared to the intensity of this emotion. He would offer his life to make hers easier.

Nothing more intimate could come of this love than had happened with that previous ill-advised infatuation. But, although he'd been able to justify marrying Charlotte when both had been willing to settle for an amicable partnership, it would be unfair and dishonourable to wed her knowing he loved, and always would love, another woman.

He tried to turn his thoughts away from how bleak that made his future. Such happiness as he could now expect would stem from knowing he'd been able to give Laura back the life she deserved. Even if there was no place for him in it.

Except…a tiny ray of hope flickered to life when he thought of the salon to which she'd invited him. When she was once again feted by Society, even after she married, they might meet again at the home of Mr Babbage or Mrs Somerville, discuss mathematical theory or exchange news about their respective families.

But, having admitted now that he loved her, would that be enough? Or would seeing her on that limited basis be worse than not seeing her at all?

A question he couldn't yet answer. All he needed to focus on now was rescuing her future.

Two days later, Laura was pacing the garden again. Her return from the disastrous Tallford ball recurred in a blur of fuzzy images…skulking down the corridor towards the ladies' withdrawing room, then abandoning plans to enter it after finding it full of gossiping ladies… Slipping instead into a curtained alcove to avoid other females coming or going until she spied Lady Swanston hurrying towards her. Intercepting that lady and towing her without a word to fetch their pelisses and return to Mount Street. Lady Swanston's quiet weeping in the carriage on the drive home at how disgracefully Laura had been treated that evening.

Exhausted, she'd immediately gone to bed and slept straight through. Fortunately, as she had no social engagements for the following day, she was able to remain cloistered at home, refusing to see even Susanna and her friends when they called.

She didn't want to see anyone until she'd calmed enough to evaluate the situation carefully herself and decide what she meant to do.

Which always brought her back to the same dilemma. Should she ease Papa's guilt by taking a husband she didn't want? Return with him to Warnton and try to persuade him she was happier remaining unwed in the bosom of family than making a prudent but loveless marriage? Escape the burden of Papa's remorse by taking a position away from her family? Although that smacked of abandonment and might result in worse servitude than a loveless marriage.

At least if she married she would have a home and perhaps a family of her own.

She'd argued back and forth with herself the whole day, but come no closer to making a decision.

Finally, last evening she'd allowed a visit from the persistent Maggie, whom she'd had turned away twice before. While she'd sat listless over their tea, Maggie had advised her to at least accept several social engagements and allow herself to get to know Mr Fullridge better, as her mother's discreet enquiries had informed them that he was definitely still interested in Laura and indifferent to the matter of her dowry.

On one hand, it felt dishonest to encourage the man when she was so uncertain of her intentions. On the other, as Maggie had argued, she couldn't be certain what her intentions might become unless she spent more time getting to know the man than had been possible in the brief conversations they had shared while dancing or taking refreshments. If Laura agreed, Lady Comeryn was prepared to invite Fullridge to dinner and allow the couple time to chat and stroll the garden together, so Laura might discover if there was some basis on which to form a closer relationship.

Laura could only think how awkward such a meeting would be. Though why should she feel more awkward at the prospect of dining with Fullridge than she had at dinners she'd previously attended with potential suitors?

Because she had such strong feelings for one who could not be a suitor?

In the end, she'd put Maggie off, telling her she couldn't make a decision yet but would let her know soon. And so she'd been walking back and forth, back and forth all morning, still no closer to resolving the matter, until she felt she must scream from frustrated indecision.

She was about to give up and return inside when a footman trotted out to halt beside her. 'Lord Carmelton asked to see you, Lady Laura.'

Immediate fear flashed through her. Her father had hardly left his bed chamber since he had given her his disturbing news. 'Is he ailing?' she asked quickly.

'No, my lady, he's in the library. Smiled when he talked to me. Seemed right jolly.'

Her apprehension eased. Whatever had happened to lighten her father's mood and get him out of his bed, she could only be grateful.

She hurried to the library, then walked in to give her father a kiss on the cheek. 'How wonderful to see you downstairs and in such good spirits!'

'Excellent spirits! After the trial we just went through, deliverance tastes especially sweet. You'll never believe the means of it—I hardly believe it myself. Seems like a miracle! Or the merciful Lord watching out for the daughter of this foolish old man. Sit, sit, let me pour you some wine.'

'This early in the afternoon?'

'Indeed. We must celebrate, my darling. We've been rescued from the teeth of disaster.'

Unable to imagine how they could possibly have been rescued, Laura tried to rein in a wild flare of hope. Stilling the questions that wanted to flood from her lips, she took the glass of wine her father held out. 'Have there been new developments, then? Tell me!'

The Marquess brought his own glass over and took a seat beside her on the sofa. 'You'll remember I told you I had taken a loan to put more money into the railway shares, then was forced to take another to cover expenses and pay interest on the loan of money that was lost? I was informed today that an investor bought up the debts and has restructured them to allow much easier terms of repayment. We'll be able to set aside some of the borrowed funds to replace your lost dowry, so you may return to participation in the Season with all your assets restored. We'll be able to keep this house as well and continue on with our life much as before. You will not be forced to marry this Season after all, unless you choose to, of course. Is that not excellent news?'

'Astounding!' She gasped. So astounding, she was having trouble taking it all in. Shaking her head as if to make sure she'd heard correctly, she said, 'Your banker was able to arrange this? As well he should, having been the instrument of the disaster!'

'Mansfield? Oh, no. He's still entangled in financial problems of his own stemming from the bankruptcy. You may view him with disfavour, as indeed I do, but he believed enough in the project that he put a great deal of his own money in it as well.'

'Then how…?'

'News of the bankruptcy apparently created a shock in the stock market, resulting in such speculation, the default became well-known in the financial community. A number of investors were affected, of course, and the names of those of us who lost capital in the scheme became known. I'm sure we owe our rescue to you, my dear—your friendship with Miss Rochdale. Her brother—what a capital fellow he is!—told me that, with our family being such a good financial risk and his sister so distressed by the change in your fortune, he felt entirely comfortable buying up the debt.'

Once again, she couldn't believe she had heard him correctly. 'R-Rochdale told you? When did you speak with him?'

'He called on me just a short time ago! In any event, he said he knew it would give his sister tremendous pleasure to have you re-join her in the social round, without any pressure that might force you into a marriage. Of course, he knows backing Warnton is a sound financial decision, for he will get all his investment repaid over time with the appropriate interest. A sound enough decision that he was amenable to setting easier repayment terms that allow us to avoid the draconian retrenchments I feared would be necessary.'

Staring at her father, Laura heard the echo of Rochdale's reassuring words from that awful night at the Tallaford ball. *'Your idle aristocratic admirers may be unwilling or unable to change anything, but I can. And I will.'*

She blinked, trying to wrap her mind around it. He must have made it a point to discover who held Papa's loans and their terms, then paid to assume the risk like… like a bank buying discounted bills. Had he made the decision on his own, or had he needed to convince a committee at his bank?

He hadn't explained the dynamics of granting personal loans, so she wasn't sure how those worked. But she had a vague idea that he must have committed a large amount to buy up their liabilities.

He had done it to assuage Susanna's distress, he'd told Papa. Was that the only reason?

'Drink, drink,' Papa said, laughing. 'We must celebrate a deliverance I never expected! Later, you must call on Miss Rochdale and add your thanks to mine with her and her brother.'

Laura took a sip, hardly tasting the wine. 'I will certainly do so.'

'But I've learned my lesson,' her father said, wagging a finger at her. 'Henceforth, you will receive from me every encouragement to apply yourself to the business of choosing a husband. I'm eager for those grandchildren, you know.'

Not wishing him to dwell on that topic, Laura steered

the conversation around to the progress of the plants he'd been neglecting while keeping to his room these last few days. She spent another half hour in her father's ebullient company, grateful for his return of spirits. When he finally let her go, her thoughts were still whirling.

Had Rochdale rescued them only to please Susanna? Because he saw it as a simple business decision, like buying discounted bills from a reputable source?

Or could he have had a more personal reason for saving her from having to make an impossible decision?

She had to know. Awkward as it might be, she meant to ask him outright. And to do that, she didn't want to see him while in Susanna's company. But how could she arrange to meet him alone?

She debated simply calling on him at his bank, but she wasn't sure how much privacy they might have there and didn't want to the create the stir that would probably result if she showed up unannounced. They'd already missed the salon at Mr Babbage's home, which had been held yesterday, so that opportunity was lost.

Then she recalled he'd told her he enjoyed riding and often hired a horse to exercise in the mornings. She'd send him a note at the bank and ask him to meet her for a morning ride in Hyde Park.

Between now and then, she would figure out how to word her questions about his reasons for buying up the loan in such a way as to determine whether her suspicion that he had feelings for her might be correct.

Even if he did harbour tender emotions, would he confirm them, knowing he was committed to Miss Dunnock? Was it wise or even honourable of her to press him for an answer when she was fully aware of that commitment? Would it make any difference in what happened next between them for her to know?

She wasn't sure of the answer to any of those questions…she knew only that she was absolutely compelled to discover what he truly felt for her—no matter how unwise it was for her to have such strong emotions about a man who could never be more than, at best, a friend.

Could he?

Laura ran up the stairs to her room to pen the note, then rang for a footman to deliver it. After he bowed himself out, she did a little dance for joy around the room. No matter why Rochdale had bought the debts, in so doing, he had lifted a tremendous burden from her shoulders.

She remembered his kiss and the tenderness with which he'd held her while she'd sobbed out her humiliation and grief. Had it been more than passion, more than sympathy for her impossible situation that had prompted his actions?

But there was still Miss Dunnock. She mustn't read too much into Rochford's gesture or indulge in secret, probably fruitless, hope. After everything that had happened, she should thank God for His mercy in sparing them and be satisfied with that.

Having her life back again should be more than blessing enough…no matter how much she might long for more.

Shortly after she'd dispatched her note, a footman came up to inform her Miss Rochdale had called and asked if Laura would like to receive her. Wondering if her brother had shared the news of his decision, Laura told the servant she would be down immediately.

When she entered the drawing room a few minutes later, it was obvious from her beaming smile and the hug she rose to give Laura that Susanna was aware of Rochdale's actions.

'Isn't it wonderful?' Susanna exclaimed. 'A perfect solution! I should have trusted Miles would find a way to handle it when I asked him.'

'You asked him to buy up Papa's loans'

'Is that what he did? I don't know the particulars. Only that he told me this morning that the situation had been resolved, your father was content with the terms and your dowry was safe after all. You'll be able to go about in Society again with your status fully restored. I'm so happy for you!'

Returning the hug, Laura said, 'I can't thank you enough. Papa said your brother told him he had done it because you were so distraught on my behalf.'

'I did ask him to do whatever he could. Honestly, he didn't at first seem hopeful that there was anything that could be done. But he came through at the last, as I had hoped he might. Now we can go on as before!' She laughed. 'Lady Margaret might be disappointed. Now she will have little leverage to persuade you to accept one of her candidates.'

'She may be disappointed indeed,' Laura agreed with smile. 'But I trust she will be more relieved that I've been saved from the pressure of having to choose hastily.'

'Yes, you may now wait as long as you like to make that choice! Continue your studies, help your father with his plants, all as you were before.'

After Laura rang for tea, they settled on the sofa together. Exuberant with joy and relief, Laura appreciated every small action she'd always taken for granted—

pouring tea in her own drawing room, being able to sit at her leisure and visit with a friend, savouring the tang of the freshly baked biscuits Cook had sent up for them.

She now had the prospect of attending balls without being cut or snubbed…though she was unlikely to continue associating with those who'd rebuffed her during her time of distress. The ability to keep helping Papa with his plants, even the mundane tasks of approving menus and reviewing household accounts, had lost their commonplace flavour and now appeared as privileges.

'What will you do first?' Susanna was asking. 'I think we should go shopping and have you order a new gown to wear to your next ball.' Susanna giggled. 'Appear in all your beauty before those jealous chits gleeful at your fall who will now have to watch you lure away their admirers!'

'A satisfying prospect,' Laura agreed. 'But I don't think I should spend recklessly. There's still a loan to repay and I have quite enough finery.' Choosing her words with care, she added, 'I must arrange to thank your brother in person too.'

'I'm sure he will brush aside any expression of gratitude. But that interview will have to wait, I'm afraid. Just after he gave me the news, he told me he was off to Norfolk. At last! Perhaps the scare of you almost being forced to marry made him realise he shouldn't wait any longer to start courting Charlotte, lest in his absence some other enterprising gentleman carried her off!'

Laura tried not to let her expression register surprise…and a stab of inward dismay.

So much for her flight of fancy that Rochdale might have intervened because he cherished deeper feelings towards her. Her face burned as she remembered capturing his mouth for that kiss. He'd rescued her from penury and now meant to rescue himself from her misguided passion by pursuing his union with a conventional, well-behaved, modest young lady.

Which she clearly was not.

But then…she knew the passion of his own response had been genuine. As was the tenderness of his concern.

She blew out a frustrated breath. There was still only one way to know for sure the true motivation for his actions.

She would engage him for that ride in the park when he returned to London. Express her gratitude, as she must. And discover once and for all if his intervention might have signalled something more than kindness and the seizing of a good business opportunity.

Chapter Eighteen

Three days later, Miles went to the bank early in the morning, after having returned late from Norfolk the night before. He would have to break the news of the termination of his understanding with Charlotte to his family sooner or later, but he'd rather avoid that confrontation and the outcry it would likely cause for a while longer.

As he arrived at his desk, he was surprised to find a note with his name inscribed on it in a feminine hand. Opening the seal, he discovered it contained a request from Lady Laura that he meet her for a ride in the park one morning soon so they 'might discuss recent investments'.

He smiled at her discreet wording. She wanted to thank him, he was certain. He longed to see her, to watch the sparkle in blue eyes that had been so dulled with misery at the ball the last night they were together…so wild with passion as she'd kissed him. The memory of it made his body stir, as it did every time he recalled it.

Which he did too often. He might no longer be obligated to Charlotte, but that didn't change the fact that prevented him from pursuing Lady Laura. She should remain in her realm and eventually wed a man who could preserve or increase her status. He hoped it would also be a man who could appreciate her unusual and sterling qualities as much as he did.

Since he couldn't bear to envisage another man enjoying her passion, he forbade himself to think of that, else he'd drive himself mad. Somehow he had to manage his feelings, put them into a small box labelled 'friend' and keep them there if wished to see her again. If he couldn't succeed in doing that, he'd better not see her at all.

Fortunately, as he wasn't yet strong enough to make the wiser choice of avoiding her completely, he had an obligation to grant her request and see her at least this once, that she might offer the thanks he knew she felt compelled to give him.

The suggested venue was good, even if seeing her wouldn't be wise. With him remaining on horseback, safely distanced from the allure of her closeness, he'd have a better chance of reining in his feelings and stifling his desire. And silencing the love that begged him to declare himself, no matter how scornfully she might afterwards refuse him.

Shouldn't he at least give her the choice of refusing?

But, as he knew only too well, when the emotions were engaged one didn't see clearly. It would be worse than a refusal, worse than never seeing her again, to have her accept him in the heat of desire and gratitude, only to regret that choice months or years later, when she realised the full extent of how much wedding him had changed her life and reduced her place in Society.

Better to remain silent.

Sighing, he took up his pen and wrote back, suggesting he meet her the following morning.

He summoned a clerk to deliver it, then sat back, the ledgers he was supposed to review lying unnoticed on the desk in front of him. He'd see Laura tomorrow. Smiling at the joy of it, he allowed himself simply to savour the anticipation.

The following morning, Laura walked her mount along the bridle path in Hyde Park in a fever of excitement and trepidation. She'd arrived early, impatient to see Rochdale again. For the whole of yesterday after receiving the reply to her note, she'd been able to indulge her delight at the prospect, since the thanks she owed him would permit her to meet him with enthusiasm.

More unnerving was the idea of determining once and for all the motivation for his generous action. To discover if her guilty hope that he might have feelings for her beyond tepid friendship had any possibility of being realised…though, given that he had just gone to visit to Miss Dunnock, probably not.

But awkward as it might be to try to find out, she must know for sure. She'd work out afterwards how to deal with the truth and what it meant for their relationship going forward—if there could even be one.

Her pulse leapt as she saw him riding towards her on a handsome bay gelding. She smiled a greeting, suddenly so overcome with emotion that the mundane words stuck in her throat.

He seemed struck too, and for a moment they just stared at each other. Finally, mindful of her trailing groom, Laura said, 'Good morning, Mr Rochdale. I hope you had a pleasant journey to Norfolk.'

'Very fine, Lady Laura. It's always good to be home, of course. Before we chat, shall we let the horses have their heads?'

And outrun her groom, so they might talk privately? Laura thought, wondering if that was in fact his purpose. In any event, she was always game for a gallop.

'Yes, my mare is fresh and eager for a run.'

He waved a hand. 'After you.'

As she had done with every small pleasure since her deliverance two days ago had made her see life with fresh, more appreciative eyes, Laura dismissed all other considerations and gave herself up to the ride, to the rush of wind and exultation of speed as the horses thundered along the bridal path. When they pulled up their mounts at the far end of the park, she threw her head back and laughed with the sheer exuberance of being alive, having her life restored…and sharing the glorious moment with this man.

A sudden nervousness made her fingers clench tighter on the reins. Now, before the groom caught up, she must ask Rochdale her questions…and try to quell the queasy unease swirling in her belly at how much the answers meant to her.

Beginning with the simple, she said, 'As I'm sure you're expecting, first let me express my heartfelt gratitude for your assistance in mitigating the financial disaster into which my family had fallen.'

He waved a self-deprecating hand. 'I'm only glad I was able to be of assistance.'

'Unlike my "idle aristocratic admirers", who were unwilling or unable to do anything?'

With a rueful smile, he nodded. 'Exactly.'

'How, precisely, were you able?' she pressed. 'You

explained before something of how loans are made, but not the particulars.'

'It's not complicated. An individual asks for a loan, we evaluate how likely he is to repay it. Your family's estate has a sound earnings record, which makes the loan an excellent risk. It was a simple decision.'

'You made it on your own?'

'Yes, I was able to do that.'

'The sum you had to invest to buy up both loans must have been rather large. I thought you didn't approve of sinking a great deal of the bank's resources into a single investment.'

He looked away. 'As a rule, I don't.'

'But you did this time? Did your father not take you to task about it?'

'Is it truly important how the loan came about, as long as it was made?'

'It's important to me.' The fact that he wouldn't meet her gaze made her even more suspicious and determined to press him. 'I suspect, to conserve bank funds and lessen the company's risk, that you used some of your personal funds to buy the loans?' When he waved a hand, as if to dismiss the question, she added, 'Please, I would appreciate very much if you would be honest with me about this.'

He blew out a breath. 'I may have used some personal funds,' he admitted.

'Not the savings Susanna told me you've been setting aside to buy a country estate, I hope! I would feel terrible if you did that. To have our banker's folly deprive your family and the lady you are pledged to marry of the home you intended to purchase for her!' she exclaimed, distressed now that he would have made such a sacrifice.

Finally he looked at her, concern on his face. 'You may be easy on that score. In using those funds, I wasn't…depriving anyone of a home. Charlotte and I have…ended our understanding.'

A wild relief it was most inappropriate to feel about the breaking of trust between two who'd been almost affianced filled her, along with a flash of hope. Would he have committed his own funds simply to help out a friend? Or did he in fact possess the deeper feelings she sensed in him?

'And with your understanding terminated you'll have no immediate need for a country house,' she confirmed.

'That's correct. There will always be time to purchase one later. My work keeps me in London for the most part anyway, so I'm in no hurry.'

'I do hope Miss Dunnock wasn't…heartbroken.'

That engendered a smile. 'Far from it. She confessed she'd delayed her return to London because she'd fallen in love with a young engineer. She had steeled herself to go through with wedding me if our families insisted on it, but had been intending to reveal the attachment to me. Of course, I assured her I would not hold her to our agreement when her feelings were engaged by another man—as long as he was worthy of her, which she assured me he was.'

Trying to hold her soaring hope in check, she said, 'So you are also free now to choose as you like. You… were not heartbroken either?'

There was a long silence, as if he was struggling what to reply, while joy and excitement tugged at the restraint she was trying to maintain.

'My…emotions were not engaged by her, no,' he said carefully.

'Were they engaged by someone else?' she persisted, feeling her face colour at her boldness.

Again, there was silence. Finally, giving her a tight smile, Rochdale said, 'You know I'm not a great believer in romantic love. It…passes.'

'And if it does not?'

'Then one endures it.'

Falling silent again, he looked away.

Torn between exasperation, despair and hope, Laura knew that was as far as she dared push him. Though Rochdale would not make any sort of declaration, with the way he avoided her gaze, with the tension crackling in the air between them and with the sensual attraction that always bound them together radiating its familiar warmth, which had dimmed only temporarily that night on terrace when she'd been so distraught, she was *sure* he must have strong feelings for her.

But if he wanted her, he didn't seem willing to admit it.

Why not? Surely he knew her well enough not to expect her to remain within proper maidenly bounds and hadn't been surprised out of making his feelings known by having her unexpectedly press the matter?

Not after she'd tried to kiss him senseless on the terrace.

She suddenly recalled the bitterness in his tone some weeks ago when he'd predicted how quickly the attention given him by maidens of the *ton* would cease once they discovered he had neither title nor pedigree. His distaste for flirting when one party could deceive the other into believing they desired an attachment when it was all a sham. And how he'd once said that love could blind one to facts that lead later to unhappiness and disillusion.

Had some female toyed with his emotions, led him on and then rejected him? Left him devastated enough that he was determined never to allow himself to develop feelings warmer than friendship? Was that resolution making him try to deny what existed between them?

While her fevered mind threw out options, casting about for some way to induce him to spell out clearly how he felt, he said abruptly, 'Shall we ride once more around the park? Then I must get to the office.'

Her time with him was dwindling rapidly. Had they not been on horseback, with her groom rapidly approaching, she might have tried to take his hand, even to kiss him again, to see if passion could break the iron grip of his control. But they *were* riding, and her groom was nearly upon them.

There would be no more opportunity for private conversation.

Laura hardly knew what inanities she might have uttered during that final circuit, all too conscious of the groom riding behind them. But over the course of that journey she did realise one crucial, dismaying fact.

Knowing that Rochford was free of his obligations to Miss Dunnock had somehow unleashed the subconscious hold Laura had been keeping over her own feelings. Though in the depths of her being she'd known the truth for days, if not weeks, the bone-deep realisation settled that she didn't just like or desire Rochford, or thought he could be a congenial partner who gratified her by admiring her intelligence and approving her interests.

As if her mind were a night sky suddenly illumined by a blaze of fireworks, as her mare trotted along the pathway, the realisation that she loved Rochford exploded into consciousness, the truth brilliantly outlined by the intensity of her emotions.

She *loved* Miles Rochdale.

She was almost sure he loved her too, and she had given him every opportunity to declare himself. That he had not done so must mean that, for whatever reason, he didn't want to.

By pushing him any harder to reveal his feelings, she would only further embarrass herself. Had she not been unmaidenly enough for one morning?

From a height of expectation, enthusiasm and wild hope, her spirits plunged to a desolation of disappointment.

He might love her, but his emotions must not run as deep as hers, obviously not deep enough to overcome his oft-repeated certainty that one should remain in one's respective sphere and would regret it later if one didn't. She suspected he thought that adage applied just as much to any relationship between him and her as it did to his sister marrying into the aristocracy.

But what of the claims of the heart for which she'd argued on his sister's behalf…never suspecting at the time she uttered those words just how true they might become for her?

He'd dismissed them then. It appeared he had just silently dismissed them again.

And, since it appeared he had, where did that leave her? A little embarrassed at pushing as hard as she had and more than a little hurt, Laura concluded her instincts about the intensity of his feelings must have been mistaken.

As they approached the park gates, signalling the end of their ride, she hardly knew what to say. Begging to know when they might see again each other again would be pathetic. She pressed her lips together so as not ask if he planned to attend any other balls, or if he might accompany Susanna when his sister called on her.

It was rather ironically amusing, she told herself. All this time since her parents' accident, she'd been assuring herself she would never fall desperately in love, so she might spare herself suffering a devastation like her father's. Fully believing that, it appeared she'd ended up doing so anyway.

The pain was just as keen as she'd feared it would be.

Despite telling herself to appreciate every detail of the life she'd been given back, Laura was hardly able to look up at Rochdale when she thanked him again and dully bid him goodbye.

She thought he meant to ride off. Instead, he looked back at her, hesitating. 'I'm afraid in the tumult of the last we days we missed the meeting with Mr Babbage you'd invited me to. Might there…be another gathering in future?'

Despite her strong efforts to squelch it, a tiny spark of hope rekindled. 'Would you be interested in attending…with me?'

'Very much. If…if you wouldn't find that an imposition.'

Finally, she let herself gaze up at his face—to find him studying her, his expression strained and a look of what seemed so much like…*hungry longing* on his face that it sent a shock through her. 'It wouldn't be an imposition at all,' she heard herself reply.

'Good,' he said, nodding. 'Ah, very good,' he repeated, sounding uncharacteristically awkward. 'Will… will you let me know when another opportunity arises?'

'Yes, of course.'

'Very well, then. Good day, Lady Laura. Thank you for the ride.'

She bid him goodbye and watched him trot off. Puzzled, confused, hopeful and a little bit angry.

If he was so determined to ignore any feelings developing between them, why ask to see her again?

The near certainty that he was *not* indifferent to her revived. Then why was he restraining himself? Denying them both what could be so glorious? She remembered the wonder of their kisses, the stimulation of discussing mathematical theories with him, the secret language of exchanging prime numbers.

When it looked so much like desperate longing might *almost* break through, there must be a strong reason holding him back. She had already probed as pointedly as she could and was unlikely to prise any more from him. How then to find out?

A possible answer occurred. She was a shameless baggage after all, she thought as she turned her horse and headed for the mews.

Just a week ago, she would never have believed herself capable of prying into someone's private affairs. But with her whole future and happiness dependent on her learning the truth, she was about to start.

Chapter Nineteen

As soon as Laura arrived back in the house, she penned a note to Susanna asking if she might call, with the excuse of wanting to discuss the ball they were to attend that evening. Though she intended to discuss something quite different: everything she could discover from Susanna about her brother's history with ladies.

Restless, torn between excitement, embarrassment at her unmaidenly persistence and dread at what she might discover, her agitation compounded by the possibility that she might encounter Rochdale when she visited his sister, Laura waited impatiently for a reply. When Susanna confirmed she would be at home and would be delighted to receive her, Laura called out for her maid to bring her pelisse and bonnet and summoned Ridley to send for a hackney practically before the footman who delivered Susanna's note could exit the drawing room.

She entered the vehicle with her mind flitting about, still unsure how best to enquire about what she needed to know. Even a shameless baggage was not shameless enough to ask baldly, 'Did your brother have an unhappy love affair?' She also tempered her impatience by reminding herself Rochdale's sister might well not know what Laura needed to discover. She suspected if Rochdale had experienced an unhappy event, he would try to keep the details to himself as much as was possible within his loving and observant family.

After tapping her fingers impatiently on the seat, nervous almost to the point of making herself ill, a short time later Laura arrived at the Rochdale townhouse and hurried into the front parlour, where her friend soon joined her. After sending for tea, Susanna came over to give Laura a hug.

'I'm so excited and pleased that you've decided to attend the ball tonight! Once again, we'll be just as we were before, except thanks to you I feel so much more comfortable, I can actually enjoy it.' She laughed. 'And what I will most enjoy is watching the short-sighted and foolish who snubbed you fall over trying to redeem themselves for their discourtesy.'

'Especially when I walk in on the arm of Lady Comeryn?'

Susanna nodded, her eyes shining. 'Exactly. Will she give the cut direct to people who were so awful to you?'

'I doubt it. The Countess is much too tender-hearted. Now, Lady Margaret may be different story…'

'I imagine she will exact retribution,' Susanna said with a laugh. 'Especially from the "candidates" she personally selected, who then proved unworthy.'

Recalling how sharp the edge of her outspoken friend's tongue could be, Laura said, 'I wouldn't want to be in their shoes. Maggie is likely to be a vengeful angel.'

'I'm glad you have such loyal friends.'

'You being one of most loyal. I might never have had

my situation resolved if you had not begged your brother to intervene.'

'I did entreat him. But I suspect he would have done something as soon as he heard the news, whether I asked him to intervene or not.'

Trying to keep her voice casual, Laura said, 'Do you think so?'

'I'm certain of it. Have you heard that he and Charlotte have terminated their arrangement?'

'He did tell me. By mutual consent, he assured me.'

Susanna shook her head. 'I warned him Charlotte might not wait for him if he continued being so tardy about wooing her. But he assures me she is completely in love with some engineer, so I cannot be too angry with Miles. Though I do question Charlotte's judgement!'

Laura chuckled. 'You are a bit prejudiced in your brother's favour.'

'And you are not?' When Laura paused, not sure how to respond, Susanna said, 'I was almost certain something was developing between the two of you. Has Miles…not said anything?'

'No. I… I confess that I do have feelings for your brother. I rather shamelessly pressed him to reveal his own. But he made nothing approaching a declaration.'

Susanna shook her head, frowning. 'I'm almost certain he loves you! I must admit, I was relieved when he told me that Charlotte had relinquished her claim on him. If you could see how his gaze follows you when he thinks no one is looking! And I may be an innocent, but even I can feel the sparks when the two of you are together.'

Grinning, she put her fingertips together and then

popped them apart, like a little explosion. 'I knew he wouldn't truly want a relationship without passion!'

'But, if he does have deeper feelings, why will he not express them? Has he experienced some…disappointment in the past? Something that would induce him to deny himself any romantic attachment in future?'

Susanna frowned, then stared into the distance, obviously sifting the question through the events of memory. 'If he did, he was very quiet about it. But then…'

Her eyes widening, she continued, 'Now that you make me concentrate on it, a few years ago, just after he came home after university, he seemed in a fever of excitement for about two months. I thought perhaps he was thrilled to finally finish his studies and begin his work at last.

'But then his high spirits abruptly faded. He became serious and withdrawn, working long hours and avoiding any social engagements. When Mama began promoting Charlotte as a suitable wife, he at first rejected the idea with some vehemence. But then, a while later, he said that making a sensible union with a girl he knew well and respected was probably an excellent idea. That if she were amenable to a convenient marriage, he might court her when the time was right.'

'So he might have experienced an unhappy love affair?'

'From what I know now about the human heart, it's quite possible…' Her voice trailed off and she blushed.

'Based on your association with a certain young gentleman from Kent?' Laura guessed.

Susanna's blush deepened. 'Yes. But you mustn't say anything to anyone! Thomas and I have reached a…private understanding, but he hasn't spoken with Papa yet.

And I truly dread telling Miles. He sounds positively me-diaeval about locking me away in a dungeon to prevent me from wedding a man not from our own social circle. In fact, last winter, he argued incessantly against my participating in this Season, despite the fact that Mama had arranged for Lady Bunting to sponsor me some time ago, and before last winter he'd never objected. In fact—' She broke off, bringing a hand to her lips.

'I didn't pay much attention to it then, but Papa made an odd remark about Miles not letting his experience with some of the *ton* colour his perceptions of them all. I thought at the time he must be referring to the men who treated Miles disdainfully at Oxford. But now that I recall it, what Papa actually said was for Miles not to let his disappointment with one *female* of the *ton* colour his perceptions!'

'If he did have an unhappy experience, that might explain the strong objections he has often expressed about you falling in love with a nobleman,' Laura said, hoping they had truly hit upon the key to Rochdale's reluctance.

But then, it might be nothing more than a coincidence.

'You mustn't give up on him,' Susanna urged. 'I would be thrilled to have you for a sister-in-law. Except—' She paused, frowning. 'One cannot deny that marrying Miles wouldn't be seen as a good match for you. And some of the same people who disparaged you when it appeared you'd lost your dowry might cut you, in truth. It would probably also see you excluded from many of Society's entertainments. Miles would have to know it too. It might well be what is holding him back.'

'The people I care about—Maggie, Eliza, their families, mine and yours—would still receive me. And I'd rather spend my time at mathematical gatherings anyway. But…how am I to find out how your brother truly feels?'

Susanna looked pensive for a moment. 'If he has for some reason decided not to pursue an attachment, he's no more likely to confess his reasons to me than he was to you. But you're so clever. I know you'll think of something!'

'We may be making a great deal too much out of your brother's courtesy and my wishful thinking,' Laura warned.

'Perhaps. But with your happiness—and his—at stake, isn't it worth discovering for sure?'

Which was exactly what she'd been thinking. What would further embarrassment be compared to the wonder of claiming his love—if he did have love to be claimed?

After all, she would mourn the lack of his love for the rest of her life anyway. She might as well take the risk of confronting him again rather than resigning herself to forfeiting his possible affection by refusing to expose herself any further.

When had she ever played the conventional maiden anyway? Putting down her tea cup, Laura rose. 'Don't say anything to your brother, please. In the meantime, I shall think carefully about how to approach him again.'

'I'm sure, if you apply that superior intellect to the problem, you will work out a way!'

Laura sighed. 'I'm not so sure, but I appreciate your confidence.'

Laura returned home, pensive. If Miles did declare himself, marrying him would change her life drastically and he would know that. Was he denying her his love because didn't want her to lose her position? If he

was holding back for that reason, he might never tell
her the truth.

If he was going to play the protective guardian and
decide on his own what he thought was best for her without letting *her* decide, maybe she needed to do something to force his hand. And show him that she, and
only she, had the right to choose what she wanted to do
with her future.

The next afternoon, Miles sat in his office at the bank.
Ledgers were open on the desk in front of him, and he'd
started several times to sum the figures, but his attention kept drifting away before he got to the end of the
column. He needed to force himself to concentrate, but
his mind kept going back to his ride with Lady Laura.

He had expected her thanks and been prepared accept
that. He'd even anticipated she might ask more penetrating questions about why and how he'd made the loan.
But when she'd begun asking about his feelings…

He sighed. If he'd been better at dissembling, he
would have flat-out lied and proclaimed he had felt nothing warmer for her than friendship. But he didn't think
he could have pulled off such a blatant falsehood.

The best he'd been able to do was evade a direct response by replying with the truthful statement that he
had never had a high opinion of romantic feelings —he
hadn't truly experienced any until he'd met her—and
that if they did exist, they would surely fade in time,
which he devoutly hoped, else the leaden dullness and
the almost unbearable ache in his heart were going to
torment him for the rest of his days.

The hurt in her eyes and disappointment in her face

had almost broken his resolve, but somehow he'd managed to avoid making her a declaration.

Some day, when she was married to a duke or a marquess or some rich baron worthy of her, someone who could offer her the correct status to augment the wealth which was the only thing he could have offered, she'd be glad he'd held to his resolve.

It wasn't the only thing he could offer, his indignant heart protested. He could have pledged to love her with all his mind, strength and soul for rest of her days.

But special as she was, surely another man would offer her that same devotion? Someone who would appreciate her brilliance, her mischievous humour, her wide-ranging interests and her boundless passion.

His brain skittered back to that kiss, that marvellous kiss when he'd held her in his arms, she pressing her delicious curves against him while she'd let him ravage her mouth and ravaged his in return. She raced through the initial steps of lovemaking with so uninhibited a passion, he could only imagine the ecstasy of fully possessing her.

But he mustn't imagine it. It was going to be hard enough living without her, without tormenting himself by remembering that another man would be tasting that passion. Hard enough living without her smile, her teasing voice, the rose scent that clouded his head with delight. Hard living with the knowledge that he was going to disappoint his parents, for he couldn't see how he could ever bring himself to marry someone else when Laura held his whole heart.

A knock at the door made him jump, pulling him from his gloomy reflections. Looking uncharacterisically flustered, his head clerk said, 'There's…um…a *lady* here to see you. Says her name is—'

Before the clerk could continue, the door was pushed open and Lady Laura walked in. 'You don't need to announce me further,' she said briskly to the clerk, making a shooing motion with her hand to urge him towards the door.

After giving Miles an uncertain gaze, the clerk hurried out.

Miles gaped at her, torn between delight at her presence and consternation at her presence *here*. 'Don't misunderstand—it's always a pleasure to see you, Lady Laura—but you shouldn't have come here to the bank. Unless your father is accompanying you?'

She shook her head.

'Your maid, then, I trust?'

'I didn't bring her, either. May I?' She indicated the chair in front of his desk.

'Please.' He waved her to it, still undecided whether to order her a hackney and send her home immediately before anyone could find out she was here or first discover why she *was* here.

'Aren't you going to offer tea or coffee?' she asked. 'It would be polite.'

He had to smile at her audacity. 'I should send you home at once—as you very well know. Whatever possessed you to come?'

'You once said you'd give me a tour, didn't you?'

'Well…yes. But I never expected you to take me up on the offer—certainly not unaccompanied. If you should come back with Lord Carmelton one day, I'd be happy to—'

'Goodness, I'm so tired of all those ridiculous rules

of behaviour. Could Susanna not come here and call on you?'

'Of course, but she's my sister. And she's not...'

'A well-born *ton* maiden?' She sighed. 'You mustn't think I'm not entirely grateful to you for arranging the loan that rescued my family's finances. And gave me the opportunity to regain my place in Society as a well-dowered marquess's daughter. But you see, during that time when I was no longer well-dowered, I did a great deal of thinking about who I am and what I really want. And I concluded that I'm not much interested in being a *ton* maiden or following Society's endless rules governing the behaviour for someone who is.'

'You're still angry about the way you were treated. That's understandable—but no reason to give up Society.'

'Of course I'm angry. I seem to remember someone saying upon viewing that hypocrisy that if he had ever been indifferent about his sister marrying into Society, the spectacle would have convinced him to urge her to avoid it at all costs. I'm inclined to agree with him.'

'You don't need to associate with those who rebuffed you.'

'I'm feeling rather combative about those who wronged me. Including that scoundrel of a trader who convinced Papa's banker to push investing in the Grand National Railway shares. I've discovered his name—a Mr Arledge. In fact, I stopped by to ask if you knew where in the Stock Exchange he does his trading. I intend to seek him out and tell him just what I think of him.'

'You intend to enter the stock exchange?'

When she calmly nodded her assent, Miles leaned

over to seize her hand in alarm. 'You must on no account do that! Don't you remember? No one but members are allowed on the floor, so you wouldn't be able
to reach him anyway. It would be thought shocking for
a gently born lady even to walk down the street outside
the exchange!'

'Perhaps I'm in the mood to shock.'

'I couldn't blame you if you were, but you must have a
care. Surely Lady Comeryn and her friends have already
concocted some story about a mistake being made in the
rumour about your lost dowry and will chide those who
believed it, but it may very well have shaken your reputation. You don't want to do anything now that might
bring it further into question.'

She curled her fingers around his hand, distracting
him, so he missed the beginning of her next speech.

'…gone to great lengths to salvage my place in Society. But the truth is I've discovered I don't care a jot
about being part of it. Instead, I find the idea of investment trading fascinating. The ability to investigate potential projects and commodities on the exchange, to
estimate percentages of gain or loss—to work with the
numbers I love in a way that could be rewarding both
intellectually and financially. It all seems much more
interesting than attending balls and routs and dinners
where the same people dance and gossip, never doing
anything valuable or useful.'

Trading? She wanted to take up *trading*? If she somehow managed to find a way to do that, her reputation
would be well and truly lost!

Feeling sweat break out on his brow, he said, 'You
mustn't throw away all the advantages of your birth
while you are still upset over what happened.'

She raked him with a scornful glance. 'Are you going to tell me that you think, like those who invested my dowry, that as a female I'm not clever enough to manage my own affairs? That they can handle them so much better? That I should remain at home…embroidering samplers?'

'No, of course not. But if you dare to do something so outside the realm of conventional behaviour, you may make it impossible to retain your proper place in Society.'

'I'll thank you again for being the means of restoring my dowry. Since I now don't need to marry someone I don't love to have financial security, I believe I shall apply that dowry to do what I really want. If that scares off potential suitors and has me cut by the *ton*, so be it. After all, I wasn't born a marquess's daughter. And I realise now I'm not cut out to be the sort of conventional wife a *ton* gentleman seeks. So, will you escort me to the exchange?'

'Certainly not! I will escort you home.'

She shook her head. 'Thank you, but no. I have a right to live my life as I choose. Once, I thought…but obviously I was wrong. I hope we can continue to be friends, though. Perhaps you will even offer me investment advice? Certainly, you are welcome to accompany me to Mr Babbage's salons.'

'You know, if you persist in doing this, you'll be ruined.'

'That's one way of looking at it. But maybe pursuing what I want isn't the road to ruin, but the path to being the person I'm meant to be. Maybe being ruined means I will no longer have to try to be something I'm not.'

'Would you truly be happy being estranged from Society?'

'I wouldn't be estranged from the company of the people I care about—my friends, my family, the mathematicians and thinkers who attend the salons. I know what I want.' She gave him a long, pensive look. 'To my great regret, I found my desires…were not shared.'

His brain was clicking through the points she'd made so quickly, he felt dizzy. She didn't care about remaining a part of Society. She was determined to pursue own course, one that was certain to see her ostracised by most of it.

If she were not taking part in Society anyway…marrying her would not destroy or diminish her. Loving and marrying her, he could share her life without irreparably harming her.

'What if those…desires *were* shared?'

She looked back at him. 'Once I thought they were, but the gentleman in question had every opportunity to confirm that. And did not.'

'Maybe he held back to protect you. So you would not lose your place. Your friends. Your status.'

'Is it not up to me what place, friends and status I wish to have? To keep all those things that mean more to me than some artificial title and position? Just as Susanna should be free to choose what she feels will make her happy? Why do men persist in thinking they know better and try to prevent women from making their own choices? Do we not know our own hearts best?'

'Maybe he was wrong to do so. Even though he thought he was protecting the lady he cherishes.'

'Does he…cherish her?'

'Absolutely.'

'Then he should know the best way to cherish her is to make her his…permanently.'

His heartbeat accelerating so he could hardly get the words out, he said, 'Are you absolutely sure?'

She looked at him squarely, tenderness in her gaze. 'I've never been surer of anything.'

'Sure as you are about which prime follows eight hundred and twenty-one?'

'Eight hundred and twenty-three,' she answered without a pause. 'So, Miles, my darling—will you let me choose? And agree with my choice?'

In a flash, he was out of his chair as she rose from hers. He pulled her into his arms, kissing her with all the ardency and pent-up need he'd been storing up since the day he'd met her, made all the keener by going through the agony of believing she could never be his.

When at last he broke off the kiss, grinning, she looked as giddy as he felt. 'Will you be mine, Laura, for all of our lives?'

'I will. I still want to confront Arledge, though. And make investments.'

'If you'll let me place them on the floor, we can calculate them together.'

She appeared to consider it for a moment. 'Very well. I suppose there is only so much revolution the English markets can stand, after all.'

Chuckling, he seized her hands and kissed them.

'You'd better tell your clerks we're to be married,' she said, gesturing towards the staring faces peering at them from the other side of the open door. 'Otherwise they are likely to be scandalised at you kissing a woman in your office.'

'They had better get used to it. I think my wife will be visiting my office often.'

'That she will.' She accepted the hand he offered. 'Shall we go and take on the world?'

'With you beside me, anything is possible.'

Epilogue

The following day, Laura gathered Maggie and Eliza in the drawing room at Mount Street, all of them exclaiming over the news she'd announced that Miles had asked for her hand and she had accepted.

'Are you sure you mean to leave Society?' Eliza asked. 'Not everyone will cut you.'

Laura shrugged. 'Why return when the only society I seek is here? I can still attend the Philharmonic, the opera, the theatre, visit the museums. Dance at small gatherings of friends. No, I will not miss it at all, and I'm not willing to give the censorious the opportunity to snub me.'

'I suppose I can't be too cross with you,' Maggie said. 'You did follow some of my advice—your Miles is rich and he's not a nobleman. I should be satisfied I got two of three.'

'I am satisfied you chose love and passion over security and respect,' Eliza said.

'I suppose enjoying the adoration of a man like Mr Rochdale makes up for not becoming a rich widow,' Maggie allowed.

Smiling as she recalled Miles's kisses, Laura said, 'You may trust me that it does! You might reconsider giving up on marriage, Maggie. I assure you it can offer... benefits.'

'Not for me,' Maggie said briskly. 'Well, I shall just have to concentrate my efforts on Eliza and hope for a better result.'

'When do you plan to be wed?' Eliza asked.

'Miles wanted to wait until the end of the Season after all the *ton* families had left town, so our union wouldn't create such a stir of gossip. But when I kissed him and asked if he really wanted to wait for more of that, he decided that getting a special licence and being wed in two weeks might be better after all.'

Eliza gave her a hug, her eyes starry. 'I'm so happy for you.'

'I'll hope for the same for you. And you too, Maggie, much as you resist it!'

Maggie shook her head. 'As long as my friends are happy, I shall be satisfied.' Turning to Laura, she said, 'You must promise to be blissful.'

'That's a promise I intend to keep,' Laura assured her.

So it was, two weeks later, that Maggie, Eliza and Susanna filed into the small chapel near Mount Street while Miles paced with the minister, waiting for Lord Carmelton to escort in the bride.

A moment later, the door opened and Laura entered.

He saw only her—the radiance of her smile that made his heart beat faster as she walked towards him. Her father placed her hand on his arm, kissed her forehead and took his seat. They turned to face the vicar and repeated in turn the ancient words of the wedding service.

Then it was his privilege to kiss her, a simple brush of his lips over hers that promised so much more.

She whispered a protest at its brevity as he walked her along the street, back to the house where a small group of friends had assembled in the drawing room to celebrate with a wedding breakfast.

'I hope you give me a better kiss than that later, husband. In length—and depth.'

'There's a high probability that I will give you all of me, as often as you like.'

'How about for ever?'

'I like that percentage,' he said, and led her in.

* * * * *

If you enjoyed this story, look out for the next book in Julia Justiss' Least Likely to Wed miniseries

Whilst you're waiting for the next book, be sure to read her Heirs in Waiting miniseries

The Bluestocking Duchess
The Railway Countess
The Explorer Baroness

◆HARLEQUIN
HISTORICAL

Your romantic escape to the past.

*Be seduced by the grandeur, drama and sumptuous detail of romances
set in long-ago eras!*

Six new books available every month!

Get 4 FREE REWARDS!

We'll send you 2 FREE Books plus 2 FREE Mystery Gifts.

FREE Value Over **$20**

Both the **Harlequin® Historical** and **Harlequin® Romance** series feature compelling novels filled with emotion and simmering romance.

YES! Please send me 2 FREE novels from the Harlequin Historical or Harlequin Romance series and my 2 FREE gifts (gifts are worth about $10 retail). After receiving them, if I don't wish to receive any more books, I can return the shipping statement marked "cancel." If I don't cancel, I will receive 6 brand-new Harlequin Historical books every month and be billed just $6.19 each in the U.S. or $6.74 each in Canada, a savings of at least 11% off the cover price, or 4 brand-new Harlequin Romance Larger-Print books every month and be billed just $6.09 each in the U.S. or $6.24 each in Canada, a savings of at least 13% off the cover price. It's quite a bargain! Shipping and handling is just 50¢ per book in the U.S. and $1.25 per book in Canada.* I understand that accepting the 2 free books and gifts places me under no obligation to buy anything. I can always return a shipment and cancel at any time by calling the number below. The free books and gifts are mine to keep no matter what I decide.

Choose one: ☐ **Harlequin Historical**
(246/349 HDN GRH7)

☐ **Harlequin Romance Larger-Print**
(119/319 HDN GRH7)

Name (please print)

Address   Apt. #

City   State/Province   Zip/Postal Code

Email: Please check this box ☐ if you would like to receive newsletters and promotional emails from Harlequin Enterprises ULC and its affiliates. You can unsubscribe anytime.

Mail to the **Harlequin Reader Service:**
IN U.S.A.: P.O. Box 1341, Buffalo, NY 14240-8531
IN CANADA: P.O. Box 603, Fort Erie, Ontario L2A 5X3

Want to try 2 free books from another series? Call 1-800-873-8635 or visit www.ReaderService.com.

*Terms and prices subject to change without notice. Prices do not include sales taxes, which will be charged (if applicable) based on your state or country of residence. Canadian residents will be charged applicable taxes. Offer not valid in Quebec. This offer is limited to one order per household. Books received may not be as shown. Not valid for current subscribers to the Harlequin Historical or Harlequin Romance series. All orders subject to approval. Credit or debit balances in a customer's account(s) may be offset by any other outstanding balance owed by or to the customer. Please allow 4 to 6 weeks for delivery. Offer available while quantities last.

Your Privacy—Your information is being collected by Harlequin Enterprises ULC, operating as Harlequin Reader Service. For a complete summary of the information we collect, how we use this information and to whom it is disclosed, please visit our privacy notice located at corporate.harlequin.com/privacy-notice. From time to time we may also exchange your personal information with reputable third parties. If you wish to opt out of this sharing of your personal information, please visit readerservice.com/consumerschoice or call 1-800-873-8635. **Notice to California Residents**—Under California law, you have specific rights to control and access your data. For more information on these rights and how to exercise them, visit corporate.harlequin.com/california-privacy.

HHHRLP22R3

Get 4 FREE REWARDS!

We'll send you 2 FREE Books plus 2 FREE Mystery Gifts.

FREE Value Over $20

Both the **Harlequin® Desire** and **Harlequin Presents®** series feature compelling novels filled with passion, sensuality and intriguing scandals.

YES! Please send me 2 FREE novels from the Harlequin Desire or Harlequin Presents series and my 2 FREE gifts (gifts are worth about $10 retail). After receiving them, if I don't wish to receive any more books, I can return the shipping statement marked "cancel." If I don't cancel, I will receive 6 brand-new Harlequin Presents Larger-Print books every month and be billed just $6.30 each in the U.S. or $6.49 each in Canada, a savings of at least 10% off the cover price, or 6 Harlequin Desire books every month and be billed just $5.05 each in the U.S. or $5.74 each in Canada, a savings of at least 12% off the cover price. It's quite a bargain! Shipping and handling is just 50¢ per book in the U.S. and $1.25 per book in Canada.* I understand that accepting the 2 free books and gifts places me under no obligation to buy anything. I can always return a shipment and cancel at any time by calling the number below. The free books and gifts are mine to keep no matter what I decide.

Choose one: ☐ **Harlequin Desire**
(225/326 HDN GRJ7)

☐ **Harlequin Presents Larger-Print**
(176/376 HDN GRJ7)

Name (please print)

Address _____ Apt. #

City _____ State/Province _____ Zip/Postal Code

Email: Please check this box ☐ if you would like to receive newsletters and promotional emails from Harlequin Enterprises ULC and its affiliates. You can unsubscribe anytime.

Mail to the Harlequin Reader Service:

IN U.S.A.: P.O. Box 1341, Buffalo, NY 14240-8531
IN CANADA: P.O. Box 603, Fort Erie, Ontario L2A 5X3

Want to try 2 free books from another series? Call 1-800-873-8635 or visit www.ReaderService.com.

HDHP22R3

HARLEQUIN
PLUS

Try the best multimedia subscription service for romance readers like you!

Read, Watch and Play.

Experience the easiest way to get the romance content you crave.

Start your **FREE TRIAL** at
www.harlequinplus.com/freetrial.